Also by Amy E. Zajac

It Started With Patton Teresa Leska's Story
A Memoir

You'll find more of Amy's stories in the following anthologies:

Chicken Soup for the Soul
From Lemons to Lemonade

Hot Dogs and Cool Cats
Animal Tales a la carte

The Guilded Pen
and
The Guilded Pen, Second Edition 2013

A Cup of Comfort for
Divorced Women

Foredestined

Amy E. Zajac

This book is a work of fiction. The events described are imaginary and the characters are fictitious and not intended to represent specific living persons.

Copyright © 2013 Amy E. Zajac

Published by Amy E. Zajac at CreateSpace

ISBN: 0988207028
ISBN-13: 978-0-9882070-2-8

Cover Illustration: T.J. Waller

DEDICATION

For two creative generations:

My dad, Alfred W. Lejman deceased and his tall
ship art which inspired part of my story, and my
grandson,
T. J. Waller, who created the cover illustration.

ACKNOWLEDGMENTS

With warmest appreciation to my daughters, Sabina Zajac and Teressa Waller, who support my life changes at every turn; to my grandson, T.J. Waller, for his artistic presence in my life; to my mother, Teri Thomas, for the spark of an idea; to my author friend, Donna Sundblad, who's guidance made me believe in my own success; to my new internet/email friend, Jeff Nunes, with gratitude for confirming the accuracy of my Hebrew translations; and to my friend Sharon Grimson for her patience, and her ability to read the same thing over and over, producing the questions I needed to develop *Foredestined* into a reality.

PROLOGUE

The asteroid slid in low from the west like an airplane attempting to land without its wheels down. Yellowstone National Park in Wyoming, part of the continental United States, took a direct hit. It ripped through the earth's crust and tectonic plates into the top of the upper mantle creating a huge tear in the lithosphere and burrowed its way to the hot rivers of magma below. The mantle's revolving movement shifted like a broken spoke driven into the gears of a working machine. Earthquake after earthquake triggered more and more rocking and rolling across the continents. In a matter of hours, the planet started to alter with super eruptions and tsunamis.

After twenty four hours the spinning blue earthly globe, no longer controlled balanced environments. As the week progressed, the skies grew dark with smoke and ash and in some parts of the world the non-breathable air lingered.

When the asteroid approached Earth, astronomers' worldwide studied its path. Headlines tracked the trajectory on a regular basis, but government controlled media minimized the event. Broadcasters reported the asteroid would pass by close enough for all parts of the world to see a great "three-dimensional-show". However, actual images, received from one of the four satellites launched in 2035, slipped through the cracks and went directly to global media centers. An ecumenical council, jumped in to confirm and prove the accuracy of the transmissions introducing scientific data to support their learned colleagues world-wide. Politicians demeaned the scientific tribunals and debates, which teachers, scientists, and environmentalists placed in front of the public. The day after, governments denounced the facts, sensational headlines read, *"Staged Pictures and Media Recordings A Hoax."*

The majority of the world's population accepted their governments' statements without question. Political leader's rhetoric prevailed over humankind rather than the logic, knowledge, and calculations of scholars of the day. Political plausibility offered an easier alternative. They stated that scientists' and educators' warnings posed an obscure non-believable threat to Earth, just like one of those ancient science fiction movies shown in the nostalgia museums.

The last minute warnings passed from government to government, received too late, made no difference. The world burned and quaked and people died. Even in the last places on Earth to erupt and quake, the populace never thought this catastrophe would move so far from the predicted point of impact. The light-weight media reports flashed into people's minds during their last moments. The extreme loss of life, though suspected, was only confirmed years later. The tragedy ravaged 194 countries and killed hundreds of millions of people.

The predicted asteroid sliced its path into the Earth's surface in 2052. Death and devastation brought agony to the pockets of survivors stretched out globally. This story introduces detailed disaster experiences, and how survivors rebuild their lives in a thirty-five year recovery.

Amy E. Zajac

ONE

Excited about her upcoming trip, Rosalie threw the dozen cruise line travel brochures up over her head and giggled as she fell backwards onto her bed. She and her mother would board the cruise ship at Boston Harbor, in just four days. Her dream to visit the University of Jerusalem and take her first cruise, all came together in celebration for an early graduation from her high school's accelerated gifted curriculum. Tomorrow will start their six-week journey as they board a plane for Boston.

To appease her parents, Rosalie set up college tours at the University of Lisbon, Universitat De Barcelona, Istituzioni Scolastiche Robert Kennedy, and the University of Salerno, all stops along the cruise route. She and her mother worked out all the details with their travel agent for Jerusalem University to be their last school to visit. By seeing all these universities, Rosalie's parents knew she would have the necessary information to support her choice.

"I just don't understand why you can't wait until August or September to go on this trip," her Dad said. "We've all heard the warnings and, we, of all people, should heed the scientists giving us an alarm. We're teachers, for crying out loud; we know they're being honest with us."

Rosalie danced around her father in the dining room, kissed him on the cheek and fanned him with the brochures she finished checking out for the thousandth time. To her father she barely looked thirteen, let alone sixteen and a high school graduate. He smiled at her happy-go-lucky dancing.

"But Dad, we've already talked this through. I'm going to tour four extra colleges plus the University of

Jerusalem, just like you wanted. Right now, I'm running to see Sally. I'll be right back if you want to talk some more. Sally's loaning me a vest. I need to get there soon, before she changes her mind. It took forever for her to say yes. I'll be back in half an hour."

"It's okay Rosalie, no need to hurry, I'll talk to your dad," her mother said. "Besides it's not the university he wants to talk about; it's the prediction."

Rosalie waved over her shoulder as she ran out the door.

"Now Tim, you know Rosalie has a chance to get into whichever university she chooses. If we wait until autumn to go, she won't be able to start until the January semester. With her early graduation complete, she's a shoe-in for this coming fall," Jane Danforth said. "Let's not go over this for the hundredth time. We'll be just fine. And besides that, Rosalie has always wanted to go on a cruise. It's a wonderful gift for her and it will give Rosalie and I some special mother-daughter time, before she leaves for school so far away from home." Jane hugged her husband to seal the conversation.

Reminiscing about Rosalie's creativity, he chuckled.

"I know, I know, I've heard it all before. Remember, she practically wrote a thesis to convince me. I just have this gnawing feeling eating at me. I'm uneasy about you traveling."

Jane folded a jacket and placed it into her suitcase, "The point of impact was predicted to be near the western border of Montana, really far away from here. Even if we were home we'd be safe here with you. But we're going to the other side of the world, farther away, and I would think, even safer due to the distance. Hand me that blouse on the bureau." She pointed across the room, until she saw that Tim recognized what she needed. "Let's just appreciate our daughter's joy. I've never seen her so happy."

Jane hugged her husband one more time and turned back to her packing, pushing down hard on the case to close the bulging sides. She smiled at him, while he helped with her bags. The plan she and her daughter put together, *was on*.

The first three weeks of the cruise to France and through the Mediterranean Sea, with its turnaround layover in Tel Aviv-Yafo, turned out to be everything Rosalie dreamed of. At every stop, they visited different schools instead of the traditional sight-seeing tours. Now that she's checked out these additional universities, her parents will accept her choice. She did what they asked her to do. All the schools offered great curriculums, but lacked the studies Rosalie dreamed about for so long. The final school tour at the University of Jerusalem, her first choice, came at the end of the first half of their six-week cruise.

The excursion through the university complete, Rosalie and her mother returned to the dormitory. Jane scanned the room slowly; "I'll be glad to get back to the ship. As small as our cabin is there, it's roomier than this dorm space."

"Oh, come on, Mom, it's not so bad. Anyway, whatever it is, I guess I'd better get used to it. This is my choice. Did you see it?"

"See what?"

Teasing her mom, Rosalie flopped back on to her dorm bunk; "Oh, I forgot, you were actually listening to our guide. In the back rooms of the library, when we were in the history archive space, there it was! My lifelong dream: the propagation study, I can't believe it. There are VOLUMES!"

"So it's all there, just as you were told. Oh

Sweetheart, that's wonderful! I guess you've confirmed your original choice." Jane turned to work on their packing. They needed to be ready when the shuttle arrived to take them back to the ship in the morning. "Have you put your dirty clothes in your suitcase?" When there was no reply, she turned to see that Rosalie, hugging her pillow, stared up at the bottom of the bunk above. Jane knew her daughter was already daydreaming about the future.

Their last day in Jerusalem, Rosalie woke at sunrise. She dressed quickly, to sneak out for a walk without waking her mother. Strolling the campus in the typical morning sunshine and thinking about what her life would be as she started her studies, took her mind off the time. She heard bells ringing on the hour and knew she'd walked longer than planned. Her stomach flip-flopped as she headed back to the dorm. Their shuttle would arrive shortly. Rosalie picked up her pace. Her adrenalin rushed; the excitement of her upcoming adventure flushed her cheeks as the rays of the early morning sun caressed her face. *I can't miss this leg of the cruise. To dock in New York City and shop for clothes is a dream. Mom is such a fabulous planner; I can't wait to get to the garment district and be totally in style for once in my life!* Just when these fanciful thoughts filled her mind, the walls next to the sidewalk toppled when the ground rocked her back and forth; she fell to her knees. Violent ground movement kept her down. Fifty feet in front of her, a young man stumbled. "Hey mister, can you help me?" but a massive new opening in the ground reached up to swallow him, right in front her eyes.

"NO, OH MY GOD..." She gripped the unstable ground, not knowing what to do next. Her heart raced and she gasped for a breath, when a wall of broken sidewalk and rocks pushed up, blocking any escape.

Rosalie's mind flashed her Dad's warning not to travel. *The old warning about destruction of the Earth; it couldn't be! Oh God, I haven't had a chance to really live yet, please take care of me today.*

The ancient historic architecture broke up into pieces all around her. Walls shattered. Old bells rang, and then wailed, when they tumbled from their ancient bell towers.

Fear and disbelief welled up inside Rosalie, *Why did I have to take a walk today of all days?* She attempted to stand, but lost her balance and fell onto a jagged wrought iron fence which appeared out of nowhere. When she fell, the ground movement threw her forward and the point of one rod stabbed through her skin at her wrist in perfect parallel with her outside forearm. The rod tore the skin off her outer arm as if it peeled an apple, with the point of the rod buried in her upper inner arm. Rosalie heard a scream, and knew the sound came from inside her, but not believing she could make a sound like that. Terror struck her thoughts when the pain from the wrought iron stopped her movements to find safety. "HELP, PLEASE ANYONE, PLEASE." Just when she believed her arm to be lost, another quake tossed her through the air and her arm released from the wrought iron. She hit her head on a granite column and felt nothing when she fell unconscious into a newly opened crevice. Incredible pain shot throughout her whole body when she came to after a few moments. Steam shot directly at her legs and paralyzed her in agony. The intense hissing from an old furnace boiler torn from its underground cellar, added to the eerie moment. Now wedged into the rocks, she lay in the hot steam, unable to move. The earth quaked again and again. Rosalie heard rumbling sounds of what she thought to be thunder. The steam hissed in her ears; the noise...so loud, no   one   heard   her   screams.

TWO

Up early to do some reading, Anatole, a young archeology professor at the University of Jerusalem, found himself a quiet spot in the gardens near the chapel. He relaxed in the early morning sunshine as he read. A huge jolt threw him from the bench to the ground. Unable to stand, he clung to the grass. *Oh my God, is this an earthquake?* "Hey, can anyone hear me? HELP!" The rocking earth lifted him into the air.

Anatole screamed when the ground below him tore open leaving him hanging from the top edge of an open crevice. His wails of fear had to be heard by someone close by. He clung to the soft grass of the garden, but his fingers lost their grip to the early morning sprinkler residue. About a foot away from his left hand a fallen lamppost extended partially across the crevice. He grabbed it and pulled hard with all his body's weight. It held. Through the unpredictable tremors, he walked up the post with his hands, threw his leg over the edge and got his balance pulling himself up, and then over, to lie on the grass once again. His body shook uncontrollably. He took a deep breath and pushed himself away from the edge, holding tight to the grass as the ground waved rocked back and forth. The crevice kept getting wider and wider. He inched away from the erratically changing opening. Leaning on newly broken pieces of sidewalk, he stretched his body as high as he could to see over the rubble. "Hey anybody...HELP!!" No one replied; all he heard ...rumbling and settling rubble.

He balanced himself enough to stand and stumbled away from the crevice. Almost falling into another one close by, he caught a glimpse of a young woman in the rubble. Injured and burned, she laid alone, dying. It took half an hour to get around the crevice and close enough to touch her neck and feel for a pulse. Anatole guessed what to do. *Since she has a pulse, she's unconscious because of pain or the head injury.* Her one upper arm, stripped of flesh and bloody, with the melted skin on her legs practically showing bare shin bone, kept her unconscious. The burned flesh reeked, gagging him. Anatole pried apart some heavy concrete, freeing her from the rocks that trapped her. When he lifted her limp body, her eerie silence and the melted skin validated the intensity of her injuries. Disrupted ground interfered with Anatole carrying her. He placed her body in a secluded spot opposite a wrought iron fence and a furnace boiler. Anatole knew she was secure. Even though non-responsive, she still breathed and hope for her survival welled up inside him. *How could she endure this pain?* "Well, at least you're alive." Her arm looked like it bled heavily at first, but it already stopped. Dried blood covered her hand and blouse. *She must have been caught here first thing this morning.* The muscle spilled out of her forearm where the skin ripped away. Her bruised forehead swelled around to her left temple. *I have to find some clean towels or sheets or something to wrap her injuries. I hate to leave her alone, but I need to get to my apartment for that first aid kit in my closet.* He climbed over piles of concrete pieces when he started out.

Anatole steered himself away from fires and erratic explosions. He tripped over and over again on the changed and convoluted ground with wreckage and bodies strewn everywhere. *Why is this taking me so long? It feels like I'm moving in slow motion.* It took time to check pulses of victims and when he found no survivors he felt more alone and driven to get back to the young woman he found alive.

When he saw his apartment building destroyed and burning to the ground, his mind screamed, *NO!* Several of his colleagues lay dead in the rubble. They jumped to their deaths, to escape the burning building. "Oh Philippe…Jonathon…God, how can this be happening? Oh please, let me wake up!" he wailed, kneeling over them, frantic to find their pulses. *Oh God…they're dead; we were going to have lunch tomorrow…a birthday celebration for Philippe…*he wept uncontrollably as he held Philippe's hand. His mind raced. *Stop, stay focused. You don't have time to lose focus. She needs help. She's waiting all alone. I need to find something clean to wrap her burn wounds…keep focused.* He closed Philippe's and Jonathon's eyes, *Oh Jonathon, your neck broke.* He wept for his friends, waiting a few moments before he moved on.

After another hour, Anatole found a clean jacket next to a dead student and grabbed it. He rushed back to the young woman's location. On the way, he found a bottle of water and a blanket inside a damaged hover-car. Grateful to see the wrought iron fence where he knew she lay unconscious, he started to run, and again fell, "good Lord, why can't I stay on my feet?"

"Yes...she's still alive," he shouted after he felt her pulse. He tore the jacket into pieces, wrapped her legs and poured water over the make-shift bandages attempting to cool the deteriorated flesh. *How can she still be alive?* The little flesh left on her legs looked liquefied and took the shape of her shin bones. *No wonder she's unconscious. The pain alone should have killed her.* Gently he pushed the skin on her arm in place, overlapped the edges, and covered it with a torn piece of jacket. After that, he placed a couple drops of water onto her dried lips, being careful not to choke her in her unconscious state.

At dusk, he covered her and sat back to rest a moment. Realizing his own thirst, he grabbed the bottle he used to pour water over her legs and drank most of what was left. He held his head back, waiting while the final drops fell into his mouth, when he stopped, remembering to leave a little bit in the bottle. *That's not enough, but I'll need more for the young woman and I'm too tired to look for water now. I think I should look for some penicillin and pain medicine; I hope she doesn't wake up too soon.* He drifted off to sleep.

Anatole slept the whole night, only to be awakened by a large aftershock early that second morning. He checked the young woman's pulse and sighed. *Yes, she's still alive... amazing.* After placing the last few drops of water left onto her lips, he set out to find more water and medicine. Since he worked at the university, locating the medical center about a half mile away should have been a simple task, but the ravaged ground and his stopping to check dead bodies slowed him down. The university streets, now in shambles, made it difficult to find his way. It took all morning to get close enough to the medical center to actually recognize where he was. The strange and uneasy quiet kept him on edge. Anatole jumped and jerked to look every time he heard concrete settling, pieces of debris falling or disruptive aftershocks. He prayed to find survivors along the way and at the medical center. The first priority was to find help for the young woman. He dug through piles of bricks and concrete pieces to get into the emergency room entrance, the logical place to find first aid medicines and bandages. *Everyone's dead here. Oh God help me!* After a couple hours, he found penicillin. Most of the bottles were broken, but he found four intact and carried them in his cupped hands, placing them gently on a blanket. *Shouldn't there be premeasured stuff like the pharmacies give out for prescriptions? Without those, I'll need to find syringes.* Close by he also saw aspirin, gauze, iodine, peroxide and water and grabbed them. He looked overhead, the ceiling hung low, another aftershock would force it down, *Come on, get out of here while you still can...NO, I NEED SYRINGES.*

Panicky to get out of the emergency room, he pushed toward the cabinets toppled over in the corner. *OH God...*he saw a man's leg sticking out from under the cabinet. Anatole touched the leg; it was cold. He jerked his hand away; his body shuddered. *OH God, how can everybody be dead? Focus, focus, syringes, you need syringes for her. Get this cabinet door open.* He tugged and pulled, then saw raised-up tiles blocking the door. Anatole kicked hard at the tiles. They broke off and the door jumped open. He kept watching the ceiling. *Please let me have enough time to find what I need.* He pulled the door up and held it open with his head. Most items in the cabinet were plastic products. His hands thrashed through. Near the bottom, he saw syringes. *Only three, there has to be more.* Rummaging again, he lost his balance when another aftershock shook the room. Thrust backwards, the cabinet door slammed shut and the ceiling yanked down, stopping just short of Anatole's head. His body stiffened expecting the impact. Silence. Wires swinging back and forth made an eerie swishing and clicking sound. His chest heaved heavily in and out. He breathed so hard he thought the movement of his chest would cause something else to fall. *Crawl, you can do it, just crawl.* He held tight to the syringes and made his way back to the blanket, where he grabbed everything. The rest of the way he rolled, holding the treasures above his head. Once out of the room, his breathing calmed, but his body shook all over. He lay crying, his face buried in his arm. *Thank you, God. You gave me what I asked for.* A few minutes later, back on his feet, he found his way back to her, carrying his cherished riches in his makeshift blanket sack.

"I sure hope you're not allergic to penicillin; we need a break here. Please God; let this work." He held his breath as he injected the needle into the young woman's uninjured arm. Afterwards, he placed the syringe back into its original bag. *I can use this one again for her.* Since he only found three syringes, he saved the others in case someone else needed penicillin in the next few days.

Because her legs were initially so bad, Anatole chose not to touch them again so soon. He unwrapped and swabbed the wound on her damaged arm. The loose skin he set in place the day before appeared to already be healing; he cleaned the dirty skin edges and upper arm, rewrapping in clean gauze. He placed water drops on her lips, and sat back watching closely to see if she reacted to the penicillin; after an hour, nothing. *If she was allergic, she would have reacted by now, she's calm and there are no rashes or changes in her.* Relief of this realization brought tears to his eyes. *Oh God, thanks for staying with us.*

For those first days, he nursed the young woman's injuries alone. They seemed to be the only two people to survive in their immediate locale. He looked for survivors, food and water. The decaying bodies out in the heat smelled very bad and inhibited his work. He covered his nose and mouth as he scavenged. The young woman lay resting in an area, away from any dead bodies. This made it easier to care for her. Anatole uncovered his face while he was with her.

On the third day, he found one survivor, a woman so traumatized she ran screaming when she saw Anatole wearing his mask-like bandana. She was afraid of him, until he showed her his face. When she calmed down, he convinced her to follow him to where he nursed the young unknown woman, still not moving. The fourth day, a little boy wandered up behind Anatole while he moved concrete away to create a place to lie down to sleep. The boy slipped his little hand into Anatole's, who jumped at the touch. The child didn't react at all. Anatole bent over to talk to the boy face-to-face. "Hey look at you...where did you come from?"

Barefoot and in shock, he stared at Anatole's face, but didn't appear to actually see him. Anatole extended his hand and the little boy grabbed it tight, but other than grabbing his hand the little boy had no emotional reaction at all. They walked over to the other new survivor sitting with the burned woman. The three of them huddled together. The little boy gripped Anatole's hand while they hugged. Neither of the new survivors spoke, but the warmth of the gentle hug momentarily calmed them; they weren't alone anymore.

On the fifth day the burned woman came out of her unconsciousness. Elated, but hardly able to believe it, Anatole sat down next to her. "Can you speak? Where are you from?" Anatole asked as he gently stroked her forehead.

Almost inaudible, she whispered and gasped a few words. "I am Rosalie...American." Other than that, she kept silent, except when she cried in her agony. The fear and pain registered in her face as she peered up at the kind stranger.

"My name is Anatole."

He poured water over the bandages on her legs to keep them cool and gave her aspirin dissolved in water. It had to taste terrible, but she didn't appear to notice. He didn't know what else to do and knew this helped only a little, if at all.

THREE

After three weeks, as if by a miracle, Rosalie began to feel better. She smiled at Anatole as he walked closer to sit down next to her. "I never thought I'd see you smiling."

"I never thought I'd feel like smiling, but when I woke up today, the pain dulled somehow. It was good." She shrugged her shoulders and winced when the skin on her arm pulled taut.

Up until that time, they only spoke in quick question and answers to get through Rosalie's healing. Other than that, she slept, cried or just stared straight ahead as if in shock. During those initial three weeks, Rosalie healed while Anatole located food and several other survivors; two of whom were brothers. They were both amateur radio operators. With them and the broken rigs they pulled from their apartment, Anatole planned communication activities even without electricity. The operators told him how they could transmit through their rig to locate other survivors and maybe find out what happened. Together the three of them searched destroyed buildings for equipment to rebuild their make-shift transmitting equipment. While the two of them built, Anatole scavenged, to locate the rest of the list of items they needed. Setting up radio operations, to transmit on daily schedules, gave the group a way to broaden their small world. This focus together kept their anxiety down a little. Reaching out to anyone who may be listening drove their every action to help build some kind of continuity of living again and away from the fear of their reality. Anatole sat awhile taking time to explain everything he knew about the devastation that occurred worldwide.

"So you see Rosalie, we had success with our very first transmission. ...our signals reached great distances! Obviously, we've only spoken with countries where amateur radio equipment is available, and more importantly, have people who know about amateur radio equipment. But sadly from most countries, there's silence...always silence. We've already created a network with regular communications during the time you were in and out of consciousness. It was during that time that I kept a supply of water close by for the other woman survivor, who helped me attend your burned legs. She gently poured water over them. Your body relaxed as she did this, so my instinct was to have her continue doing it, while I looked for more survivors. I've never heard her say a word. Does she ever speak to you?"

"No. She's sad and lost, but she is so gentle with me."

Only this limited HAM communication existed. All the past advances in technology were unsustainable with no experts and no electricity. The sparse population left on earth knew nothing about the remaining miniscule bits of working technology to make a difference. Therefore, the old style "HAM" communications became the main communication line with Anatole their organizer and coordinator.

During her many hours of recuperation Rosalie began to remember what occurred on the day of the catastrophe. At first, she had no memories, she only endured pain. *Now I remember,* she thought. *I was out walking and as soon as I completed my walk I would go back to my room to pick up my mother...Oh, Mom....* When Anatole checked on her again mid-day, Rosalie asked him to locate the dormitory she and her mother stayed in, to see if he could find her or...her body.

The next day Anatole found the building burned down and returned to tell her, but struggled with the words. Rosalie helped him. "I can tell by the look on your face. I know, you didn't find her," she said. Anatole held her hand while she wept again, different this time because she began to grieve.

After several more weeks, there being no word one way or another, Rosalie stopped hoping her mother survived. Lying in her makeshift bed of rags, a couch cushion and a couple blankets, she stared off into space lost in her sorrow and her ongoing pain.

Communication extended through amateur radios. Anatole called the two men working the radios, "HAM" operators.

"Why 'HAM' operators?" Rosalie asked Anatole.

"I'm not sure. A couple years ago I was curious and I looked it up on Filter-net. I found so many variations of why they're called HAM. There were several theories out there. I liked one of them; it stood for "Help All Mankind". I finally chose that one to remember it by. It suited me. With the extended history of amateur radio operator's service for people suffering adversity from natural and civil disasters, the acronym became H.A.M., similar to S.O.S. I do know that the expression is old, from about the 1920s or 30s. Now when I think about what's happening to us, I know I made the right choice, because I truly believe our communications can help all mankind."

The HAM operator survivors worked with Anatole to coordinate activities through regular communication schedules, first only short distances with people in the Middle East and Russia. But soon after, their broadcasts reached the United States by using a technique called a moon bounce, radio waves between the moon and Earth. Challenged by the need for batteries, they argued in their anxiety and fatigue. *We can't always use the batteries for HAM transmissions. That's a waste. There are other things we need batteries for.*

Resting close by Rosalie heard the frustration in their voices. "Does it matter if we save anything or not? We just want to find out what happened and about other survivors for now. Today, now, is what we have. Tomorrow will take care of itself."

Her calm voice steadied them.

The tension eased. They agreed to use some batteries for a makeshift first aid area, and after that for the transmissions. Able to talk calmly again, Anatole and the HAM operators talked about old technology and built a hand crank generator like the ones used during WW II to power field radios. They were no longer limited to the life of each scavenged battery. The internal part of the generator, a spinning magnet, provided a simple enough power source to create energy for their communications.

Through these regular nightly schedules to the United States, Rosalie received word about her father.

Colorado's damage encompassed the whole state. Where mountains stood, there used to be valleys. Cities like Denver, Rosalie's hometown, Colorado Springs, and prominent regions like Pikes Peak disappeared or were destroyed. Many of these places were swallowed up by the large crevasses, which opened and devoured almost all existing life, leaving wasteland. Colorado's picturesque panoramic landscape ravaged by the earthquakes laid unchanged for eons prior to that day. The old NORAD facility at Cheyenne Mountain, with its artificial tunnels and massive shafts in partial use for the last seventy five years, melted and collapsed, which catapulted the effects of the massive lava flows and quaking ground.

Colorado's population peaked at 10,000,000 in 2030; now almost 100 percent of the population died. The way the descriptions of the changed lay of the land came through a transmission from Ren, an officer cadet at the Air Force Academy northwest of Colorado Springs, Rosalie understood her home no longer existed.

FOUR

The man, Ren, saw no other survivors even after a month. When he heard the inquiry about Rosalie's father, he took a day to get to the area where his third grade teacher, Timothy Danforth, lived with his family. He taught Ren all the important lessons about life. This man needed to be found. His daughter, alive in Jerusalem, wanted to know if he survived.

Anatole received the reply to Rosalie's inquiry. He hated to deliver the sad news, but he knew Rosalie expected it. "Tim Danforth died during the quakes." An additional message came through at the same time, "Please arrange for Rosalie Danforth to be in attendance at the next transmission." Anatole told her, but at the time didn't think much of it.

"I hope I feel well enough to talk. I'm so tired all the time and my shins hurt so much."

Rosalie never met Ren prior to hearing him on the amateur radio transmission. "It's so good to meet you, Ren. Why don't you just talk through as much as you can for this transmission with me? Next time we'll build into Anatole's format for our calls."

"Oh thank you, Rosalie. I'm so lonely. It will be good to talk and just ramble on knowing someone is actually listening to me. I've been thinking a lot about what I'd say to you. First of all, I'm so glad you survived. Your dad talked about you all the time. I don't understand why we never met over the years, but I guess that's just the way it was."

"Your dad, my third grade teacher, taught me the simple concept of the Golden Rule. I grasped what the Golden Rule meant and wanted to believe the ideal followed through, not only for my life, but also, for everybody else's. I accepted this ideal as part of my identity, and it just stayed with me. I believed so much in the idea, even at that early age, so I decided to build a relationship with your dad. Every autumn when school started, I stopped by to visit with him and by the time I graduated from high school we enjoyed a solid mutual friendship."

"Your dad was my mentor and most trusted friend. I took his advice setting myself up for positive growth through college, and then I advanced to the Air Force Academy, my dream."

"Even though I learned about the Golden Rule at that early age, it took me a long time to accept that all humanity didn't practice the beautiful concept. Most people looked to politics for mentoring and advice. They looked for immediate gratification instead of understanding the inner warmth they could feel if they simply helped someone, eventually receiving something in return."

There was quiet on the transmission.

"Ren, are you there?"

She heard him; he was crying.

"Oh Ren...I'm sorry we're not closer."

"There's nobody Rosalie...nobody. It's like I'm supposed to clean up and create the world all alone. Until I knew there were other survivors, everything was so big and overwhelming. When I heard the question about your dad, I cried the whole night in disbelief before I was able to get myself out and down the hill toward the city to look for him. Someone literally asked me to find out something, and the names were familiar. It made me feel alive again."

"I got lost so many times; there was so much rubble in the destruction. I kept getting cornered between new ravines; I guess they should be called crevices. When I thought I got to the area where your family lived, there was nothing there and more specifically, there was no one there, just bodies and death all around me."

"Oh Ren... You're not responsible for the whole world, just for a little piece for yourself. Just focus on you. Do you understand what I'm saying?"

"Yes...I think so. Right now though, I can't even begin to tell you how wonderful it feels to be talking to someone, just rambling on. This is my first year at the academy. Just when I started my overnight peaceful duty in the radio room at the far end of the campus, I felt the first quake. I did everything we were told to do so many times, ever since I could remember. You know, standing in the door jamb or get underneath a table. After two minutes or so, I realized this earthquake shook longer than the minimal ones I experienced before. To keep my balance, I crawled away from the door jamb and dodged falling pictures, maneuvering around floor tiles which broke up under my knees. Electronic equipment crashed all around me and the last hallway before I reached the door to the outside, the ceiling collided with the top of my body, pinning me down. The floor below me bulged up, knocking the wind out of me. After that, there was barely any room to breathe or move around. I felt no pain and relaxed a moment to catch my breath. The quaking rocked me back and forth. I hit my head over and over. The building collapsed. I heard explosive sounds of plummeting debris and screamed and screamed for help. No one answered me. I yelled; I'm stuck under the ceiling, help. Then I remembered no one else was on duty. I had to get out of there on my own. Hours went by. It was so hard to breathe. I stopped pushing myself and fell asleep. I think it was when the noise from the constant quaking stopped that I woke up."

"I didn't know how long I slept. I just knew the panic of being trapped made me struggle. I shoved my arms up over my head to push on and loosen the ceiling pieces that trapped me. I expected fresh air to hit my face, but instead, smoke burned my eyes and choked me. The debris and the building were on fire. Again, I panicked...I pushed and strained to get out. I gasped for breath and felt worn out right away. To make head-way I squeezed through crawling to what I thought would be outside. My fingernails screeched on the tiles, there was nothing to grab onto. I choked and choked with little breathable air left. I had to get outside. My head hit a loose 2x4 piece of wood. I pushed it under my chin to get leverage, and then squeezed my arm to bend it close to my side. Holding it with my chin, aiming at the wall ahead of me, I jammed the heel of my hand against the end of it. It moved a couple inches, breaking through the debris in front of me. Unfortunately, it slid against my chin. The splinters I got really hurt, but I was grateful to feel air hit my face. I took a deep breath of the little bit of air left in that space. I pushed through the broken walls, and thought to myself, *it's dark outside, but it's still day.* Ash filled the air and made easier breathing impossible."

"I covered my mouth and nose with my hand. That helped just a little. I needed to get to a place where I could breathe. As quick as I could, I squirmed back to where I came from."

"Every breath felt like sand paper scratching my throat. I burrowed under the rubble, driving myself into a stack of loose wallboard pieces; this allowed me to get away from the ash. The very small space gave me a chance to create an air pocket around my head. To keep the ash away, I wriggled out of my shirt, and stretched it over the opening. I pushed against the rubble above and behind me to make more room. This gave me a secure space to wait out the time needed for the ash to settle. I slept a lot. That helped to keep me calm with lighter breathing. When I'd wake up, panic pushed into my thoughts. I knew if I waited as long as I could, I'd be able to get out safely, so I kept talking to myself. After two days' time, daylight began to show through my shirt. I pushed it away, but as I did, ash slid onto my face. I brushed it off as fast as I could, but some of it got into my nose and mouth. I choked and spit and coughed horribly hard."

"I needed to find water, but my muscles were sore from being confined and I'm sure from not having any water in two days. I was dehydrated. I had to get my body moving and dug through the rubble by kicking wood and scratching the ground. Miraculously, and I truly mean that, the old antique bubbler machine everybody always joked about, managed to stay upright wedged against a portion of a wall. I was so grateful, Rosalie, I drank for a very long time. That was the last blessing I found. Being trapped and burrowed under the rubble saved me, but I never found a single person alive. The bodies I found close by had their hands gripped over their mouths and chests. They choked to death. Their faces contorted when they gasped for breath with their mouths stretched wide, suffocating. Many with their eyes opened, as if to search for a solution to their tragic last moment dilemma. Finding victims buried in the ash were the encounters easiest for me to deal with. I never saw their eyes."

"The remnants of the campus were burned and toppled and laid in the abyss that devoured most of it. The air, filled with residue from the ash, hampered me from searching for survivors. I covered my mouth and nose while dragging a cot into one of the six buildings I found. This gave me a place to live temporarily. I've kept my face covered ever since, because of the dead body smell."

"From my location, I saw the destroyed Colorado Springs with most of it swallowed by the earth. Being higher, gave me a good vantage point. Like a huge shelf, these rocks pushed up through the ground and kept the few buildings partially upright. For the next couple weeks, I scavenged for food, water and survivors. I found the food and some drinks, but like I said earlier, I never found anyone alive."

"My mind played tricks on me. I'd see shadows, and I'd run to check if it was a person hiding from me. I tried to rationalize why I survived and no one else nearby did. So much loss on every level caused me to go a little crazy. I talked to myself and one day I just said right out loud, I HAVE TO TALK TO SOMEONE ELSE. That's when I remembered the amateur radio."

"Remembering one of the first lessons I had in the academy's standard curriculum, I now had a focus, to build a rig for myself. Do you understand about these transmissions, Rosalie?"

"Well, very little, but I'm learning fast; Anatole has been very helpful, explaining to me."

"In our class we learned about the Amateur Radio transmissions, a simple communication style used since the mid 1900's. Each of us built a receiver. I learned a lot and actually got it to work to get an A in the class."

"I searched for parts and worked night and day. Please let me find someone alive, I repeated over and over.

I about jumped out of my skin when I heard Anatole's transmission after listening to many different frequencies for about three days. I listened almost constantly after that. I learned about other survivors by following the regular transmissions from there in Israel. Your friend Anatole talked about the clean-up they wanted to do and so many other things. It made me feel like I was right there with them talking, so when I broke into the conversation being transmitted, they were shocked to hear me. Holding onto hope became easier after I spoke to other people even though they're on the other side of the world. My relief after that first transmission eliminated my bad dreams."

"Once I heard Anatole talk, I knew I needed to begin a job which I kept putting off. I needed to take care of the dead bodies. Shortly after the quakes, I dragged them by their arms and rolled them into piles. It was gruesome, but it was the easiest way. That was when the bad dreams started. Their hands so lifeless as I grasped them, I gagged and several times threw-up what little fluid I had left in my stomach. The piles strategically placed, out of my line of site where I walked around every day. This helped me not to dwell on the death all around me. I covered the piles with tarps I found in one of the damaged maintenance shacks."

"The stench overwhelmed me; I barely ate anything, not even my favorite candy bars I broke out of a vending machine. With no air conditioning because of no electricity, I smelled death, even inside my temporary home."

"Day before yesterday, I took care of the closest pile. I wore gloves, and kept my nose and mouth covered with a towel. Uncovering the fifteen bodies, I said a prayer over them and added some broken lumber pieces. After that I sprinkled some lighter fluid onto the wood, I lit a match and tossed it. The bodies badly decayed already, the fire quickly raged and burned many hours into the night. I knew I needed to do this for the other two piles, but became depressed; I put off the task for later."

"My feeling of loss after I burned the dead bodies surprised me. I never expected to feel so alone. They'd been dead so long already. It drained me. I stopped sleeping. My last hope of someone seeing the new distinct fire and seeking me out dwindled after that."

"The transmissions gave me something to live for. I closed my eyes to listen to the melodic rhythms of the different speakers to let their words drip over me like toffee syrup for the purest of comfort. That brings me up to date, Rosalie."

"Oh Ren, thank you. I'm so glad to hear about you and my dad. This gives me thoughts to hold onto while I heal from all these injuries. Anatole told you about how he found me, didn't he?"

"Yes, he told me. It's amazing that you survived."

"There's a group of us now, and I know you'll find people to be with again, too. I'll pray on that for you. Well, Anatole is signaling me to sign off with you. They need the rig for another scheduled transmission. We'll talk again soon. Bye-bye Ren."

"Bye Rosalie."

I have to remember Rosalie's words. What were they...I'm not responsible for the whole world, just for a little piece for myself. Yes, that was it. I need to remember this. But the length of time to the next transmission overwhelmed Ren with grim anxiety, even with the simple words to focus on, his hope faltered.

While listening to another transmission, he heard that a new U.S. governing body started up in Spokane, Washington. The former U.S. capitol, Washington, D.C. and its population was lost on the day of the quakes according to the person speaking. With only a few participants on the east coast of the U.S., sketchy descriptions of the destroyed shoreline were available. So far it is known that the east coast now followed the highest points of the Blue Ridge, Pocono and Catskill mountain ridges dramatically shifted from the past coastline.

An aging senator from Wyoming, who just happened to be vacationing in nearby Spokane, and Spokane's city council, began talks to set up emergency services and a new governing system. Since the rampage of the asteroid's impact forced its way eastward following the low trajectory, Spokane's damaged areas were less because the eruptions and quaking slowed down by the time they rippled around the world. When the quakes started in the Spokane area, a few of the oldest buildings were lost, including The Davenport Hotel Memorial to the floods of 2035 and the old bridge across the Spokane River.

The city council for this stable community prided itself in its twenty year old motto, the "last hold-out for reason and caring in the United States". This motto attracted many large families and teachers to the community during the same time period. The twenty years prior to the cataclysm, Spokane leadership and its populace grew their city into a moral and studious place where families thrived and politics of the "new age" of technology were left at the city limits. Belief in people, not machines, remained strong. Struggles with philosophies, to keep the libraries open seven-days-a-week and the music programs in schools won over the dominant extra-curricular sports programs. The retention of sports only through the physical education programs inside the curriculum remained. The city council members, mostly educators and doctors by trade, used this challenge to resurrect ideals long left behind by all other governing bodies throughout the world since the 2020's and before. The thousands of Spokane citizens lost that day were like family members for everyone. Definitely less than the rest of the world, but tragic, none the less, for this close knit community.

At first, when Ren heard the transmissions and spoke with Rosalie about her dad, he sounded positive under the circumstances. However, on the last transmission, everyone heard Ren's impatience and anxiety. His depression grew after burning the dead bodies. He never talked about it, but being alone, made his mind trip up and caused erratic behavior. His comments followed suit. It concerned all who spoke to him, because he interrupted the transmissions by cutting off people during their scheduled time to speak. He sounded agitated and nervous. Hearing the positive words about Spokane, which focused on a moral life style Ren understood; he began to feel hopeful again. The thought of staying alone in the lost Colorado Springs area, limited any hope for his future. His loneliness bred fear. The thought of isolation for the rest of his life terrified him. He made a decision to leave Colorado. Even though walking through a shattered countryside to Spokane would take a very long time, he knew Spokane offered survival. This became his focus. *I'll think about what Rosalie said. I'm only responsible for my little piece of the world. No matter how long it takes me to get to Spokane, my world will encompass me every day.* Ren knew where he belonged…Spokane. No point for him to wait, he left right away.

His regular messages stopped the next day. No one knew what happened to Ren and although he managed to make portable equipment to take with him for transmissions, power sources became a problem; no one ever heard from him again. The other scheduled transmission participants presumed and accepted that he died. From then on the other operators referred to him as a "Silent Key", a dead HAM operator.

FIVE

Enrico, surprised to book last minute vacation reservations so easily, told his wife Katherine, about his success. She expected it.

"Remember all the warnings about the asteroid hitting Earth sometime around now? I've been hearing about people actually believing the scams and people are traveling less here in Europe. Funny thing though, news programs on PDS say that people in the United States appear to be ignoring the predictions. Travel is at a normal rate. Hotels are filled at their spring and summer high levels. I don't know what to think. All I know is, we'll be together, wherever we go, so if it's true or not, it doesn't matter." They held each other and Enrico caressed his wife's cheek as he gently kissed her.

Enrico traveled with his family to the City of Milano for their vacation. Katherine liked a view from high up, so he arranged for a hotel room on the fortieth floor of the new Milano Arms International Plus properties. From that level, the view overlooked the whole city and beyond.

Katherine fussed over the twins clothing for the day, so he decided to go down to the lobby to arrange for a couple tours of the city.

"Take your time, after all we got up earlier than planned; I'll arrange for everything during the time it takes you to finish dressing Marnia and Terenia. We're on vacation, so there's no need to rush," he smiled over his shoulder when he left their room, and realized he was the one with the impatience, not his calm and beautiful wife.

He took his own advice. Enrico daydreamed and walked to the elevator. As he rode down to the lobby, he closed his eyes and enjoyed the serenity of the ideal vacation. He knew Katherine needed extra time to finish dressing the girls, so he slowed down to a snail's pace.

At the concierge desk, Enrico waited for the tour tickets to be printed. He looked around and saw the large picture windows which faced the street; however, at that very moment, the windows looked strange. They were rounded half bubbles. Two other hotel guests stood near him with their dogs, returning from their morning routine. The dogs began to bark, just before the windows burst outward into the street spraying minute pieces of shattered glass like glitter tossed on New Year's Eve. The crashing and explosive sounds and the immediate screams of the other hotel patrons became thunderous. Quaking threw Enrico abruptly to the floor. The constant shaking and the slippery marble kept him down; he crawled to the now open windows and out onto the sidewalk. The rougher concrete helped him to feel a little more stable, but the glass from the broken windows cut his hands and knees. Screaming pierced his ears. The rumbling sounds of the shaking buildings roared. The street in front of him opened up into a huge crack, the moving cars crashed and fell in out of control with the parked cars disappearing right behind. It broadened even more. The laundry in the hotel's basement exploded. Bleach and detergent permeated the dusty air. Clouds of steam draped the confusion with annoying hissing it's accompaniment. The hotel swayed and bricks shot like mortar shells when they exploded outward. Parts of the hotel tumbled to the ground. Unable to move, Enrico never got to his feet to run. His mind raced, *why did I always have to be so impatient? I should be with Kat and the girls.*

An older man grabbed Enrico's arm at the elbow and dragged him away from the building just when the thunderous hotel started collapsing. He pulled Enrico into a stairwell at the edge of the sidewalk and screamed as both men fell down many steps. Enrico's body painfully came to a stop when he hit his head, knocking him unconscious. He knew he came-to quickly because the quaking still tossed him violently. His forehead felt like an explosion of throbs, and blood ran into his left eye. When he tried to wipe it away, he couldn't. Debris of all kinds fell in on him which made it impossible to move. A jagged piece of concrete made a direct hit on the back side of his upper left arm, just above the elbow. Pinned underneath it, the pain stopped him from moving. The ground kept shaking, "Why doesn't it stop?" He yelled to the old man who fell with him, "Are you okay mister? Hey, can you hear me? I think my arm is broken. I can't move. Hey, can you hear me?"

No reply made Enrico believe the old man saved him, but died during his last courageous act. Just when Enrico felt the man's leg underneath him, the hotel exploded again. The loud blast pierced Enrico's hearing as if someone turned on a light switch and the heat wave hit his body like a sharp slap on the face. His back burned with the constant heat. He fell face down, that's how the concrete pinned him. While he pushed his face into the gravel to keep it covered for moments away from the heat, he prayed, *please save me God.* Debris toppled everywhere and the powerful blast shot right over the stairwell where Enrico remained almost buried. Pieces of gravel spit at him and stung the back of his head. Smoke and dust choked him. He screamed when something stabbed his leg and became agitated when he couldn't see what it was. He knew he needed to free his left arm, to be agile enough to help himself sit up.

Enrico twisted around and moved his right arm to touch the concrete piece still on top of his other arm. He could barely see, because of the murky smoke. The concrete piece appeared to be standing on end. One good push with his shoulder would tip it enough to fall away, freeing his upper body.

"AAhhh...there," he boosted himself up with his right arm and the concrete fell downward a couple more steps toward the other side of the stairwell. *Maybe I can sit up now, if the shaking ground doesn't stop me.* He pushed himself around to see how bad his arm looked. *HHHmmm...not so bad,* surprised not to see more blood everywhere.

Enrico heard building parts fall to the ground. People's screams rang in his ears. *Please don't let any of those screams be my family. How will I ever be able to find them?* To keep the gravel and dust out of his eyes, he buried his face in the curve of his arm. He wept; fear overtook his thoughts. *"Oh Kat, where are you? Please God help me get out of here."*

The shaking ground tossed him over and over again and each time he tried to move up one more step away from the depth of the stairwell and the expanding wreckage. Additional quakes packed the debris down harder on top of him. He managed to stay close to the edge of the opening now that he moved. More debris fell into the deep part of the stairs. He called out to the man below, but still no reply.

When the violent quaking stopped, the stairwell contained broken cement, brick and splintered wood pieces. Unable to move, with his legs and most of his torso severely confined, Enrico was trapped. The fumes and the thick dust filled the air like a stirred pot. His throat burned from choking and coughing. The dust he breathed in tasted like smoldering charcoal, gagging him. His only thoughts were about getting free, so he could find his family. *No more crying. I have to focus. Where are Kat, Mari and Teri?* He tried to scream, but gasped for air when more smoke and dust constricted his throat.

Being near the higher part of the stairwell, he knew rescue would be imminent. His shoulders, arms and head showed and confidently he relaxed a little with the thought that he would be easily seen. He looked at his watch still attached to his wrist, but the crystal was smashed and it was no longer running.

After a long time, probably several hours, Enrico didn't hear the hopeful sounds of the rescue he expected. It took what seemed like forever for the dust to settle and even though it settled, it was still not clear air. With so many fires, the smoke billowed high in the sky scattered by prevailing winds. Steam still shot out of the ground, and Enrico heard lingering building pieces fall helter-skelter.

There should be sirens, he kept telling himself. *I read about the City of Milano, which completed state-of-the-art police and fire emergency systems two years ago. Their response time was down to under three minutes anywhere in the city.* The most positive news headlines released in a long time became one of the reasons Enrico and Katherine chose Milano as their vacation spot. *Why don't I hear any sirens? It's been hours.*

"HELLO, CAN ANYONE HEAR ME?" Over and over he yelled, but with no response, he panicked and strained to move his body, stopping when pain struck in his legs. *I'm caught; how can I get out?* His thoughts raced with fear for himself and his family. `

Crackling embers close by and loud enough to hear made him stop writhing around. He smelled wood burning. Enrico never thought much about the sound of fire, but the recognizable whirring sound scared him deep inside. *With no fire department response, burning to death would be a horrible way to die. Stop that, think about something else.* That last thought triggered a dazed feeling, like a rush of adrenalin; fatigue took over. He drifted off to sleep and dreamed he found his girls.

Shaking woke him. He knew he'd only slept a short time and remembered the dream, *oh God it was only a dream, oh God, where are they?*

"There's that annoying sound again." *Why is the*

steam pressure still so strong? After so many hours, the pressure should be less, so I wouldn't be hearing it anymore. He listened, but heard no other sounds, just the steam. *Well, at least it's not fire like it was earlier.* The ground shook every few minutes, after-shocks from what he guessed to be a massive earthquake.

His legs felt cold and numb from the pressure of the debris. He squirmed around as much as possible with his torso hoping to loosen some of the objects which still buried his lower body. His left arm looked very swollen and already began to bruise, so his right arm became the tool to remove everything that encumbered him. After he moved a couple pieces of concrete and able to twist a little more to the side, he saw what held him down. Nothing too big, just bricks and wood, 2 x 4 pieces, which gave him hope. All the debris which lay on top of him, jammed in very tight as the hotel fell. Every single movement caused him pain. He screamed over and over again. *Why doesn't anyone come? Someone should hear me.*

Slowly he moved the bricks off his legs. During one of the rest periods he allowed himself, he heard a scuffing sound, and intermittent whimpering, almost childlike. At first far away, but it became closer as the day progressed.

Enrico tried to be patient, and yelled to see if anyone answered, but still no reply.

Working backwards he agonized to pull each piece of debris off his legs with only one hand, grunting and moaning with each action. During his next rest period he dozed off, and woke up after a couple minutes. Above him, on the opposite side of the stairwell, a small dog, dirty and bleeding over his eye, stood looking down at him. It looked like a dachshund, but so dirty his brown coat looked dusty black.

"Hey there, are you here to rescue me? I sure hope so. What, no reply? Maybe we'll take care of each other. You stay right there. I'll be out of here by tomorrow," he spoke to the dog like a friend who would wait.

The dachshund lay next to the top of the stairwell and watched while Enrico made progress with the rubble. The little dog kept its distance. Its eyes never left Enrico as he worked to free himself. After all the work that day, Enrico lay exhausted. He fell asleep right at dusk and woke up at dawn to find the sweet little dog snuggled next to his body, just underneath Enrico's stretched out arm. The dog's warmth against his cold body comforted him.

"Today I will move my legs," he said, as he reached out to pat the dog's dirty coat, but the action startled the dog and he scrambled away. He stayed just far enough away that Enrico couldn't reach him. "Okay, I know, you're as scared as I am. I'll take it slow with you."

The discomfort of the numbing in his calves became almost unbearable and kept him from any true rest as the day progressed. About noon time the second day, Enrico managed to remove the last of the bricks, but the 2 x 4 pieces landed as if a dagger jammed into the ground. Enrico's minimal body movement slowed his excavation, and, being face down, although a blessing at first hindered his removing the debris which trapped him. Each time he rocked a 2 x 4 piece back and forth, he tired more quickly. The third one he pulled from the debris came out so suddenly, it threw him sideways hard, hitting his head on the wall of the stairwell. As he slid his hand down the wood piece to give him leverage to toss it away, his hand felt wet. Enrico looked at his hand. It was blood. In the split second realization that it wasn't his own blood, he knew it came from the man below him in the stairwell. The old man that saved his life; "Oh God, why doesn't this nightmare end? How do You expect me to continue, if every step I encounter more tragedy." Enrico's tears streamed down his dirty cheeks. He laid forward and sobbed, and prayed for his family and the old man.

Already forty eight hours with no water or food, his body's weaknesses slowed him considerably. With the last of the wood discarded, Enrico was free to move again. He rolled over. His legs shook when he tried to lift them. Barely able to move his left arm, his right arm served him as he rubbed his thighs to get some circulation back. His back ached as he turned over and leaned forward to rub his calves. He moved his legs very slowly, but his left leg hurt much worse so he stopped. He twisted his lower body to the right to see. A piece of a mirror, shaped like a dagger, protruded from his outer calf. "CAN ANYONE HEAR ME; I NEED HELP. HELLO, PLEASE HELP ME." With no reply and the little dog disappearing when he heard Enrico yelling, he knew he had no one to rely on except himself. *I hope the little dog will come back. I didn't want to scare him. Now I'm alone again.*

Somehow the bleeding at the point of entry for the mirror piece stopped; blood scabbed around the edges of the wound. Enrico never heard of that happening before, but didn't dwell on it. He worked on. The mirror needed to be removed.

The little dog returned to the back end of the stairwell. "Hey you, I'm so glad you came back. I see you're staying farther away from me. I guess I don't blame you. I didn't mean to scare you away by yelling like that. Please stick it out this time. I don't want to be alone and I don't think you do either."

"You know, I should have worn long pants today. Maybe then this dagger piece might have slipped off my leg"...*Oh, brother, will you stop with the 'should-a could-a' scenarios!* As Enrico spoke to his new friend, the little dog laid it's head on its front paws with a big sigh and watched. Luckily that morning, Enrico grabbed a bandana from the suitcase. He reached into his pocket, "I'll need to wrap my calf tight after I remove the glass, don't you think?" He spoke out loud to the dog.

Enrico wrapped the bandana around the glass piece and held it with his right hand. "Okay, on three...one, two, three...aahhh." He passed out. When he awoke, the bleeding already stopped. He knew he lay unconscious for a couple hours, because the sun, lower in the sky, moved dramatically during that time. His little friend licked Enrico's wound. The ticklish feeling of the dog's tongue brought him around. "You'll be a handy friend, won't you?

I wonder if your licking my wound saved my life. Will you help me find my girls? That would make me feel like my life is saved for sure."

From the stairwell, he saw smoking rubble everywhere he looked. After he tied his leg wound, he carefully stood. Enrico's legs shook and his back ached from being pinned down so long. His calf started to bleed again.

Now on his feet, he saw the hotel, destroyed and still burning. The trailing smoke moved skyward in endless waves. The foreground which faced Enrico looked like a bomb went off leaving piles of rubble, bricks and broken concrete. Although he knew their burial places were right in front of him, he fought to keep that thought of his family out of his mind. The aftershocks kept knocking him off his feet. Each time Enrico fell, the little dog ran away, but only far enough to keep him in sight and easing back to Enrico's side after only a few minutes.

When Enrico saw the vast crevasse in the road, only three feet away from where he lay trapped in the stairwell he grabbed his head and screamed. "Can anyone hear me? HELP!" Everywhere he turned all he saw were piles of concrete and destroyed cars, but no people. Most of the hotel toppled into the crevasse which ran up the distance of the famous boulevard. The new hotel had been built on ruins of an earlier hotel, attached to the Teatro Lirico theatre, burned down in a horrific fire many years before. The stories of this neighborhood were part of historic Milano near the Royal Palace of Milan and one of the reasons Enrico and Kat chose to vacation there. Since the hotel fell away from him in the stairwell, Enrico survived. This blessing ate at him. Seeing the hotel destroyed, literally in piles of concrete, bricks and erratic broken rebar, his thoughts ran wild with the horror his wife and daughters experienced in their last moments of life. "Oh Kat, I wasn't with you after all and we just talked about being together if something happened over this vacation. Oh God..." He fell to his knees, sobbing.

He slept, but when he woke, focused on the destruction around him. It wasn't until then that Enrico saw dead bodies and body parts, almost everywhere. So caught up in his own situation until that time, Enrico's reality of the tragedy began to set in. *"Oh Kat, I miss you My Love."* The little dog lay next to him. Enrico's shoulders heaved in and out as he cried. He could barely catch his breath. Wave after wave of crying kept him immobilized, until he realized he had no more tears. He needed water.

"Where should I go?" he asked the little dog. "There must be others who have survived; you and I can't be the only ones." Enrico decided on a name for his new little friend, "I'm going to call you Rubble. After all that's where you came from, out of the rubble," he smiled at his friend and patted him. Rubble didn't run away this time; he stayed close to Enrico as he stumbled through the ravaged streets, with bodies strewn everywhere. Every once in a while when someone's body wasn't ripped apart, Enrico touched their wrist or neck for a pulse, but found no one alive.

Enrico located a destroyed pharmacy and crawled through the piles of broken rows of shelves. He found water in the older style plastic bottles only recently outlawed in Italy and poured out water for Rubble into an upside down broken picture frame. After that he proceeded to drink down four bottles himself. It tasted so good, and relieved the scratchy feeling in his throat. He looked through piles of damaged tubes of products, managing to scavenge a tube of topical antibiotic. He medicated his throbbing leg wound. Keeping the wound clean became difficult with so much dust from all the fallen buildings.

He searched and searched for his family. His hands bled from all the rough edged bricks he pulled off bodies, each time hoping to see the face of his wife or one of his daughters. After days of foraging through the destroyed hotel and enduring the dead body stench, his anxiety grew. Enrico had no logical thoughts of what to do and one afternoon he walked away from the hotel area for no particular reason. He ended up near one of the demolished old canals connected to the Po River. The debris looked like it had been through great flooding. Near an antiquated dike, broken down and entrenched with debris, he heard crying. He lifted a couple pieces of aluminum siding and the crying became louder. Underneath, he found a rowboat filled with blankets and pillows, which encased a young girl. She sat up and shielded her eyes from the daylight, even though the sky was overcast and still smokey. At first she wouldn't speak to Enrico, but Rubble warmed her heart and she spoke directly to the dog after several hours. The young girl, whose parents placed her in a boat at the edge of one of the old canals, covered her with blankets and pillows and went to get her older brother who had been playing in the park. They never came back. She stayed in the small boat, just like her parents told her to and the eight year old miraculously survived. Her name was Cristiana and after Enrico found her, she followed him and Rubble everywhere they went.

Enrico spent time trying to get back to the destroyed hotel to look for his family. He never found his way and never found his wife and twin daughters. After a short time, he stopped talking. Rubble stayed close to him, but Cristiana wanted to talk and when he stopped, she wandered off alone. Depressed, his only solace was his new little friend, Rubble, who stayed loyally at his side. When he encountered a group of survivors about a week later, he was very happy to see Cristiana there. Their reunion jarred Enrico's reality. "Why did you leave us? I'm so glad to see you. I was worried about you, but felt frozen and unable to look for you. It was too much. I'm so sorry."

Cristiana listened while she hugged Enrico, "It's okay, see over there." She pointed to some of the group stacking food supplies to be organized. "That lady in the orange shirt is my mother. I found my way back to my neighborhood and I found her there. Together we buried my dad and my brother and then we started walking and found these people. So you see, what happened to you helped me. I'm so glad to see you again, though. I wanted you to know, I found my mom."

To overcome his loss, he kept busy looking for food with the group of survivors and Cristiana. They also disposed of dead bodies. Finding Cristiana gave Enrico a new outlook. She reminded him of Teri and Mari, even though they were several years younger. He realized that good things can still happen even though the sadness overpowered him in waves.

To escape the horrors in Milan and get away from the area which every day triggered the painful memories of the last day with his family, he decided to leave the city. He walked west toward, Monesteroli, the coastal town of his youth near the Cinque Terre National Park. With Rubble at his side, he left Cristiana behind, safe in her mother's care.

After several months of difficult walking and sporadic times with minimal food, Enrico arrived back in the area where he grew up and found it very different, almost unrecognizable. With the whole countryside ravaged by the quakes, there were hardly any survivors. His family moved away more than thirty years before, so he had no ties there any longer, exactly why he wanted to return. After looking around for a couple weeks, he met a group of survivors who offered him work and a life-line to food stores they scavenged since the quakes occurred. His little friend, Rubble, was a hit with everyone. They wanted him to stay close to their encampment at the top of the cliffs, but Enrico was determined to be close to the water. "Don't worry about me and Rubble; we'll come to work with you often. I've dreamed of living close to the water, but never had the chance. Now it's time for me to act on what I want for myself. It will help me through missing my family." His new friends nodded in agreement and all looked off into the distance as if realizing they were doing the same thing, all in their own ways.

The rocky coast, now very disrupted by the quakes, provided ample supplies to build steps to the beach from the steep terrain above. That's what he tackled first. The local teams supported his idea. They found lumber for Enrico to use and surprised him the first morning after he finished building the steps. "We can help you get the wood down to the shoreline, Enrico."

"Oh no, this is my endeavor. You're already so great to have found wood and building supplies for me. I will take the wood down, as I need to. Keeping it away from the moisture from the sea water, will make the wood easier to work with. I'll be fine and come to work with your team every Tuesday."

Enrico chose a space in a cove with a view to the north and started to build. It took him a long time to get the wood down the steps to create the small building, but once complete, their new home kept them safe from rain and wind brought in by coastal storms. Rubble flourished and regularly chased the sparse population of sandpipers through the sand. Enrico kept to himself, except for working weekly with the small population of the Liguria Region who lived in the encampment above, about a mile south on the cliff. He kept his mind and body occupied and drew up plans to build a boat.

SIX

Named for an American cousin, Doug Magnusson suffered relentless teasing year after year growing up in Norway. None of his classmates ever heard his given name before. His anguish tugged at his grandfather's heartstrings. The teasing followed Doug from class to class. To help shift his grandson's minds focus, he started teaching Doug to scuba dive on his seventh birthday. From then on, Doug vacationed every year with his grandfather, at his Oslofjord coastal summer home in Moss.

When the tidal wave hit from the west and rolled around the southern tip of Norway raising the level of the Skagerrak Sea, it also raised the waters of the Oslofjord. Doug and his grandfather dove off the coast, just south of

Moss. This was the first excursion on the new twenty five foot motor boat Doug's granddad bought with all new equipment. Recognizing the shifting water, Doug's grandfather tried to stay calm and not scare his grandson, "We can't dive today, Doug. The currents are too erratic. It's too dangerous." Underneath his calm exterior, panic grew. In his experience, the water flow and rolling level of the waves told him, tidal wave. He saw this same thing ten years before. The more Doug's grandfather kept watch of the closest landmass, the more his agitation showed. Doug never saw him this way before.

"Granddad your face is pale. What's wrong? Are you feeling sick? Do you want to eat some lunch?"

"NO, not now," he said, "I'm okay right now. You don't need to worry."

Even though his grandfather said no, Doug knew something was wrong. *Granddad never yells at me; not even a single word.*

After half an hour, his grandfather tugged at his shirt near his collar and started to breathe erratically. Leaning forward he grabbed Doug's shoulders. They both hit the floor on their knees. The boat rocked wildly, while Doug tried to get his bearings. "Granddad, can you breathe? Relax. Come-on…just relax. Try to take a deep breath."

He clutched his chest. Tears came to Doug's eyes. He offered his granddad a drink and helped him unbutton his shirt. Nothing helped. Doug found pillows and a blanket in the boat's storage cabinets and pushed him on his side, covered and propped up with extra pillows. His granddad clawed his chest even more with his right arm; his left arm lay limp. Doug knew about heart attacks, but never saw one before and lay down next to him. His grandfather coughed as he spoke. His voice, barely audible gave the horrible facts to his favorite grandson. "It's a tidal wave, Doug, and it's very big. It has already covered a lot of our country. It started earlier this morning; I saw it start as we were preparing to dive. While I watched the high water currents raise at the shore, they took over the land." Coughing again his granddad stopped to take extra breaths. Barely able to get air into his lungs anymore, he tugged at his shirt. Tears in his eyes, "I'm going to die here, Doug."

"No Grandpa, no, no, no, please don't say that," Doug leaned over and hugged him.

"Don't cry, my sweet boy. I need to tell you things." Again he gasped for breath. "Listen close to what

I say. After I'm dead, every few hours until you're rescued, sprinkle ocean water on my body, and be sure to cover my head. It will be too difficult for you, if you don't," he whispered into Doug's ear. *Oh Doug I can't tell you to place my body in the water for a burial at sea. It's too drastic an instruction.* "If you drift to a landmass, be sure to stay in the boat as long as you can. It is the safest place to be right now. Wait for rescuers to help you."

When his grandfather spoke those last words, Doug stood up to look toward shore. He turned in every direction; no land anywhere. He fell to his knees sobbing unable to catch his breath. Lying down next to his grandfather, Doug held him tight in their last loving hug. His whispers became weaker and even less audible, so Doug started to talk to give him relief. His grandfather's body relaxed and he listened to Doug say, "I love you, Granddad. I'm glad we were together today." After that Doug felt his granddad's arm fall away from his shoulder and he knew his grandfather died.

"NO...GRANDDAD," He cried and sobbed for a long time, and fell asleep nestled up to his grandfather's body.

Doug woke as the boat jerked from the erratic

waves. His mind crashed into reality when he felt his grandfather's lifeless body next to him. He sat up and looked over at his grandfather's face. His eyes were closed. He looked asleep and it made Doug think that his grandfather may still be alive. Doug's heart started beating fast and he placed his hand on his grandfather's chest, pressing down to see if he felt his heartbeat; nothing. He picked up his hand, and felt around for a pulse, like he'd seen in so many old movies and read about in stories; nothing. Reality returned. *Yes, I'm sure this time. This strong man, who taught me how to dive and to love the water, will no longer share a future with me.* With tears flooding his cheeks, he covered his grandfather's head. He found a drinking cup and over and over again scooped sea water to pour over the body. Once finished, Doug gently laid the cup on the floor of the boat, as if trying not to wake his granddad.

Doug felt numb all over and stared out over the water, still seeing nothing in any direction. He cried again sobbing hard. After he sat for a bit, he felt his stomach growl. He needed to eat. The picnic lunch still sat untouched. *Now what was it Grandpa whispered near the end. I could barely hear it. It was something about the food. Oh, I remember, eat and drink as little as possible; make it last. Oh Granddad; I'm so scared!*

Doug followed his grandfather's instructions, but even doing that, the food ran out at about seven days. The drinks and water lasted longer, to the ninth day.

He tried to stay at the opposite end of the boat away from his granddad's body and out of the sun as much as he could. Sunburn became an issue after the first week, when he ran out of sun screen products. Since he was drinking so little, his muscles hurt, and he cried so much, he had no tears anymore.

Doug first saw a tiny dot on the horizon the thirteenth day. After an hour it was larger and he knew it was a ship coming toward him. When he thought it was close enough, he stood up and waved a seat cushion back and forth over his head. After a few minutes the ship looked like it slowed down. The horn blew three times. Doug knew they saw him. He sat down and cried, "Oh Granddad, they saw me. Thank God. I've run out of food; I'm so scared, and I'm so weak."

Doug maneuvered his motor boat next to the ocean liner loaded with travelers from the United States. He was twelve years old.

The ship's captain said a few words over his grandfather in a short funeral service. Doug listened to the words, but didn't understand what he said. The captain's deep voice, along with the fact he spoke very slowly, frustrated and upset Doug. Although he learned English in school since age six, Doug never heard it spoken by Americans before; it sounded different and very slow. The captain spoke the slowest of everyone he heard so far. Many people came to the service even though Doug was a stranger. When each person spoke to him, he could tell they focused hard on what he said. One boy about his age said, "Why do you talk so fast? It's hard to understand you." Doug just shook his head in disbelief and smiled.

At the end of the service, his grandfather's body slid into the water, for the sea burial. Doug stood at the railing for a very long time. He watched where his grandfather's body went into the water and thought, *now I understand why you didn't tell me what to do in more detail. I wouldn't have been able to put your body overboard. Oh Granddad, I know you loved the water so much, this must be right for you.*

Most everyone he encountered during the first days on the ship, were kind to him, but there were a few people who were upset when the captain picked him up. He overheard their conversations. They talked very loud and didn't care if Doug heard them. The reason for their anger, food rations needed to be shared with an additional person. Doug was not the first person picked up since the disaster, so people were on edge. They were worried about food. The captain followed the standard international rules of sea, and to rescue survivors became a priority.

Several kind people on the ship took him under their wings; they attempted to console his loss and prepared him for the understanding that everyone he ever knew was now dead. They listened to his heartbreaking story. He told how his grandfather died and about their last conversation. Doug found it difficult to tell, because when he told the story, he relived it all over again.

One family comforted Doug; he stayed with them in their cabin. They were kind to him offering gentle hugs, treating his sunburn and giving him daytime privacy to nap and heal. When the water subsided in Norway, the ship docked in the Oslofjord southeast of the destroyed Oslo. The crew and the passengers decided altogether to stay in Norway, even though they were torn by the tragedy and missed their homes and families. With no pumps working to refuel the ship, it stayed moored and remained everyone's home for several years. Doug's new family treated him well and although they were always kind, right from the beginning, they never connected with him. They were from New York City and didn't understand why he always wanted to talk about diving and fishing. He just never fit in. As a result, when he turned fifteen, Doug ran off to find his own way. Most of the time, he walked, scavenged and moved south. Several times he came upon groups of people, where he tried to make his way in their life pathways, but Doug chose not to stay long. Those groups didn't focus on a new start; they lingered in the sadness of the past.

Doug moved south to warmer weather. He knew living near the water would provide a good life for him.

One night walking near a rocky beach on the west coast of Italy, a fire blazed in the distance. Its glow drew him closer where he saw only one man in its light enjoying the lazy evening. "Helllllooo, may I approach? You're fire acts like an invitation."

A dog barked and the man jumped to his feet, startled by Doug's greeting.

"Are you alone or do you travel with others?"

"I'm alone…just passing through. My name is Doug. May I come in closer?"

"Absolutely, come have some dinner with me. I was just about to cook my catch of the day." The man smiled as he saw the traveler's face and bent over to quiet the dog with some comforting pats. "You look as if a good meal would be perfect right about now."

"You have no idea. I always try to walk a little farther every day, and put off eating, then fall asleep hungry." Doug reached out to shake hands, but instead received a big bear hug.

"Welcome to Monesteroli! There are only a few of us around in this region, but we've put together good lives. My name is Enrico and this is my friend, Rubble. I'm sure he'll get used to you in a few minutes. You're our first visitor to come along alone like this in a long time."

Enrico rambled on while Doug got comfortable next to the warm fire. They spent hours that night speaking about the past. "Where were you when the quakes occurred?"

"On a boat with my granddad, he was my best friend. He taught me how to dive. I spent every summer with him for five years, until I was twelve."

"Oh, where's your grandfather now? Did he stay in Norway?"

"Well, no, not exactly. He died on the boat with me. He knew the tidal wave hit land all around us and he didn't want me to know at first. I think he was so upset inside, trying to keep it from me; it was just too much for him. He had a heart attack and died in front of me... a cruise ship rescued me. I think it was after two weeks. The captain of the ship worked out a service for Granddad and put his body to rest in the water off the side of the ship. I remember at the time thinking Granddad would be glad to be buried at sea. He so loved the water. I try not to think about it too much anymore."

"I'm sorry, Doug. I know we all have sadness to leave behind." They both stared into the fire and fell asleep next to the crackling embers.

It took Doug five years to get there and now at twenty years of age, for the first time since his grandfather died, he found friendship in their immediate good rapport.

"You should consider staying around here, Doug. You sound like you love the water like I do."

"It would be nice to rest and not always be on the move. It's been a long time for me." Doug relaxed as he ate the fish Enrico cooked for breakfast.

"Sure. At least you could stay awhile and see how you like it here. I can be pretty good company, just ask Rubble." They laughed. Doug stayed.

Enrico told Doug about the amateur radio communications that began coming through from Jerusalem, a few years before. To build a new future and to work, felt good. In their limited spare time, they finished the boat Enrico started. Together they dreamed about a better future.

SEVEN

Directed to turn in early by their sailing trainer, all twelve scouts from Texas, agreed that getting up at 4 a.m. would be a challenge. No one fought the suggestion; they were ready for sleep after their long travel day. Adrenalin kept them going up to that point. Excitement raged when they talked about learning how to work on and sail a tall ship, the newest program attached to the marine biology teaching center in Norris Point. The twelve were awarded three-weeks training with free round-trips to Newfoundland, for their exceptional work completing the wilderness first-aid and sailing badge programs.

Slumber came over all twelve of the travelers the moment they fell into bed. Their accommodations were cottages on the northern side of Bonne Bay. This part of the package endowed through the International Maritime Historical Society was near the ancient Viking Trail, Route 430.

Explosions woke the scouts. They all emerged from their cottages at the same time, several tripping when they ran down the wooden steps in their untied sneakers. The darkness engulfed them with only the explosive sounds piercing the night air.

TJ looked for Don, their troop leader. "Whatever this is, it's big. Quick, grab your gear, there's no time to dress. We need to get to another place," TJ screamed as the ground started to shake. "GET RIGHT BACK HERE IN ONE MINUTE."

They welcomed TJ's words. Glad to have direction, all the scouts scattered. The oldest of the scouts, TJ turned fifteen on his last birthday, a couple days before Christmas. The first to complete the badge requirements, he challenged the rest of his friends to do the same. They could enter the contest together, if they all finished by March 1st. The whirlwind of successes produced their winnings at the presentation ceremony in Dallas on April 15th.

The youngest scout, Sammy, turned twelve the day before they left for Newfoundland. His parents gave permission to go, since their troop leader would also go with them. They departed from Dallas May 11th.

Angus, the first back to their designated place with his gear, yelled for their leader, Don, but there was no answer. The other scouts ran toward him. The ground shook, and there was a rushing and crushing sound over toward Bonne Bay. Scared, he yelled for the others to hurry, "Where are you TJ? Come on, we gotta get out of here! Something's coming; it's getting closer. I can hear it."

TJ and Sammy came out together, with TJ pulling Sammy's backpack strap over him arm, as they ran down the steps. "Did anyone see Don?"

All replied, no. "I yelled for him, but he didn't answer," Angus said. "Maybe he went to that bar we saw when we drove through town. After all, we were settled in bed, four by four by four, so no one was alone."

"Yeah that's possible," TJ said. His mind raced, *what do we do next?*

"SSHHH, listen," Angus said. "Do you hear that

rushing sound?"

They stood absolutely still. An explosion made them jump and their heads jerked to see. About a half mile away down the hill, the sparks flew like fireworks.

"What's doing that?" TJ said out loud, but not meaning to.

"That kind of explosion happens when an electrical transformer breaks down," Glenn said.

"I don't know about that, but listen there's that rushing sound. Do you hear it?" Angus said. They were quiet again.

"Its water," TJ said, "Come on, we need to get to a higher place. Find your flashlights. Let's go over to the main hall where we registered."

"Run." Angus said. "Come on everybody, and watch out for rocks. Remember our wilderness training."

The rocking ground catapulted their steps through the darkness toward the main hall.

TJ was the first to run up the steps. Surprised by the locked door, "That's strange. They said we'd have access

24/7." Banging on the door, "Anybody there?" he yelled over and over. *The manager did hit it off with Don as we checked in. They talked about getting to know each other. Maybe they went somewhere together.*

"Hey TJ, that rushing sound is louder now, and there's crashing, too...listen." Angus' voice grew panicky.

TJ turned around in a circle, checking the whole perimeter. Too dark, to see anything, he ran around to the back of the main hall. The others followed. A spotlight pole 500 feet from the back of the building stood next to rowboats stacked on a rack.

"Over there, come on," pointing to the spotlight. "Faster you guys. Run. The water is right behind us. We need three of those boats to get all of us in." He was out of breath.

Before they reached the boats, there was another explosion. The flood light ahead of them went out.

Even with no lights their teamwork proved efficient in getting the boats down. Two were rowboats, about twelve feet long. The other two on the rack were the same, but each with a removable motor at the rear. They only had time to get three of the boats down and only one of them had a motor.

TJ looked over his shoulder, "Oh my God, everybody, quick, get into the boats. Sammy, get in the same boat with me. Come on, come on, the water is rushing right toward us, past the hall already," TJ yelled louder now. "Hold tight to the sides of the boats. Keep the oars inside, so we won't lose them. Stay as close to the center of the boat as possible. Hold on for your life."

Pieces of wood hit the boats first, throwing Jake, Scott and Joe over the side with the initial jolt. They grabbed the sides of their boat hoping to get back in, but the water crashed too hard with huge momentum. The wood pieces hit Scott on his head; he had no chance to hold on. The other two, yanked out of sight, disappeared in the raging water and dark night. After Jake, Scott and Joe were lost, Mikey Two and Rob were alone in one boat.

The first wave of rushing water capsized the boat with Angus, Mikey One, and Walt. They screamed in the early morning blackness. Broken trees, mixed in with pieces of wreckage, pushed along by the water took their lives in seconds.

Glenn, Sammy, TJ and Jeremy were in the boat

with the motor. The extra weight kept their boat stable when the raging water hit.

"Whatever happens, meet back at Bonne Bay near the tall ship." TJ yelled to the other boats at the top of his lungs. The water raged so loud and pushed them along so fast, he didn't know if they heard him. They were separated and alone.

The debris and rushing water's noise terrified Sammy as the small boat tipped and rocked wildly. TJ forced him to the bottom, holding him as tight as he could with only one arm. He knew Sammy wouldn't fall out. Sammy sobbed; TJ felt his body shudder as he pushed him to the floor with his backpack still strapped on. Sammy lay on his side with the sack toward TJ. This allowed TJ to force his foot onto the backpack, to stabilize him. Jeremy already on the floor near the bow of the boat grabbed Sammy's arm. He calmed down a little after TJ and Jeremy secured him. Sammy reached over his head and grabbed a bow's seat leg. He closed his eyes and held tight.

TJ looked back at Glenn who already shifted to the floor. He saw Glenn's shadow and moved to the floor next to him. TJ reached underneath the middle seat. He released his foot, then seized Sammy's backpack with his hand, and found a seat leg to hold on to through the raging ride. *How could so many things happen to us in a matter of minutes? What will be next?* TJ's frenzied thoughts kept him alert. The darkness engulfed them.

TJ woke to the tapping of something on the side of their boat. He opened his eyes, but lay still until he got his bearings. The boat rocked gently. The rising sun barely lit the sky. Overcast and murky from clouds mixed with smoke, he remembered the night before. When TJ jumped up, Glenn grabbed his shoulder and whispered, "SSHHH, Sammy and Jeremy are still sleeping."

TJ nodded and scanned the perimeter. The boat, trapped in a small pool of water, rocked as if tied to a dock during the gentle days of summer. This odd picture of their boat surrounded by gigantic pine trees now torn up into pieces caught in a massive log jam, created an impossible image to fathom. Garbage, lumber pieces of ravaged buildings together with the pine trees were bunched all around them. TJ stood to see past the debris in what looked like an inlet or a bay.

"Where is land?" he yelled out waking Jeremy and Sammy. "I can't see any land."

The other boys jumped up, almost capsizing the boat.

"Okay, okay, let's all sit down." They followed TJ's direction. "We have to think smarter than that, after all we're wilderness scouts. Come on let's have breakfast. Check your backpacks. We all packed food by the lists we made. There should be enough for a couple days. We can put it all together and plan how much we can eat until we find more food." The boys got busy and stayed focused until after they ate.

Eating helped. No longer agitated by every thought, they looked in every direction.

"We're stuck. It could be a long time before we're spotted here, so we need to get ourselves out," TJ said. "What do all of you think?"

"That makes sense," Glenn said, "But it won't be easy."

"Which way will we go?" Jeremy asked.

Glenn perched himself at the side of the boat. "That looks like the shortest route to the edge," he pointed. "I can work here at the bow and steady the boat. TJ and Jeremy can be on each side. We'll pull the boat out of the water onto the trees. Sammy, you can stay in the boat. You'll stabilize it for us and it's safer for you since you're younger than we are."

They worked from early morning until dark to get close to the moving water current. Glenn's leg kept getting caught when he tested each next step to move forward. When that happened, they backtracked a couple feet finding a more stable spot.

"I'm hungry," Sammy said. "The crackers we had for lunch didn't last long in my stomach. Can we eat now?"

"Sure, Sammy; we're all hungry," TJ said. "Let's get into the boat for the night. We'll eat, and stay seated to go to sleep early. I don't know about any of you, but I've never been so tired. I'm sure I'll fall right to sleep." *I want to think more about our next steps. Where would the rushing water take us? Where are other people? Where can we find more food?* His drifting thoughts stopped when he bit into his granola bar, their planned supper.

As soon as they finished eating, even though the boat straddled and rocked on the trees jammed together, the boys slept. At first light they woke and began their last task of moving the boat toward the rushing water. They had about twenty feet to go.

The boat hit hard near the water's edge. The unstable debris dented the rowboat as it dropped down and away. "Hey, you guys, we need to be more careful or we'll sink once we're back in the water." Jeremy ran his hand over the dent, "I don't feel a hole, but we have to be more careful. This hull is pretty light weight."

Glenn moved a piece of a roof out of the way, the water rushed over their feet and they jumped back into the boat. Within seconds the water grabbed the boat and once again moved as part of the deluge. Steadier than the night before the boat resembled a white rapids amusement park ride, as the boys rode the flow of the raging waters.

TJ yelled over the noise, "Now that we're moving again, don't forget to watch for the other boats. They should be caught in all this junk, too. I hope they're okay."

After an hour or so, the boat slowed down. The water looked like it needed to move back to where it came from. "Hey it's like a wave or maybe this is how tsunami waters retreat. We read about that in history. Remember, TJ? Mr. Hobbs added it to our world history class last year.

We talked about how the waters in Southeast Asia retreated, and the count of the dead after was like, over 200,000. Remember that?" Glenn said.

"Well, I guess we don't need to hear about that right now." TJ made a face at Glenn and tilted his head toward Sammy, to indicate not to scare him.

Glenn nodded his head and dropped the conversation. They drifted with the loose debris for several hours more. Toward evening, they took a chance by using the boat oars to maneuver themselves toward some rocks which looked stable. The water moved around the boulder type rocks standing firm.

"Sammy, switch places with Jeremy, then get the twine out of your backpack. Jeremy when we get close enough, reach out to grab those weeds by that largest rock over there." TJ pointed to the specific spot. "Try to hold us next to the rock long enough for Glenn to attach some of the twine from the bow's end. He can make a large loop to throw over the rounded top. That should hold us in place over night."

They worked together managing to get the doubled up twine over the boulder. With that in place, they decided to secure the back end with a second loop. Once finished, they settled down for another granola bar dinner.

"TJ, I have a half bottle of water left," Sammy said. "What happens when we run out? I'm really hungry, too. It's only been a couple days and I've already moved my belt over a notch tighter. I haven't eaten this little in…well ever. Mom always calls me a 'bottomless pit'." He stopped talking. His thoughts drifted to his family. Everything happened so fast. He let go with some tears and sobbed after a couple minutes.

"I know Sammy. Tomorrow…we'll talk about it all tomorrow." TJ slid down to the floor of the boat to get comfortable. They sat in silence, as their own personal thoughts comforted them. Sammy cried for a while, the others left him alone. TJ heard all three of his friends breathe that steady sound when you drift into a slumber. Glad that they were calm enough to sleep, he followed their lead.

Grateful the twine held them in place over night, they needed to find solid land and search for water and food.

The receded waters reversed their deluge patterns

overnight. TJ dug through his backpack, "Hey does anyone have their compass. Mine's not here." They started searching and Sammy found his first, waving it over his head. "Great Sammy, how about if you keep us on track, we need to continue in one single direction. Rowing in the water is difficult to follow a straight course." TJ looked around. He stood up. In the distance he saw what appeared to be some land, and not just rocks or piles of junk. He pointed. "What do you say if we row over that way?"

They all agreed and Sammy noted the direction on his compass. "It's northwest. We need to go northwest."

"I'll row first this morning," TJ said. "Jeremy can take over after that. What do you think?"

"Sounds good," Jeremy said. Everyone else nodded and sat down to eat half a granola bar, their rationed breakfast.

After they ate, they saw trees standing upright in the distance. "Now why didn't we see that before?" TJ said, pushing down hard with the oars hitting pieces of junk and trees, not water at each turn.

"I think it was just too far before, they looked like they were laying down like all the damaged trees," Glenn said.

"I guess you're right," out of breath from rowing and talking, TJ inhaled several times. "My shoulders are sore, can you take over Jeremy?"

"I'm ready, TJ," Jeremy said. They switched places.

"Before you start rowing, Jeremy, wrap your hands in something. Glenn, can you help him rip up a t-shirt? That should work good. See, look at my hands, they're very blistered and they really hurt. I should have wrapped my hands, it just didn't occur to me. We can learn from my mistake." Jeremy changed places with TJ. While Jeremy rowed, TJ poured water from his last bottle onto his hands. It stung. Glancing at the open blisters, "Boy, that was smart," he said out loud, but really intending the sarcasm only for himself.

Jeremy rowed hard. TJ laid back to rest and Glenn and Sammy watched for the other boats. A couple hours passed when they decided to have their half granola bar lunch. Jeremy sat resting from his rowing and enjoyed the food, even though it was so little.

While they ate, they talked about their location.

Everything looked so different after all the flooding ravaged the area. "How can we possibly figure out where we are? We saw so little during the daylight that first day, because we arrived so late. I don't know about you guys, but I'm scared. Don't you think we need to find local survivors who can help us?" Glenn said.

Sammy whimpered and tried to hide his tears. Glenn's words mirrored his thoughts. He leaned over with his hands covering his face. His sobs and tears helped him to release what had built up inside for the last couple days. He couldn't act like the older boys any more. He just let go.

"Oh, come on, everybody! It's only been a couple days. We will do everything we need to do. Don't we always? Hey, can you believe it?" Jeremy smiled, "We didn't drown through all that flooding. Thank God we found the rowboats."

TJ stared off in the distance. "Hey, look over there, just next to those trees." He pointed ahead to where the trees were right up next to the water's edge, many of them hung over the shoreline. "See, there's something behind the trees. Look close. Jeremy, let Glenn row for a while. You've been rowing long enough." They shifted positions. "Glenn, head over to those trees. If it's what I think it is, the tall ship is right there. Oh my God, I think we've found our tall ship."

Sammy wiped his eyes on his pajama sleeve and stood up to look.

Their focus on the trees intensified. They were back in the area where they first arrived and now actually saw something to give them hope. Everything else was underwater.

Glenn rowed hard and the rest of the scouts watched the treed area. Their boat bumped into heavier wreckage. Glenn hit something with the oar. "Oh God." Sammy saw a women's face. Her body, bloated and bluish, and her eyes wide open. Sammy threw-up over the side of the boat. With little in his stomach, he gagged several times bringing up what was left. TJ leaned over and held Sammy's shoulders.

"It's okay, Sammy; it's okay." TJ consoled.

So far there were no other people around; at least they didn't see any. The woman was the first dead person they saw up close. A few minutes after, nearer the trees, Sammy screamed when he saw two more bodies floating face down. He wasn't prepared for it. Hysterical, TJ grabbed his shoulders again.

Still standing and rubbing Sammy's shoulders, TJ saw the bow of the ship. "There it is. Oh my god, can you believe it?"

Jeremy stood up shouting. "Wow, just look at her? She's still afloat, not like all the other boats we've seen capsized or sunk. It's intact and upright."

They all stared. Glenn rowed on, eager to get close enough to secure the rowboat. About twenty minutes later, next to the tall ship, TJ reached up and held the ladder to keep the rowboat steady. Glenn pulled debris out of its rungs. They needed a clear way to get up the side.

The rowboat dwarfed next to it, TJ pulled himself up to the first step and climbed to the deck. "Glenn, throw me the twine."

"Okay, here it comes." TJ caught it and tied it to the top of the ladder.

"Glenn, you're the tallest next to me; you stay in the boat until after we help Sammy and Jeremy climb up. You should be able to make it by yourself, just like I did."

"Okay TJ." They all went to work.

Sammy needed both Jeremy and Glenn to help him

get up the ladder. "I didn't know the tall ship was so big. I'm glad we found it, but I'm so scared now, I don't know if I can get up there this way." Uneasy with the height, he panicked, sat down, crossed his arms, and refused to try. Jeremy sat down next to him.

"I get it that you're scared and I know its high, but we can't stay on this little boat. We're not safe." Pointing up, "That's our chance." Seeing that Sammy wasn't convinced, "Okay try this. There should be food up there. I know I'm really hungry and you said you are, too. Just think about the food up there. Can you do that and don't think about anything else?"

"Okay Jeremy, I'll try. I am very hungry."

"Glenn, if you hold the boat steady for us, I'll push Sammy's leg up to the lowest step, so he can get a good foot-hold. Ready, Sammy?"

Jeremy's steady voice and confidence helped Sammy to get started, but he made a face and sighed. "I wish I'd stay home," but still followed Jeremy's every word. Once up a couple steps, he saw TJ's hand reaching down to him.

"Come on Sammy, grab my hand." TJ lunged

slightly and latched onto him. Once Sammy was on board, Jeremy made it up the ladder pretty easy, Glenn pushed him from behind to get him started. He carried two of the backpacks. Glenn followed carrying the other two with the extra rope from the rowboat.

The scouts stood in awe of the spectacle in front of them. The deck was dirty with leaves, pine branches and needles, but their dream lay at their feet, literally. The masts and the tied down sails were still intact and all the ropes and equipment were also in place. Obviously, the tall ship rode out whatever happened, and ended up dragged into the trees where it got caught.

TJ broke the silence. "Hey, this boat should have been ready to sail. After all, we were going to be on board very early the next morning after all this happened. So, if it was ready to sail, there should be food on board. Remember, we were going to be out for three weeks." He smiled for the first time in three days.

Glenn said, "The last one to the galley does the dishes." They all scattered. No one knew where the galley was, they just looked for any downward steps. Sammy found it, "Wow, look at all these shelves. You won't believe it."

The cupboards in the galley were loaded. Jeremy already started to pull out everything, when he heard Sammy, but Sammy was nowhere near the cupboards in the galley. TJ, again the voice of reason, said, "WAIT A MINUTE YOU GUYS, we need to talk about what's going on and our situation; we'll make a nice meal for ourselves in a little while. "Hey Sammy, where are you?"

"Down here; I think I'm near the middle of the boat!"

Just then Glenn found Sammy. "Hey, everybody, Sammy found the "hold", there's all kinds of stuff stored down here. And, wow, there's lots of food!"

The four of them sat down together at a table in the mess hall. TJ poured each of them a large glass of water from a five gallon container. "Something very big has happened. We need to talk about it. Since the other night, we haven't said much, because we were just trying to save ourselves, but something is very wrong. You saw those dead bodies, and look where this boat is moored. Well, it's not really moored, it's just caught here against the trees and we haven't seen anyone alive on any of the shorelines. Norris Point is all under water."

"Do you think everyone drowned, TJ?" Glenn asked, "What's going to happen to us?"

"Come on Glenn, that can't be; can it, TJ?" Sammy whispered, barely audible, not able to grasp the whole situation.

"Yes, Sammy. I'm afraid Glenn's right." TJ sat down after he put away the water container.

They were all quiet. Jeremy put his head down on the table. He said nothing. Glenn put his hand on Sammy's shoulder. TJ's mind raced. *What will we do now?*

Dinner that first night was heavenly. TJ cooked together with Jeremy while Glenn and Sammy cleaned up. The four of them settled in on-board and together they discovered the whole ship. A two masted 37 foot brig style ship called the Dream Catcher, built in 2041. The four boys slept in the crew's quarters, grateful for the warmth of the enclosed place after sleeping three nights in the cold and cramped rowboat. The large space for crew members allowed for twenty four people in pocketed separate berths. There were several cabins which held three people, set aside for officers, empty for now, but may be used later once they found more survivors.

Glenn located the manuals originally planned for the scouts training. With all these new circumstances and if no one survived who could give them instruction, they needed to teach themselves how to work the ship. Glenn gave a book to each one of them. When they started to read, they were discouraged. The required crew to handle the tall ship, a minimum of twenty people plus officers or masters, left them feeling even more baffled on what to do. *How would we be able to sail this ship with so few people?*

After a couple days reading, and also looking through binoculars to find survivors, TJ started to check what actually worked aboard the ship, besides the propane stove and lanterns. There was a radio room with equipment he didn't notice at first. He'd need to work with Glenn to learn how to use everything. Glenn was the mechanical one in the group, and already spoke about how to teach them about the diesel engine and other equipment he knew about. Luckily, most of the equipment looked new!

EIGHT

For a second year, Thomas earned a scholarship to the Greek-style theatre summer camp near Sochi on the northern coast of the Black Sea. He traveled to camp by train from his home in Volgograd, Russia.

Thomas' summer flew by. He rose early for his hike to the barn on the opposite side of the city away from the theatre. During his walk he passed the athletic arenas, which were built for the winter Olympics in 2014. Neglected and run down after so many years, the local populace held proud to the old stories of glory from the games. One of the songs to be sung during the final celebration referred to the golden days of the winter sports success and the acclaimed winter wonderland.

Thomas wore shorts, the summer heat stifling, in contrast to his thoughts about the winter wonderland which would explode onto the scene in a short couple months. The old barn, although well ventilated with fans, always overheated upstairs where he worked on prop repairs. He liked this assignment when it came up, because it gave him a quiet and restful day. Usually, four students received this daily task; however, that morning, the list of chores changed due to a celebration for the summer's final performance. Today he worked alone, where he repaired some damaged table legs for the last show. The other three people took on tasks for party set-up in the new theatre annex. Everyone looked forward to the program's closing events. The party will last all night, in the new building with more room for the always exuberant crowd.

The costumes swung back and forth high in the rafters. Thomas looked up when he heard the gentle creaking sound above his head. Dust got into his eyes and he sneezed again and again. His work on the second floor, didn't allow him to feel the earth shake except for the dust. When he looked up and saw the costumes swinging, he thought, *that's strange.* With no warning, the building weaved back and forth. The floor gave way and he dropped twenty feet to the room below. "AAAAHHHHH," his right leg pinned underneath him at an odd angle. He broke into a sweat as the excruciating pain mounted. The walls wavered back and forth. The motion cracked and popped wall boards, which snapped in half. The barn collapsed like a house of cards trapping Thomas. He pulled his arms up near his head to push the smothering fabric away from his face. Every breath constricted by the weight of the costumes and the growing pain in his leg, he lay helpless and alone. *Oh God, how will I get out of here?*

The shaking ground compacted the costumes on top of him; the weight making it harder and harder to breathe. He clawed and pulled himself forward by grabbing onto the fabric over his head and pulling down. Dragging his leg against the floor with the extra weight caused it to throb from his ankle all the way to his thigh. After every two or three pulls, he had to stop, gasping for breath.

A little air hit his face, cooling him slightly. Thomas burrowed toward it. He pulled on several white shirts, and a space opened above his head. His movement brought him underneath a table and he felt air rush around him. He pulled himself between the table legs and lay with his eyes closed. He breathed evenly and calmed down.

Those white shirts, clean and light weight, would

make good strips to tie around my shin to keep the broken bone from moving. Oh god it hurts. He spent time ripping the shirts and kept a couple to wear, to keep his elbows from getting scratched on the barn floor. The small space under the table limited his movements. Barely able to bend forward to wrap his lower leg, Thomas strained to create support for the broken bone. Bending to the side allowed him to put on a couple extra shirts and a jacket. Tackling the addition of long pants over his makeshift bandages took longer. Encased in the long pants gave the injured leg a more secure feeling. He needed to move around in the mound of costumes. With his leg wrapped, the shooting pains stopped, allowing him to pull forward dragging his leg a few inches at a time. It took him a whole day to get out from under the costumes. Finding the table gave him his bearings to efficiently get outside. *I wonder why no one's come to find me.* Thomas rested when he finally got free of the mountainous pile entombing him, about sixteen hours later.

With the barn collapsed, Thomas wasn't sure of what else to expect. There were no lights in any direction. The extra clothing he put on earlier now kept him warm in the cool night air. The still air hung over the eerie calm summer evening.

Amy E. Zajac

Thomas stayed next to the barn and tried to make a comfortable bed; however, his frustration mounted. The pain shot through his whole body every time he moved. Exhausted, he fell asleep and slept through aftershocks, not waking until daylight.

All the dust from the barn the day before didn't help his very dry throat, plus it was more than a day since he'd had anything to drink. *I need water. Apparently all the dust from the whole barn lodged in my throat and mouth.* He chuckled out loud, *how can I even joke at a time like this?*

I wonder why no one's come to find me. Thomas knew something major happened. Barely able to prop himself up on his forearm, because his broken leg gave him no leverage, terror ripped through him at his first sighting of the fallen buildings. He scanned the wreckage all around him in disbelief. His panic forced him to stand, despite the agonizing leg pain. He hyperventilated. It took only seconds for him to remember to curb his breathing. Placing a piece of his sleeve over his mouth, he focused. *Breathe slow and steady.*

His breathing calmer, the reality of the destruction he saw and his almost disbelief of it, stripped Thomas of his energy. He drifted to sleep again. After only a few minutes, he woke and sat up to get a better perspective of the wreckage. He still couldn't move very well. The swelling caused his whole leg to throb with every heartbeat.

The rolling countryside, now torn up and battered, confirmed his initial theory. During a history lesson the year before, he viewed similar ground disruptions of an earthquake in Haiti which destroyed most of the island country. The pictures looked like piles of concrete and metal pieces stirred up in a large mixing bowl and then dumped out. In the middle of the road in front of him, piles of broken up asphalt, left no easy way to get around a displaced portion of the road shooting up from the ground. Smoke drifted upward from burning debris inside a crevasse in front of the jagged asphalt pieces. The small theatre grounds vehicle buildings, which were right next to the road, all collapsed and one, looked like it was up-side-down.

This type of destruction could only be an earthquake...*No wonder no one came to find me.* His mind raced in every direction. He didn't know what to do or how to do anything; the pain in his leg stifled his every movement.

Under normal conditions he experienced a forty five

minute walk back to the ridge above the city, but now he endured a week of setbacks to get there. Crevasses everywhere, over and over again he retraced his footsteps to find a way past the opened ground. Of course, it took him twice as long because he hobbled with the makeshift crutch, he created for himself out of a 2x4 piece from the toppled barn wall. He didn't see a single person in all that time, not even a dead body.

Thomas worried about his mother in Volgograd. *She must be going crazy not knowing what happened to me. She worked extra hours to purchase me a sleeping compartment ticket for the day after the celebration closing ceremonies.* When she met the train and he wasn't on it, Thomas knew she'd panic. They were all each other had. His grandparents and his dad were all dead. Since their deaths when he was just a baby, over the years he came to understand her love of work, and how teaching Thomas to be a good person, drove her. *I need to get home.*

Even with all the destruction Thomas saw over that first week, he was not ready for what he saw when he got to the ridge to start down on the other side. Completely under water, the city no longer existed. Even though some water already subsided, the sea now engulfed everything up to the ridge. Thomas dropped his crutch and fell over. The renewed pain in his leg made him scream out. He broke down crying. The terror of his reality caught up with him.

Thomas froze. The enormity of what he needed to face kept him immobile. He stayed at that spot a week. His thoughts and prayers gave him no comfort. His panic raged. Before he left the barn the week before, he managed to find the snacks he brought for that day's work, which included two bottles of water. With half a bottle of water left, he needed to ration better. *What will happen to me when I run out of food?* He functioned better before he saw the city under water. *What should I do; where should I go? Oh God help me.*

After he dropped his crutch and the pain ripped through his body, Thomas thought he broke his leg again. He rested; the pain eased. His leg already started to heal. It didn't hurt as much at the second week mark and only hurt if he twisted it. He taught himself a new walking pattern dragging his leg and still used the make-shift crutch when he walked northwest towards Tuapse. A logical direction to take, that's where he should have transferred to a different train on his way home to Volgograd.

While he slept early the third morning of the walk

toward Tuapse, he opened his eyes and jumped when he saw a little boy's face about three inches from his own. Their heads hit and the child fell back surprised when Thomas opened his eyes. Five survivors walking together saw him lying next to the damaged road. They shared water and what little food they had. Thomas eagerly accepted their generosity, overwhelmed with gratitude not to be alone anymore. Now their group was six.

Not under water, Tuapse's earthquake damage looked like a bombing. Fires, dead bodies, and crevasses were everywhere. The stench from the already decaying bodies repulsed Thomas and the other survivors. After a few days they found food in a small grocery store not yet hit by other scavengers. The treasured canned food, bottled water and other essentials carried by everyone, even the children, gave them a curious comfort, since they didn't know when they'd find anything again. When they got out of town and built a fire to cook some food, they appreciated their first real prepared meal in more than four weeks. Up until that time they managed with soda crackers and beef jerky.

The small group stayed at this site two days, deciding what to do next. They were Thomas; Moira and her two sons visiting Sochi from Svetlograd; Boris actually from Sochi his whole life; and Krystyna from Tuapse.

Boris and Krystyna decided to stay in Tuapse to be as close to their homes as possible. Moira and her sons, traveled with Thomas northeast toward their homes in Svetlograd and Volgograd. It took them ten weeks to get to Svetlograd and another week to find their neighborhood, because of the extensive damage to the city. Moira found her husband dead where he lay trapped and killed by a fallen brick wall at the side of their house. His body was decayed and deteriorated.

Moira recognized the wristwatch still on his wrist. She and Thomas buried his remains on her small property. The kitchen in her house still had a roof and the walls appeared to be stable. Thomas, able to clean up and fix the old fireplace, set it up for Moira to be able to cook and heat using the same space. He never did any mechanical work before and learned as he went remembering a book he read about how fireplaces worked. This gave him a place to start.

Thomas spent extra time helping Krystyna before he started out again for Volgograd; he cut enough wood for her to get through the winter and stacked it close. It felt good for him to do the physical work. His leg healed during the walk to Svetlograd, but the broken leg emerged with a permanent limp. He favored it during the whole healing time. Even though they walked so far, he still needed to build up the muscles in both his legs again.

With winter coming, Thomas left Moira and her sons confident all she needed to do would be to build a daily life for her boys. Her very old well-built house had a good solid door to the outside. It closed well with a good seal to keep the cold out. He knew they would be warm. Moira expressed her gratitude to Thomas. He helped her with things her young sons could not do.

They sought out local survivor teams to let them know, they were back in Svetlograd. When they walked into one of their work areas, all were astounded. Thomas, Moira and her sons were the first "new" survivors to come around since the early days after the quakes. Now that these people knew Moira and her sons were there in Svetlograd, Thomas prepared to leave for Volgograd. Moira planned to start working with these teams, even if all she did was provide cooked food for them during the upcoming winter months. Moira and her sons were home.

Thomas walked toward Volgograd. He moved

faster now, without Moira's small sons holding him back. His leg, stronger with all the work he did for Moira, only the limp showed as a telltale sign of what happened to him.

Moira gave Thomas a winter coat found in her destroyed house. An old coat which belonged to her husband, she shared knowing he stayed longer than he planned and cold weather was just around the corner. She also found gloves and a hat and some old work boots which fit him pretty well.

Once on the road again, Thomas scavenged food wherever he could, in empty houses, stores, or from people he encountered and were willing to share with him. He managed to survive the seven weeks it took him to get to Volgograd. His mother, always first and foremost in his mind, needed to be found.

Volgograd, destroyed by fire, quakes or floods, matched everywhere else. Although small clean-up crews worked steadily, their slow progress appeared exaggerated with no working machinery and electricity. When he recognized what appeared to be his old neighborhood, he broke out into a run. *Will she be there? Has she been looking for him and worried just like he's been for her? Oh no, there's our apartment building...*

Burned to the ground, he found no one around. In the small yard near the end of the burned out shell, his neighbor's sons swing-set stood strangely upright and intact with an eerie stillness. It's motionlessness a sign of the deaths of his friends and his...mother. Survivors must already be in action. There were no dead body remains anywhere around the area. He wept uncontrollably and sat on the remnants of the concrete steps without moving most of the day and through the night. His sadness overpowered and paralyzed him. The scavenger team found him the next day. They took him to their community team home where everyone gathered around to welcome him.

It took him twenty-one weeks to get home and find nothing. He never found his mother, or any record of her burial. After seeing the apartment building and making inquiries, he accepted she died in the fire at their apartment on that day.

Thomas stayed in Volgograd, sharing stories about what he saw in Sochi, Tuapse, and Svetlograd. He joined a team to begin the rebuilding. The five month trek to get home to his mother changed him. Numb and abruptly an adult, it felt good for him to get to work. It didn't matter what he did. Focusing on something other than chaos helped him to get past the sadness and loneliness of all the loss.

Joining the library and religion team, his education began again which made him feel closer to his mother even though she died that horrible day. He followed her footsteps as a teacher.

NINE

Global communications reached farther and farther through Anatole's creative HAM schedules which bounced off the sunburned atmosphere to Canada, Brazil, Northern Poland, China, and Australia. All the new countries participating, described similar devastation with only pockets of survivors.

Comparing the current circumstances to past catastrophes became a pattern during the transmissions. The last two prior disasters occurred in the Southeast Asia part of the world, aside from the many wars humanity inflicted upon itself. The first, tsunamis occurred in a single day in the year 2004. Undersea earthquakes in the Indian Ocean triggered these tsunamis along the coast of most of the bordering landmasses. The second, an 8.9 magnitude earthquake just off the east coast of Japan, caused huge water displacement and spawned a ferocious tsunami in 2011.

Since the extended transmissions corroborated the global event cataclysm, the tsunamis and earthquakes in the early 2000's, although catastrophic, now appeared to the survivors to be miniscule in proportion.

Three years before the disastrous global event, a scientific study became a popular subject for conversation. The study began in the 1990's, covering information which started back in the 1950's. World renowned scientists at multiple universities compiled their findings globally, validating the accuracy of the data for several generations of scientists. This monumental new calculation of all species on Earth made headlines in every corner of the world. Rosalie found all the chatter by adults everywhere she went, fascinating. Her biology teacher relented to her persistent questions. He provided an explanation of the study's findings, keeping it simple enough for a thirteen year old, the brightest student he ever taught.

He explained the population patterns of all people on Earth, less by approximately 30% from the population numbers in the timeframe 1950 to 2040; this surprised everyone. Not only that, all other living species of animals, plants, and insects diminished by the same percentage during the same time frame of history, which elevated the surprise to shock. This made the outcome of the long time study even more mysterious. The great scientific minds associated with the study could not provide any logical, chemical or biological reason for the reversal. Simply put, fewer babies were being born, fewer plants were reseeding themselves, and fewer animals and insects were propagating.

With the explanation from her biology teacher, Rosalie tried to understand why this caused all the adults to be talking about the subject all the time. She titled her year-end science project "Propagation of Species and Why It Is So Important". She took First Place; however, more importantly, it became a driving force in Rosalie's life. By the time she finished high school, Rosalie read the hypothesis of the "2049" study twice, and both times stumbled through the reading when she got to the end. The questions were staggering, and the summation, empty, from all parties involved in the study.

Rosalie, the epitome of a popular geek, loved learning. The intriguing study challenged her. Energy and enthusiasm helped her lead high school classmates by example. This filled her life with all different types of friends even though she attended for just two years graduating early. Her charismatic personality along with her dark brown hair, brown eyes, sweet round face, and happy rolling giggle, painted a person very recognizable.

When the quakes occurred, Rosalie plunged into a solitude she never before experienced, not only by losing her family, but waking up badly injured in a totally destroyed world.

TEN

At the university, Anatole became the catalyst which brought everyone together. Tirelessly, he worked day and night. During the early weeks after the disaster, Anatole found scores of people who looked to him for comfort and consolation. Rosalie, excited to see more and more survivors, got to know everyone, which kept her spirits up during her slow recuperation. The burns on her legs healed slowly with obvious scars. She worked hard to minimize in her mind how bad her legs looked. Her right arm lost most of its muscle mass, but it functioned well. Thanks to Anatole, she focused on living.

Among the search for survivors, Anatole found a young woman; a recent brain chip implant recipient. The AX Book Brand tattooed below the surgical area identified her. The implant embedded in her temple barely healed; the calibration of the chip never completed because the quakes interfered with her scheduled procedure. Without the final intricate calibrations, her wound hemorrhaged internally.

Anatole brought her back to the group and asked Rosalie to comfort her with quiet conversation. At first Rosalie didn't understand what happened to the young woman. Her injuries didn't appear to be earthquake related, yet survival was doubtful because of the hemorrhaging. The incision didn't bleed; however, her nose and her ears bled ongoing. Once Anatole explained about her condition, Rosalie grieved because this woman would die due to the controversial idealist 'easy-fix' for education. She remembered her Mom's words about the controversy; *it's a sign of the times.*

"An implant clinic placed near the university became a political statement made six or so years ago," Anatole said. "Simply by placing their manufacturing facilities and surgical clinics so near twenty universities globally, they drew potential students for the implants 'quick-fix'. This action caused riots and dissention similar to civil rights movements in the U.S. during the late 1960s. But instead of civil rights, the ideals in question were education. The riots weren't in a single country; they broke out all around the world."

After hearing Anatole's explanation, Rosalie remembered back to when she was ten years old and how her parents spoke about the controversy. They believed in developing the human mind through teaching and learning, not through the artificial implantation of an electronic chip. Brought up in the traditional world of educators and scientists, Rosalie's ideals grew similar to her parents; always ready for the next step, looking for something new to embrace.

Sadly and as expected, the young woman died after two days with Rosalie. With so many people dead and the need for burials in immense proportions, Rosalie begged Anatole to officiate this young woman's funeral, as a symbol for so many deaths. Still unable to walk, Anatole carried Rosalie. Even with her legs incapacitated she wanted to attend this service. Anatole set her down on a large broken piece of concrete where she sat to view the service. He chose this site for the grave because it was near most of their recent activities. A few other survivors created a mini park-like area around the grave, where they planted different size pieces of Yucca plants. A small piece of granite with her first name, Anya, and the year, 2052, marked the site. Everyone attended, to honor the young woman and all people dead from the recent catastrophic horrors. All were comforted by the closure Anatole's gentle words provided.

ELEVEN

Rosalie started to feel better, but after-shocks made her wish she never woke up. Every time the ground shook, her mind raced to the morning walk and the last time she saw her mother. She watched the children as she recuperated. Their obvious sadness, coupled with their whimpering and crying made them look like mini-worn-out-adults, not children. They lacked inner joy. Only one of them had a parent survive.

Many survivors argued with one another; they broke down crying and frown lines on their faces showed they were on edge. No one wanted to be told to do anything by anyone else. Anatole's determination to save everyone was his primary job. Rosalie rarely saw him during the day and she knew they had to come up with a single plan to help everyone. He showed up exhausted and hungry, just before dark. Selflessly, Anatole turned into rescuer and caregiver for everyone found, as more survivors joined the ranks. Rosalie worked out the plan to move them in the right direction.

"Anatole, would you please look for paper and pens, enough for all of us. I have an idea and having everyone's input, will speed the process." Rosalie stared off into space. *Okay, it's just us. We're all we have. We need to eat and drink and have shelter. If we're sick, we need to care for each other. We need to learn to trust one another and we need to take care of the dead. Focus on these details. How can we succeed? There must be something simple.........teams.*

Anatole scavenged for pens and found old hospital reports in disarray near the university hospital headquarters. *I'm sure the unprinted back sides of pages will accommodate whatever Rosalie wanted us to write down.* He gathered up a stack of the old paper and organized a meeting place. With the recent good weather, he decided to find a place outside. The university chapel garden space would accommodate everyone. Since the walls of the chapel fell inward, the garden remained open except the crevice he almost fell into that first day. He made a bed for Rosalie near the back of the garden. With Rosalie's healing wounds, Anatole carried her to the makeshift bed made up of a couple torn couch cushions and towels he found at the hospital. Everyone could see and hear her well. The children gathered in close, several sitting in the bed with her; the rest crowded in, grateful to have the momentary distraction. They passed around paper and pens. The quiet crowd shared the pens and each grabbed a piece of paper.

"Okay, everybody, my idea is for us to work in teams, with everyone working on a team as if it's your own personal job." *Okay, good... a few people are nodding their heads in agreement. That's a relief.* "I know quite a few of us are struggling with moodiness, and...agitation. I'm pretty young, but I know some of these traits are part of trauma and grief. If we work together and rely on each other, we'll learn about each other. Building a bond as friends and co-workers will help us pass time and heal. Please write down all the teams you feel we need. Since I can't do much yet physically, I'll coordinate your ideas and arrange the teams appropriately. If you have a preference to serve on a particular team, be sure to write it on your paper." She glanced over at Anatole. He smiled and nodded in approval. She smiled back.

Rosalie saw smiles on many faces and felt grateful to see this immediate reaction. Everyone wrote their ideas. Rosalie played a patty-cake game with two young girls seated on her makeshift bed. She waited for everyone to finish. While they wrote their ideas down, several quiet whispers began, almost the first consensus since they came together. Building this team idea instilled a focus in everyone, happy to be part of a new endeavor. Anatole sat to the side, appreciative for this successful beginning. He closed his eyes and listened to the voices while they whispered. The familiar sounds comforted him, easing his quake-related anxiety.

Work started right away. The teams organized how to guide everyone and make progress in an efficient pattern. With so many things to do, all agreed Rosalie's plan worked and provided confidence in the new idea. Only the amateur radio operators requested they continue their work with the same team; everyone else welcomed their direction from Rosalie.

The teams agreed upon: water, food/cooking, dead bodies, first aid, electrical, plumbing, amateur radios/ communication, clean-up, living quarters/reconstruction, library and religion, childcare/classroom set-up and teaching, hazard/clean-up, runners and food delivery, clothing, and storage set up. Rosalie organized the information in a few hours' time and proceeded to tell everyone their assignments. All teams were set and ready to begin.

Forty people were assigned to the dead body team with fifteen people each for all the other teams except library/religion, and classroom set-up/teaching, both included fourteen people. The twenty seven children were part of the childcare/classroom set-up/teaching team, the older children helped take care of the younger children.

Rosalie's adult life started that day. With her parents dead, her new friend Anatole, and now her plan implemented, she became a person for the other survivors to rely on. After Rosalie's leg burns healed, she worked with the dead body team. They identified, documented and built a count of the dead in Jerusalem. This team, an immediate need, because bodies were everywhere. Most of the bodies, already deteriorated and decayed, made the job grisly and took a special group of people. Empathy and compassion were the most important traits for this team's members. It helped them to honor the dead.

TWELVE

The first team organized before Rosalie regained consciousness was the Amateur Radio team. It provided hope for all. It opened a window to survivors around the world. When Rosalie pushed to organize after that, understanding they were connected to other people globally eased the panic among survivors in Jerusalem. The planned work pattern helped them to progress.

"Anatole, we need to share our "team" plan with everyone on our daily communication transmissions. It's working so well here; we can help survivors in other countries to have the same." This thought hit her like a slap in the face and when Anatole agreed, she wondered why she didn't think of it sooner.

Rosalie wrote down a more detailed plan than before, because she knew the amateur radio team members would read everything. They didn't need to rely on memory of what was going on in Jerusalem; it needed to be a specific script of the teams and how they needed to start right down to the pens and paper found to build ideas from the local survivors. The document also described how each person focused on a single job. It included how working in the teams would help teammates to deal with grief, get over the horror, adjust to the change, plus helped everyone through the inevitable waves of panic. She added the details about what each team did daily, especially the dead body team because they learned early on that burying the bodies became detrimental to the team's health. Burning the bodies, led a more efficient and thereby productive team for the clean-up of the dead. The plan also provided many details about how all the people regarded the team work for their individual jobs, taking pride in their daily routines and successes.

"We need to include as many countries as possible. This way the information the Amateur Radio team members read during the scheduled transmissions would get out to more than one country at a time; hopefully, it would help the other countries to communicate through their own chaos and panic."

This sharing promoted local explosions of activity around the world and kept simple teams at work; immediate progress occurred. Because there was a team to take care of food, a team to take care of water, and a team to take care of clothing, other teams were free to work hard and not worry about how to feed and clothe themselves. This unity created closeness as the first step toward recovery.

The teams became their own small communities. Now with the new focus, their lives again began to grow meaning. Everyone on each team lived a simple life; they allocated salvaged items, being cooperative, and being good to each other. Conflict did not occur because everyone remained confident with no reason for fear; personal ambition no longer existed in this changed world. Each person helped their own team to be successful in their daily endeavors. Everyone was grateful. Truly the golden rule came back to life.

When Rosalie thought about how the teams' strategy worked so effectively everywhere, it reminded her of the story her dad loved to tell her as a small child; the story about when Jesus destroyed the marketplace in the temple. With the marketplace now destroyed, the temple again became used for worship. The whole earth cleansed on the day of the quakes, with commercialism destroyed in 2052, leaving the world ready to begin again. The few people left on earth never prepared for this mammoth devastation as it evolved during the major calamity. Now humbled by what they learned, humankind lived simple, caring lives.

Each time they located a new pocket of survivors, Rosalie helped to get the same teams set in place. Work, an important key to help forward movement, allowed the teams to evolve and produce positive results.

THIRTEEN

Anatole worked the Jerusalem clean-up, reconstruction, first aid, and amateur radio teams. With no tools at the beginning, clean-up remained crippled. After three months, searches through the city rubble revealed a destroyed hardware store. Like gold, the tools found in the debris, produced more efficient clean-up. Shovels and pitch-forks gave the scavenger team and reconstruction team wings. Their efficiency more than doubled during their daily tasks. The gloves found, replaced the rags which wrapped the workers hands. These precious treasures now protected the team members against cuts and infections, always a concern during those early months.

At first, most everyone slept together in a cleaned out dormitory with no wall on one end. Luckily the end of the building where the hallway and stairways led to different floors retained its sturdiness, allowing the stairs to be usable. Surprised by this find, Anatole reinforced the entry way to be able to walk up and down. The space, large enough and usable for the 263 survivors, provided living quarters to get organized and allowed all of them to live together like a large family. Minimal clean-up was necessary. Anatole only found eight dead bodies nearby.

Family atmosphere built for all, especially for the lonely and traumatized children. This living arrangement gave each person a sense of home again.

The new living space held another surprise. Anatole stumbled over it at the bottom of the stairway. The first of many to be found, saved, and stored, a PDS (Poly-d-sensory), a new viewing communication technology developed through the use of diamond dust during the 2030s. When Anatole lifted it and stood it up at an angle against the wall, he brushed his hand over it. It's perfect surface, still as smooth as glass, didn't have a mark on it...not a single scratch. The advertising everyone heard about this product over the years was all true.

Anatole tried the PDS, but it did not turn on. As with other destroyed technologies, the one backing PDS throughout the world no longer worked. The PDS phenomenon lay unusable at his feet.

During the next years' time, the salvage team cataloged more than 2500 PDS devices. They stored the equipment in train boxcar containers, part of the first storage places created by the salvage team.

Rosalie's injuries were the worst of all the survivors, except for the young implant patient who died. Rosalie needed a separate place to recuperate. Anatole modified an efficiency apartment with no steps close by the dormitory, so he and several other survivors were able to easily look in on her. The dormitory and Rosalie's new space started a new community center of activity for everyone. The reconstruction team focused on this area for their first task as a team creating a homey atmosphere from individual beds, dressing rooms draped off with scavenged fabrics, washing basins, and a community style kitchen stocked with all kinds of edibles found by the food team. Rosalie's space, stocked high with bandages and bottles of aspirin, had a cozy bed with a portion of a mattress built up to promote her sleeping as much as possible. Anatole found another place close by for him to start to gather documents and objects which needed to be saved. He felt responsible for Rosalie, since he found her first and nursed her nearly fatal burns. Rosalie surprised him and everyone when she survived.

FOURTEEN

Anatole moved to Jerusalem from Greece with his parents the week he turned fifteen. Miserable and lonely, and to get over his home sickness, Anatole turned to his studies. The only child of the two educators who took Greek, Hebrew, Arabic, and Farsi translator jobs at the University, Anatole became part of the educational and intellectual world of the Middle East. He left behind his quiet childhood in Greece. During the next ten years he worked and studied, while his parent's notoriety grew locally in Israel. Their translation abilities proved to be important, not only at the university, but also in government affairs, especially for state dinners. At first,

Anatole attended these social gatherings with his parents; however, his indifferent attitude and distaste for the commercial ideas his parents emulated during those years, drove a wedge between them. When they began to travel and participate with these social and governmental responsibilities, they were gone months at a time. Anatole once again turned inward to his studies. Both his parents were from single child families and all Anatole's grandparents died when he was a child. Though he planned to start college in Israel, he had momentary thoughts about moving back to Greece. With no family to join there, he decided to stay in Jerusalem and move forward in his life, not backward.

Because of all the changes he experienced with the move in his teen years, and later with his troubled parental relationship, Anatole craved solitude. He made few friends and repeatedly explained about his accent and where his family came from. Even though he faded in and out of feeling depressed and alone, he reached down inside himself and found an inner strength and independence. This consoled him, as he grew into adulthood. *I will rely on no one and no one will need to rely on me*, he reasoned. Even though he still needed to complete his high school credits, he enrolled in an archaeology university class at age seventeen. He fell in love with the archeological ideology and craved the solitude of excavation work. Quickly, he worked through the class requirements, while he also worked to finalize his high school credits. Upon graduation, he registered at the university, in the archeology curriculum. These classes included a lab required to work at a nearby excavation site in the desert. Anatole excelled in his classes, but his relationship with his parents deteriorated. Their involvement with the commercial side of government and its politics took them away more and more. Anatole's life grew into a single purpose, with his focus on himself. His solace became learning. He became an added value to the university and the excavation. The one-on-one guidance he provided the students helped them to produce and move into paid field work immediately upon their graduation. His stamina grew and he worked extended hours resulting in many university team-discoveries. With his own graduation accomplished, the archeology department dean and professors created a new position, a "field-professor" to accommodate Anatole's specific talents. Honored by their offer, he accepted the position a year prior to the devastating earthquakes.

His parents returned to Jerusalem after more than a year, working with the new government hover-car dealership, established in south Palestine. They barely spoke to him, and didn't understand why his work became so important to him. After a month they stopped talking altogether. Anatole stayed at the university away from their family home.

On the day of the quakes after he found Rosalie and then found his friends dead, Anatole made his way to his family's house. They lived very near the university campus and once the earthquakes settled down a bit, Anatole became frantic in the need to see them.

Most of the house lay collapsed. Miraculously there were no fires, as in so many other places. He found his parents dead in their bedroom, having never left their bed that horrible morning; their bodies crushed by the walls falling in on them. He pulled them from the rubble and found a small space to bury them near their house…then, grief overcame him. So many regrets rushed into his thoughts, while he sat next to their makeshift graves and realized he just buried his own parents. At first tears flooded his cheeks and soon after that, sobs exploded and his chest heaved in and out. He could barely pull oxygen into his lungs.

I just spent the last two hours interring my mother's

and father's bodies. I worked so hard to remove them from my life, because they were so caught up in shallow global politics. Now they're gone. Who really was the shallow one? He cried and reflected on his life's moments with his parents. The feeling of remorse grew inside him. *How could I have been so callous and indifferent these last years? Did their politics really change the fact that they were my parents? Now they're gone. I'll never have my mother's hug again. Her hugs never changed, even though I became so hardhearted.* He never spoke to anyone about finding them.

Anatole walked back to the survivors grateful to be alive and knowing he just experienced a life changing moment. More than the earthquakes tragedy in the last hours, he finally understood what his life should be. *I have a chance to be different to fellow human beings; now I will wear compassion on my sleeve.*

Caring for Rosalie the way he did, built within Anatole a family like closeness for her. Different from the past, which was all about him, somehow he needed to help, protect, and be responsible for her and for all the Jerusalem survivors. The loss of his parents pushed to the lowest possible place in his psyche. Now he would be part of a new world with a changed passion. No more regrets for Anatole. He didn't run away from the terror and the confusion, he stood up and found someone to help and then went right on to help, work and sacrifice, to create ways for others to build new lives. Little did he know his new reliability and his good deeds supported the virtuous new world attitude. Respect grew for Anatole. His concern and fatherly image spread to his teammates. They learned quickly to emulate him. The survivors in Jerusalem became a family.

FIFTEEN

"Demi, Demi," Rosalie crept toward the barely audible sound. Behind a pile of concrete pieces, lying on the ground, staring straight upward, a woman laid repeating the words. Her calloused and raw bare feet bled with dried caked-on mud. The filthy and ragged clothes she wore, matched her deteriorated physical condition, with her hair matted and her eyes swollen.

No matter what Rosalie said, this woman, looked right through her, as if in a daze. She didn't even react when Rosalie wrapped her arm around the woman's shoulders to guide her to the make-shift Jerusalem Hospital, several blocks away. The first aid team members manning the sign-in desk greeted Rosalie and the sad disheveled woman in her care. Anatole worked on the first aid team at that time and heard Rosalie's voice around the corner. "Hey, what's going on?" He blurted out as he came up behind them. His face changed to concern the second he saw the woman with Rosalie. Anatole took charge, "Now don't worry about a thing; we'll take great care of your new friend, Rosalie." The woman spoke nothing at all during the activity at the sign-in desk; she just repeated the name, "Demi", over and over again.

Anatole and others on the first aid team, after searching for symptom descriptions in anatomy books kept as resources for diagnosing, determined she suffered from exhaustion, shock, and malnourishment.

"Once she's feeling better, someone needs to keep an eye on this woman, and utilize her on a team. Rosalie, your team has some duties, which don't require special skills. Plus, she could stay with you or me, just until she starts to be herself again."

"Okay Anatole that will work. Since I haven't moved into the dormitory with everyone else yet, she can stay with me for now. If she needs to be alone, we'll arrange for assistance in that healing apartment I have, and then my team can use her as an extra person. We have a perfect job for her. She can deliver the books we find to our storage."

"Great! That will be simple to teach her, even in her diminished capacity."

"I think I'll call her Red. When I stopped by the hospital on my way home, I saw that someone washed and cut the mats out of her hair. It's a beautiful auburn color."

Anatole and Rosalie embraced a new family member and an extra team member for rebuilding Jerusalem.

Rosalie visited her at the hospital the three following days, after that, Red came to stay with Rosalie. She still did not speak, but understood requests and acknowledged the people who attended her, by her actions. The wounds on her feet already began to heal and she ate when meals were served by the food team.

Even though Red remained non-communicative, Rosalie talked to her as if she would reply. When she explained to Red why she decided to call her "Red", for a moment Rosalie thought she acknowledged with a faint smile, but it immediately diminished.

Rising with the sun, the survivors also settled in for sleep near dusk. The only generator powered by batteries, found a year before at the Jerusalem Airport, directed all electricity to the hospital. This electricity accommodates the needs for the make-shift hospital only. The salvage team searched for batteries to keep the old generator operating and found candles and battery driven lanterns and flashlights for local team daily living. These small items were kept close by for daily retrieval. During their search and excavation in the northwest corner of Jerusalem, the electrical team discovered the remains of a destroyed propane company. The sparse supply of propane worked as the alternative for cooking, plus heating the hospital, a true blessing. The teams worked in an organized cooperative pattern and kept everything moving forward.

Buried in trash, sand and rubble, the electrical team unearthed a working solar-charged automobile. Solar powered batteries became the standard when gasoline run automobiles were outlawed worldwide the year Rosalie was born. All cars manufactured since 2036 were either battery run or solar charged only. The new technology of government regulated hover-cars was introduced in 2049. All the team leaders agreed the automobile would be used by the hospital, at least, until more working vehicles were found.

Word spread very quickly between all the teams. Everyone expressed enthusiasm when they heard and all were in agreement. *A working car, how wonderful is that?* For the first time in three years, they planned a celebration!

Half the fun of the upcoming celebration turned out to be the preparation. The clothing team provided new clothes for everybody. The food team worked together with the water team to prepare a wonderful feast. The reconstruction team surprised everyone with a renovated building to be used for the new library, a perfect place for a party since no shelves or tables were set in place yet. The amateur radio/communication team created magic with music for the evening. The library and religion team decorated and set the tables. The runners served and entertained. And last but not least, of course, the clean-up team cleaned.

The party started and everyone kept commenting on how all the teams together became a well-oiled mega-team. Since the earthquakes occurred the survivors came together and learned to rely on each other once they worked on the teams. In the beginning when they got to know each other, they cried together, shared in their grief and consoled one another. When differences occurred, they argued, but were swift to realize the argument made no sense. They learned a new tolerance and warmth for one another, which turned into a solid love all around. Rosalie's team idea brought continuity.

When the children got up to sing, everyone cheered, which gave them confidence and comfort. As they sang their last melodic song, they dispersed into the audience to hug everyone. Red sat next to Rosalie when a beautiful young blonde singer came over to hug them. She hugged Rosalie first and then moved to hug Red. It had been a month since Red wandered in to meet Rosalie's team working in the university rubble and still she never spoke. The young girl tapped Red's shoulder and sang as she reached around Red's neck. Rosalie watched and smiled. Red stood up, literally picking up the young girl hugging her tight. As tears ran down her cheeks Red said, "Demi, Demi. It's you; it's you."

The young girl, not afraid, returned Red's hug intensity. Standing, Rosalie embraced both of them. Other people at the table stood and joined the group hug. A minute passed, and to everyone's surprise, Red spoke for the first time since she arrived.

"But...you can't be Demi. She's not a child anymore. She's grown. She got so sick. I couldn't help her. We were all alone. I buried her."

Red released the young girl. Tears streamed down her cheeks as she turned to face Rosalie.

"You've been so kind to me. You just kept taking care of me, but I never spoke to you. I don't understand why I couldn't speak. It felt wrong and it felt like I was living someone else's life, not my own. I kept thinking Demi's death was a dream, and then finding all of you was a dream, too. But tonight, seeing this sweet child pulled me out of the daze. Demi was blond with a sweet face just like this child."

After Red spoke and everyone wished her well, the children sang one more song to finish the evening. Red and Rosalie walked home. Neither spoke.

Over the next couple days, Rosalie learned more about Red. Her real name was Madeline. Her daughter, Demi, also survived the catastrophe. Together when the quakes started, no one else in their area survived. They were on a short vacation in Beersheba, and up early for a walk by the Monument to the Negev Brigade near the eastern entrance of the city. They drove several miles to the site for their walk and being tourists were unfamiliar with the area. The monument, a popular tourist attraction and a precursor to land art, drew them there for Demi's educational path of learning Israeli history. The watchtower portion of the monument fell in front of them, as the earth first quaked. Thrown into the air about 30 feet apart with the next huge quake, it took more than an hour to get back to each other. The ground shook so constant as the quakes began; they were thrown farther and farther apart. They kept yelling to one another to keep their bearings, but even though they yelled, neither heard the other's voice. The ground movement gave off thunderous sounds which made their screams sound like whimpers.

Demi crawled toward the spot she last saw her mother. The quaking hindered her progress. Huge cuts on her legs bled heavily, and tore when she moved over broken pieces of concrete. Exhausted and unable to crawl anymore, she screamed out one last time. "Mom where are you; where are you?" Madeline heard Demi; she knew Demi was close by. She crawled the last few feet to her daughter.

They hugged for several minutes, comforted they

were back together. Madeline ripped up her shirt to wrap the gash on Demi's calf. The other minor scratches could be cared for later. With the ground still quaking so violently, bandaging Demi's leg proved to be very difficult. She started over several times. Finally, the fourth try she finished it enough to close the gash. Madeline got on her knees to look around, but the quaking kept throwing her back down. After several tries, she caught a glimpse of a metal staircase, which already fell. They crawled about twenty feet to get to it. They dug into a corner near the fallen staircase and stayed there clinging to each other until the quakes stopped.

Once they got past the horrible day of the tragedy, they found food supplies and water at small markets when they walked back toward the city. It wasn't until then they saw dead bodies everywhere. They tried to find their motel, but the rubble and crevices were too restrictive and cumbersome to get through. After they found additional food, they decided to walk back to the monument, since there were no bodies there. Madeline believed they would be found by rescue squads eventually. She kept up Demi's spirits by focusing on being rescued and continuing to talk about her studies. Madeline redressed Demi's wounds with clean gauze and hydrogen peroxide found with the food.

When no one ever came searching for them and they found no one alive during their searches into the city, they settled in to what they believed would be their lives forever, alone. After two years, Demi got sick. Since they were alone, with no medical treatment, she just deteriorated. After six months, she died in her sleep. Her illness remained a mystery to Madeline; however, she suspected cancer.

The undisturbed hard desert ground was difficult for Madeline to dig a traditional grave. She buried Demi in one of the small crevasses close to where they lived for the last two and half years. She covered Demi with rocks and scratched her name in one of them. Once Madeline's focus on Demi ended, she did nothing. She remained isolated. Most of the time she slept and after about four months, food ran out. One day she just started to walk.

At first she followed railroad tracks away from the city and she walked until she needed to sleep. She just dropped right where she was and slept. Since life meant nothing she stopped eating and drinking. Her health deteriorated after she lost her shoes. Her feet bled and infections started when the cuts went untreated. The blood on her feet collected dust which caked on with the blood moisture and then would dry while she slept.

She stumbled many times and when she fell each time, became very dirty and injured, but never bad enough to stop her though. She just wandered on. After three weeks walking she came upon Rosalie and her team quite unexpectedly.

In her prior life she taught elementary children, so when recovered from her walk she started to help by organizing books from the library and religion team. Drawn to the work and to help right away, Red transferred to the childcare/classroom set-up and teaching team. The move, a logical switch, benefited the children.

The change in the teams promoted new excitement. Within six months, the first school opened thanks to Red's ideas and direction. The children separated into grade level classrooms. This new classroom environment now promoted learning instead of the semi-chaos the children tried to learn in before. No one ever called her Madeline after she explained her history. Even the children called her Red from then on.

SIXTEEN

The dead body team worked together, at least in the Jerusalem area, for three years. The tasks changed as time went by, because after an extended time, only skeletal remains were found and disposed of. At first, smell and decay horrified everyone. The dead body team kept working and cleaning in a circumference expanding around the living area created by the original team. As this space grew, everyone moved around without encountering bodies, odors, and bugs.

While Rosalie worked with this team right after the tragedy she learned to deal with many aspects of death. Empathy for the people lost, exuded from her every pore. In the beginning, the work involved identification. This occurred by finding something which belonged to the person on or near the body. As time passed, bodies decayed and deteriorated. The team learned forensics and dental identification to keep records in case someone came looking for a relative or friend. However, searches never occurred. The documentation of the dead became part of the historic record, almost a negative census count.

The dead body team's work ended, Rosalie decided she wanted to work to rebuild the university. She transferred to the library and religion team shortly before Red arrived. Rosalie first came to Jerusalem to determine if the university could be her home for her four years of college education. She decided on Jerusalem University the day before the disaster; now three years later, to help rebuild this wonderful place of learning became a powerful motivation. Life took a dramatic turn away from her plan to work on the propagation of the species theory. The global calamity, gave the whole "theory" a morbid kind of twist. *It probably just didn't matter anymore.*

Everyone worked all the time. They rested in shifts and cared for each other. The teams turned into family units, with strong camaraderie and warmth between all. When Rosalie decided to join the library and religion team, her co-team members moved on to other teams, too; the ongoing newly named Morgue team needed only for minimal work. Their solemn last day of working together finished up with hugs and good wishes. Although they would see each other every day because they all lived in close proximity, sealing their success with good wishes brought closure for everyone.

Rosalie's new team excavated for buried books, cataloged materials found, and their condition, for use later on, to help with duplicates and sharing in a library and for schools. The books shared by the elementary and high school classrooms became part of the Jerusalem University Library. The university started to recover due to the diligence of their team. Rosalie thrived on the work. She spoke regularly with Red about what education used to be worldwide. In the decades prior to the catastrophe, political priorities which took away educational funding from all levels limited learning growth globally. The standards of education deteriorated. Politics minimized the need to raise the bar at colleges and universities. Anatole jumped in to confirm all Red's statements to be true, because of everything he experienced through his own education process. Rosalie considered all the technological shortcuts to learning, which Red explained existed up until the cataclysm. Ordinary people no longer involved themselves with organizations like NASA, Green Peace, and the International Water Preservation Society. Learning what these organizations were all about and what they offered humanity, didn't matter to them. In the 2020's, fifty percent of humanity took shortcuts using the old internet advertising, telepathic machines, and the controversial surgical brain chip implants.

When the International Epidural Axiom Corporation contracted the brain encyclopedia chip for retail sale, the government lobbyists worked against the past higher education subsidies established many years before. The argument stated "since human augmentation is so simplified, costly traditional education is no longer warranted. Global governance over the chip will change education everywhere." The lobbyists' success resulted in new government regulations for the commercial encyclopedia chip. This opened doors for other products, such as the hover-car, for governments to regulate.

It took years for Axiom Corporation to build global facilities with attached surgical clinics. Once the momentum began, the populace bought into it, proving once again, the easy way blended into the political ambivalence of the times. The clinics became so busy, with assembly lines of patrons, proving their success. With outpatient surgery implants completed in a single day and the chip calibrations adjusted and monitored for several weeks following the healing process, people made governments rich. The chip calibrations concluded the process so well, no adjustments over each person's lifetime were necessary. If a person noticed a malfunction during day-to-day knowledge use, the chip correction process was taken care of long distance via their personal Visimag, without the person coming into the clinic. A serial number, registered to the Axiom Corporation, identified a name with each chip. Similar to the old cell phone technologies in the early 2000's, depending on the owner complaint, a code was entered into a computer and the chip reprogrammed. Visimags, which replaced cell phones starting in 2030, no longer worked since the disaster. Corrections for the knowledge chip were no longer possible.

Traditional education was lost to a strange mix of science fiction and political liberalism. People who chose the implant, versus the people who didn't, had opposite viewpoints on politics, their religious beliefs, and, of course, their ideals about education.

Red's knowledge of the liberal lobbyists of Axiom Corporation provided a historic model to be eliminated. Yes, the former traditional education plans gave the education team a solid plan to follow. Rosalie and her team built the old ideals back in as they went along. Lost technology brought back the classic learning style which fit in with the team's philosophy of rebuilding. Red explained many of the details about the government's involvement with the corporations which pushed the encyclopedia chip. These explanations helped Rosalie learn the reasons for the changes which came about in her early childhood years. Her conservative parents kept her life traditional. She loved learning and discovery. Rosalie's education background made her the perfect choice to lead the rebuilding of Jerusalem University.

After the initial discussion with Red, Rosalie started to formulate an idea. Remembering how good she worked in school when she competed with someone, gave her an idea. *We can compete, university team against university team. Whichever university opens first is the winner. This will help us to pick up the pace, because everyone always wants to be "first". This is perfect!*

The idea required a discussion with the other

university library and religion teams working together through the amateur radio regular transmissions. Rosalie scheduled a time to talk to the representatives from all the other universities in the U.S., Germany, Russia, Australia, and France. She chose an off-time empty schedule space, which allowed Rosalie to talk longer through her idea and brainstorm. The simple idea, start a competition to reopen one university in each country, will consolidate efforts. "This competition will promote camaraderie and idea exchanges. Together we will write the new world-wide-standards for education. Each university can specialize in a relevant global series of occupational groupings. We'll keep all the universities linked with the same principles and guidelines through a single organization. Unless we determine a better allocation we can plan as follows. Israel will take archeology and associated sciences, Germany will take the Law and associated roles, the United States will take medicine and associated sciences, France will take the Arts and all associated roles, Australia will take agriculture and associated roles, and Russia will take electronics with technical and mechanical associated roles. Later, once each university established the essentials for these assigned curriculums, additional curriculums will be added, and will become the amended standards worldwide. The first country to open a university with the programs planned out through our coordinated work using the new world standards, will win."

The excitement in everyone's voice when they voted, assured Rosalie they received her idea with enthusiasm. The competition began.

SEVENTEEN

TJ taught himself about the radio room equipment by reading the manuals Glenn discovered that first day when they found the tall ship intact. It gave him a focus, because the foursome needed to get their minds on something other than being alone in Newfoundland.

Glenn did the same; however, the task he gave himself, "learn how a diesel engine works". He spent most of his time learning the terminology. That took him six months.

Sammy's job, to learn how to climb the rigging and masts and to search for survivors, was perfect for the agile boy. At first he hesitated to climb up the rigging. After the first day getting onto the tall ship, he was scared. TJ encouraged him, "We really need someone to be able to be high up on the masts to watch for the other boats still lost. It would be a perfect thing for you to learn. There are books all about it down in the documentation room with all the other manuals. They were supposed to be for our three week training, but now you can use them to learn how to climb and work the sails." When Sammy thought about being able to do that, excitement showed in his eyes for the first time. He took a deep breath and volunteered. He carried the binoculars constantly and watched for survivors and his friends still out there in the small rowboats.

Mikey Two and Bob showed up in their damaged rowboat about three weeks after TJ's group located the tall ship. Their boat adrift, Sammy spotted them from the top of the main mast. "Hey, you guys, there's a boat down there." He pointed out past the trees at the point.

"Okay Sammy, we'll take the motor boat over, it still has a little gasoline." TJ yelled and waved. They maneuvered over to the drifting rowboat. They found Mikey Two asleep, propped up holding Bob's head in his lap. Not conscious, Bob looked very sick. When the motor turned off, Mikey Two woke up.

"Oh TJ, thank God you found us. I thought we were going to die," he said as TJ hugged him. Mikey Two cried all the way back to the tall ship, about a half mile. So dehydrated, he had no tears, but his sobbing somehow brought him relief.

Bob didn't move on his own, but he did have a pulse. Glenn created a rope stretcher to pull him over the side of the tall ship with a pulley rigging. TJ helped Mikey Two. He complained that all his muscles and body ached. "When was the last time you had water to drink?" TJ asked him.

"I think it was four days ago. I kept the last for Bob. He had a fever. I knew he needed water. The water in the river was so filthy; I knew he'd get sicker if I tried to give him that."

"Let's go down to the First Aid room. I need to check you over for bug bites. When you take a drink of water, drink slow...very slow at first, okay?"

"Okay, TJ. I'll drink slowly. That will be easy to do. My lips are sore." He tried to smile.

The small First Aid room, located next to some crew berths, made it convenient to take care of Bob and Mikey

Two. After Mikey Two drank two glasses of water and had a cup of warm chicken broth, he climbed into a top berth. He fell right to sleep when he closed his eyes. TJ covered him; he knew Mikey Two would sleep a very long time.

Glenn and TJ carried Bob to the lower berth next to where Mikey Two slept. They didn't know what to do for him. His fever raged. They knew he needed fluids. "Glenn, look up in that medical book you found about dehydration and fever, if someone is unconscious."

"Okay, TJ, but I think we'll need to give him something intravenously. The First Aid room has what we need, but I don't think I could do it...could you?"

"Oh Glenn, if we need to do it, we will, together, we can do it." TJ said it out loud, but he tried to convince himself more than he was trying to convince Glenn. *If only Bob would just wake up, then we could give him some food and some aspirin or penicillin.*

Jeremy popped his head in having heard their conversation as he came to help. "Hey you guys, don't you remember, I took that course last summer and they taught us how to give injections and how to insert an IV. I did plan to go to medical school someday. I loved that class!"

"Thank God," TJ said. "I forgot all about that. Look at Bob, he hasn't moved, but he has a pulse. He's really hot, too. I don't know what to do for him. Glenn's reading to try to find out."

"I know that we should give him an IV with saline solution. If he's sick, it's probably complicated by dehydration. Then, after that, his symptoms should lesson and maybe he'll regain consciousness," Jeremy said. "The First Aid room has everything we need for now. I'll stay with him to watch for any changes after I set up the IV."

Jeremy did everything for Bob. Confident in his actions, he inserted the IV and after a several hours, Bob spoke. Jeremy fed Bob some chicken broth and crackers, then gave him some aspirin.

After 24 hours, Bob felt much better. He slept calmer after he ate the soup. When he woke up the next day, he wanted to hear about the tragedy.

TJ explained everything they knew, which was very little, and then they all got into a pattern of living and learning about the tall ship. But now there were six of them, instead of four.

As time passed, TJ read the amateur radio manuals

over and over again to become their expert on board. Sammy became the great student of climbing. At first unsure, but then climbed the mast so many times, he made it look as easy as breathing. Jeremy reorganized the First Aid room and took care of everyone's little accidents, which were mostly rope burns, becoming proficient in their medical care. Glenn set up the class room near the bow and created class work schedules so all of them could attend class every day. Mikey Two cooked dinners every night and Bob created schedules for daily jobs needing to be accomplished, with a very special food schedule for rationing.

The scouts never understood what happened in the world. They just knew they were alone and no one ever came to look for them. When they went ashore to find additional food and water, they found no one alive anywhere.

Loneliness became their enemy. Sammy especially suffered. Many days he lingered in his berth, wanting no part of the regimens the older boys built into their daily life. When TJ was on watch one night, he found Sammy at the farthest point of the bow, sobbing to the point of his not being able to catch a breath. TJ hugged him and held him tight. "I keep…hhahh. .hhahh…dreaming about Mom… hhahh. .hhahh… She keeps calling…hhahh..hhahh…for me."

"I'm sorry Sammy, why didn't you tell us. Even though we don't talk about it, our dreams are bad, too. We all miss our mothers." Holding him tight as he sobbed, TJ talked on, "You know what, starting tomorrow we'll sit together and talk about our families and how much we miss them. We can also talk about our dreams. I think that will help all of us. What do you think Sammy?" TJ felt Sammy's body calm down, so he let the hug go.

"O.K., TJ. That sounds good. Maybe it will help."

They started the next day. After a few more days, Sammy started to rest a little more at night. The dreams of home dwindled and his energy to do more things during the day came back.

They listened to the radio on the different frequencies suggested in the manuals. TJ tried a couple different frequencies every night. Finally, they heard other survivors. They talked about earthquakes, volcanic eruptions and tsunamis that ravaged the whole Earth. It took them a little while to realize their families were probably dead. They built a fire pit at the edge of the shoreline, near Dream Catcher. When they sat around the fire, they reminisced about their families and what they missed most. Many times silence overcame the troop and their tears helped cleanse the sadness which belonged to them all.

TJ never got the radio to work correctly, so they could speak to the people they heard in Israel, Russia and the United States. He thought it may be their location. Up to that point, they never moved the tall ship. Now that they were older and stronger, he decided to talk about it with everyone. In three years' time they learned everything about how to sail. Moving to a new location became their new agenda. It was time.

"What do you think about putting our knowledge to work and sail our ship to a new place? Maybe then we'd be able to speak to some of the people we hear on the radio each evening. After all, we've kept the sails in good condition by drying them out on a regular basis. The ship looks as good as the day we found her."

Sammy jumped to his feet, "Yes, yes, yes. This will be great and so much fun. We should have done it long ago, but I guess it's better late than never. Where should we go?

I vote for somewhere warm. Last winter was so cold. What do you say to that?"

"Whoa, Sammy...I was just thinking about going a short distance, say to over where St. John's used to be. We'd be at the coastline and maybe Israel could hear us from there." TJ said. "Then after we do that we could talk about moving on once again. Who knows, maybe we'll be able to find more types of food in St. Johns, the way they talk about it on the radio, you know by scavenging. I know I'd like to eat something other than the fish we catch." They all agreed and decided to leave in two days.

Mikey Two stood at the bow alone gazing out over the water. TJ came up behind him. "Hey, you were really quiet at breakfast. Something wrong? Don't you want to move from here?"

"Oh no, that's not it. I'm glad we're going. I was just thinking about Mikey One and how we never found him, Angus, Jake and Walt. I should have been with them in the boat; after all, they were my best friends. We joined the scouts together all those years ago. I know they're dead and I'm sad for them. It's my name I'm thinking about. Does that sound selfish to you?" TJ shook his head "no", but not really understanding what he was referring to.

"Since Mikey One is gone, I've been thinking you guys should just call me Mike. I'd like that. Mikey Two seems kind of silly and tiresome, especially now that we're older."

"Of course, Mike. It's a great idea. I'm glad you decided. Let's go tell the others."

"Wait a minute, TJ, there's one more thing. I've been thinking about it a lot lately, probably because I was thinking about my name, and Mikey One. We lost a lot of friends three years ago. I know I kept thinking they would just show up one day, but, well, they didn't. Before we leave here, can we put up a stone or build something as a memorial for them? What do you think?"

"Oh Mike, that's a great idea. We should have thought of it sooner. I'm glad you said something. Let's get the others."

TJ explained their task and all agreed with great enthusiasm. Through the afternoon they found numerous rocks along the shoreline, which allowed them to build a pyramid shaped mound in a small meadow near where the tall ship stayed moored for the last three years. Bob chipped and scratched the words, Scout Troop 776, into a rock with a smooth flat face, and adjusted it about half way up the side of the mound.

Jeremy wrote a few words to say as part of a short service. He gave the paper to Mike to read as they finished their work.

"Today we honor our friends who were lost when we first came to Norris Point. From Troop 776, Angus, Jake, Joe, Mikey One, Scott and Walt, we hope they didn't suffer and we hope they rest in peace. We place this monument in their honor, because they were our friends. And Lord, thank you for saving the rest of us, we promise to take care of each other. Amen."

"That's very good," TJ said. "Seal it in a plastic bag and tuck it just behind the plaque that Bob carved. Now we can remember that we had a memorial service for them. Let's get back to the 'Catcher. We need to get to sleep early, but not 'til we've secured everything to be ready for our sunrise departure time."

They rose before sun-up, because they knew it would take extra time to get underway their first trip and also using minimal sails. Sammy, at the top of the main mast, saw the ravaged coast and even after the three year gap, felt his stomach flip-flop. The disturbing sight of destroyed buildings never cleaned up or rebuilt. He thought, *How could the six of us survive and no one else?*

TJ directed the team to stay close to the coast. This slow and controlled movement of the ship was their test of ability with everything they learned from books. They modified all the procedures in the books to work with only the six of them, almost like changing a card game to work with only a couple people. Testing themselves on the working tall ship during the several years since the disaster helped to pass the time. It kept their minds off being rescued and the sadness of not knowing what actually happened to the world.

They arrived in the St. Johns area after eight days. Directed by the charts on board, they hugged the coastline. To get to shore they used both their rowboats. Scavenging for food was first on their agenda. Speaking to the people on the call schedule with Israel came next. There didn't appear to be any survivors in this area either, but they were always on the lookout.

Encountering decayed never disposed of dead bodies changed excitement to revulsion, when they walked through a neighborhood-like area. Encouraging each other they forged through, knowing food was close at hand.

Several hours later, the rowboats loaded, canned goods mostly, they headed for the tall ship.

After the scrumptious dinner with the new foods from their scavenging, Sammy watched the shoreline from high in the rigging. His night to keep watch until midnight, Sammy jumped to a rigid attention when saw a light start to blink on shore and yelled for everyone to climb up the mast. He wanted to make sure he wasn't imagining it.

"TJ, look...there." Sammy pointed at the intermittent light. "It started a few minutes ago. I yelled to you as soon as I saw it. It's right where we went ashore earlier."

"Holy cow, TJ, look at that. Sammy's right. We were there just two hours ago. It looks like it may be a flashlight, because it's a pretty weak light. Mike and I can go back to the spot to check." Glenn started to climb back down the rigging.

"Wait a minute. Let's talk about this a little bit. I know we want to find survivors, but it's been almost four years. We need to be careful and consider a way to protect ourselves." TJ said. *Whoa, I sound just like my dad. I guess that's logical, I am older now. Trippy...* "We've been isolated for so long; we don't know how anyone else perceives our appearance here."

They all climbed down. "Okay, I see your point, TJ." Glenn said, "What about this. I'll take Mike in one rowboat, and Jeremy and Bob can take the second rowboat. They can follow us, but they'll be off to the side out of sight. They'll have our shadows in sight. All four of us will have flashlights. I will use one as we get to the shore, so they can follow us."

"That sounds a lot better. " TJ said, shaking his head. "Let's go with that. Sammy climb back up. You can track their shadows and Glenn's flashlight. Glenn if there's a problem, erratically flash your light. If all is okay, with a flashlight, send the Morse Code "ok'. Sammy will see it. We'll get to you as soon as we can and remember Jeremy and Bob will be right behind you.

When they got to shore, Glenn turned on his flashlight and walked with Mike. Too close to see the signal light, Glenn yelled, hoping whoever needed them would hear him and approach. "HH-ee-llll-oo, we're from the tall ship. You probably saw us this afternoon. We needed food. Can we help you?"

At first, just silence, but after about a minute, they heard a man's timid voice, "Y-Yes, I'm here. Please don't leave me. I'm here."

The voice gave them direction. He was behind them.

The man limped and walked slowly out from behind massive plant overgrowth, next to a destroyed building. Although just a shadow, the scouts felt no threat from his tattered and sad demeanor. Mike turned back to the ship and sent a Morse Code message, "OK" while Glenn hugged the man. His body shook and trembled while he sobbed and cried. He held onto Glenn all the way back to the tall ship.

His nickname, Friday, came from an old boss who teased him, because he was always in a rush for Friday to arrive. The night of the destruction in St. John's he was aboard his newly purchased cruiser. He spent every waking moment on it. "You see I should have been a fish. I loved the water and spent all my time working on the water or in the water when the temperature was right."

"Did you find anyone alive after you survived the disaster?" TJ asked, "We never did, but we know there are survivors; we've heard them on our Ham Radio. They are in Israel, Russia and the United States."

"No, I was alone. When I saw you today, I thought I was asleep and dreaming, especially because of the tall ship. I've read hundreds of stories and articles about tall ships. It seemed logical when you came ashore from a tall ship that you were here to rescue me. That's what a dream is. Then when you left without me, I realized I was awake and that the nightmare I was living would continue. I started to panic. I thought for sure you'd leave without me." He coughed hard, probably triggered by his speaking and as if he was sick with something like bronchitis. "I've ridden up and down the coast in my boat, but never saw anyone alive. The tsunami was huge and because it came in at night, we were not prepared. Everyone I ever knew was gone." Friday started to cry again. Apparent to all the scouts, he suffered from exhaustion and a huge amount of stress or maybe he was sick.

The scouts cared for Friday. They made him dinner, helped him ready himself for bed because his body shook so much. When he fell asleep, he slept for two days.

While he slept, the scouts made many trips ashore. Scavenging, they found more food, bottled water, propane, penicillin and medical supplies, batteries, and clothing. All the boys grew in the three years' time since the disaster.

The few clothes they found in Norris Point were already worn out and didn't fit. Thrilled with shoes that didn't have their toes ripped out and covered with rags, helped all of them to feel very festive. They all wondered why they didn't move the tall ship to another place a long time ago.

When Friday woke, they celebrated with warm food. They ran out of propane for the stove over a year ago. The grand dinner felt like a holiday celebration.

The wonderful evening closed with listening to the schedule of talks on the Ham Radio, where Israel survivors spoke. With a quick break in the radio conversation, TJ flipped the switch to speak. "This is St. John's, Newfoundland. Israel can you hear us?" He flipped the switch back to listen.

The thunderous reaction over the radio waves blessed the scout's ears, "Yes, we hear you. We're glad you're there. How many are you?"

The scouts and Friday screamed and danced and hugged each other. Their plan worked.

TJ yelled, "Israel heard us! We did it!"

After that Bob took over the regular schedule, to

speak and learn what the scouts should or could be doing. TJ worked with Friday, because Friday's experience of the seas around Newfoundland helped with the next step of their plan. They were going to spend the winter in a warmer place. Friday helped them to get there by moving down the coast of the United States. The changed coast slowed them down. It took them eight months. During that trip, Friday documented everything. He decided to work together with TJ to capture geographic changes that occurred during the disaster. They drew new maps to share with all the survivors' globally.

EIGHTEEN

Rosalie's team, hot in pursuit of the first place prize, led the way by finding several intact rooms in the destroyed university rubble. Since a huge crevasse encapsulated the found rooms, this miraculously saved its contents. Originally, the crevice opened, outside the university walls. After that, the earth shifted sideways, it moved the open crevice over the basement storage rooms and didn't displace the room's ceiling. The contents of the rooms sealed inside were not destroyed by the jarring quakes. The buried rooms, covered by the shifted broken ground, kept them concealed.

Delicate excavation twisted and turned below the

ground, through which Rosalie's team found the amazing rooms. They lay undiscovered for over three years. Concrete, jagged rocks and rebars, removed with the old style bulldozers, gave way to an opening to the buried library rooms. Once they revealed the opening to the first room, huge disappointment for the team followed. The room presented millions of destroyed Terabyte Memory Nanic-threads, technology's most recent storage style. The nanic-threads held terabyte volumes of data dehydrated through the liquid form of carbon dioxide. Nanic-threads arc a brainstorm of the Green Age when multiple global corporations collaborated to develop the disposal storage units. These miniscule threads could be re-hydrated at a planned time for one-time use of the data stored within. The need for carbon dioxide turned into such high demand, an atmosphere clean-up war, almost like a contest, began by siphoning the gas from the atmosphere into major cities around the world. The action of the natural gas was twofold. The gas removed from the atmosphere as an overdue necessary clean-up, and the retrieved gas converted to liquid form for hydration and re-hydration of the nanic-threads.

Once they cleared the Thread Room of the massive debris, they found the Thread Cases. The fused threads became lost to humanity once the air-conditioning went off and fires throughout the library and around the area drove up the temperature for an extended period. The fused threads were irreparable. A devastating blow for Rosalie and her team; lost forever were the details stored in this destroyed room.

Earlier in their searches, the team located university blueprints, which acted as a map to a second room. It was only upon finding the first room that they understood how the earth moved and where a second room may still exist. This second room, buried deeper in the ground within the crevasse, appeared to be intact. Since the sealed room stayed buried after the disaster, all the ancient books and multiple rows of file cabinets emerged retrievable. The cabinets held thousands of converted older records on CDs and DVDs placed in these formats many years before to save space. At the time of the quakes, transfers of the older data to nanic-thread technology never occurred.

This windfall by the library and religion team gave Jerusalem a huge advantage for the competition. The local electrical team helped with some stored away batteries and portable DVD/CD players. These items, found earlier during scavenging activities, became tools for all of Rosalie's team, to review the "old" forms of historical records.

Within this discovery, the team found the copy of the endangered species study, which originally brought Rosalie to Jerusalem University. This part of the discovery became her most cherished treasure of all. She came to the university with hopes to be involved in the ongoing study and learn more about the empty summation. Her long-term plan to rebuild the summation and hypothesis into a formal thesis for her degree, stayed tucked away in her future thoughts. However, the earthquakes occurred which changed the world and everyone's lives. Rosalie, sure the paper manuals of the study she saw during her university tour were lost in the gigantic library fire, rejoiced in the discovery of the old CD/DVD copies, even though it only meant something to her and no one else.

With so much loss of documentation throughout the world on that day, this valuable discovery catapulted the library and religion team from Jerusalem into first place for their opening day.

An added incentive for the competition occurred, when the scouts from Newfoundland promised to provide passage for the winning team to wherever they wanted to go. These positive young men just showed up on a scheduled call one evening after almost four years. They brought new insight for all who heard their dramatic story of courage and hope and they fit right in to support the competition. The Jerusalem University team won the competition by opening first. The scouts took Rosalie's team to the ruins in Greece. A joyous trip tying new ruins to old ruins, and faraway teams to Jerusalem teams, which introduced lifetime friendships.

The trip took place immediately upon winning notification. Rosalie's interest in the endangered species study found again was so intense, she took it with her to Greece. Even though everyone else relaxed and laid on deck enjoying the sunshine on the exciting tall ship excursion, Rosalie sat in the onboard classroom and read and listened. Rosalie absorbed every word when she viewed the study's documents. The recorded notes from the ancient scientists, with their cryptic words, fascinated her and jettisoned her back into learning mode, even though she needed to stay focused on the university opening. The passion of her youth brought back to life. During the first weeks of the discovery she expressed her disbelief; she thought the study lost forever when the catastrophe occurred. With this turn of events, she began to understand and learn more about the details, hopeful to teach about the changed propagation worldwide. However, since so many species were wiped out during the quakes, this may now be a moot point.

The documents stated certain species began to decrease in numbers starting in the 1950's. The specific species: Marine Turtles, Gorillas, and Tigers. These species diminished by 1990 and were completely gone by the year 2030. The details of why were sketchy. Determined to clear up the mystery, Rosalie kept the study close by, to read, re-read and evaluate in every spare moment. Volumes of scanned scientist's notes provided her insight. The speculations in the personal notations prior to the published study, gave her an odd perspective of the fact, the summation showed empty.

Always in the back of her mind were the details about the human censuses covering over 100 years placed in the study. As she read, this puzzled her. *Why was this information placed here?* Rosalie hoped to find an answer to this question somewhere within the thorough study because of the longevity of its existence. *There must be answers buried somewhere in all these volumes.*

When the two week Grecian trip came to a close, Rosalie had to give up her reading. She wanted to spend all her time working with the study; however, the university start-up needed to be a priority. Her focus turned to the preparation of the opening day festivities once she returned to Jerusalem. To open its doors for public classes, remained the perfect beginning.

NINETEEN

Although Rosalie worked primarily with the Library and Religion team, she and Anatole communicated regularly about the Jerusalem Hospital and about the worldwide network of new hospitals. Anatole worked with the hospitals just like Rosalie worked with the universities. Over the early years Anatole became privy to a fact about the hospitals that at first was only curious, but over time needed to be recorded and tracked. This began one of the first "studies" since the day of the quakes.

At first, hospitals were makeshift and helped with minor first aid only. With limited doctors available, if any at all, the teams for first aid did the best they could to cleanse wounds, treat burns, and set broken bones. As time passed, the first aid teams grew the facilities, building into departmental groupings, including pediatrics, orthopedics, internal medicine, maternity, and family medicine.

These departments were just shells; however, over the years, the first aid teams acquired enough knowledge to function for them. Eventually, the facilities would require doctors.

The university in the United States, which specialized in medicine required many books. It began slowly with the classes for the first year of medical school and a nursing program. To open the university doors required at least enough information to fit a basic curriculum. These initial classes guided by regular volunteer teachers, and where possible, a professor who was a doctor. As in every other profession, doctors died in multitudes during the earthquakes world-wide. Details required to teach new doctors challenged the university team builders. The first classes to graduate would set a standard for every new department needed at each facility for the town where the student came from.

After their graduations, the new doctors came into each of their home town facility's very enthusiastic; they checked makeshift records the first aid teams set up for tracking, and then they began to create new procedures.

The records for most of the departments were as expected; however, one department did not show regular patients, maternity.

Anatole involved himself with the Jerusalem Hospital right from the onset. He participated in Rosalie's transmissions which introduced the teams work patterns. These conversations around the first aid teams and the plans to re-open new hospital teams worldwide helped everyone globally. Since hospitals grew in individual cities, the new procedural directions came from the U.S. University in Spokane. This sharing helped humanity with simplified newer health standards required for the worlds changed condition.

When the newest doctor for maternity told Anatole the records showed no births since the hospital opened, he became curious. *Are women not coming in for guidance or deliveries?* He pondered the idea.

One day he again listened in on a scheduled transmission with the leaders of the first aid teams, in Canada and the United States. The participants explained the progress with new doctor graduates starting in all departments at their facilities. When Anatole explained the one department in Jerusalem with unusual records for maternity, everyone tried to speak at the same time creating chaos on the transmission. Once the commotion cleared up, all participants agreed the same thing happened in all the facilities globally.

All teams decided to set up a necessary survey for all the family medicine departments. This would track:

1. Were sexual relations occurring with married couples?
2. If yes, was contraception being used to prevent propagation?
3. If yes, how many child births?
4. If no, how many child births?

This would be tracked for a year to begin with. After six months, a progress report would be sent to Anatole by all teams.

When Anatole told Rosalie about this incident, something in the conversation tugged at her. Somewhere in her mind she knew something about fewer babies being born. Rosalie went back to the CD/DVD archive room to again review the Endangered Species Study. *Yes, there it is.* She forgot what she saw there during her earlier reviews. Human propagation also showed to be depleted just like the other species. Rosalie searched through the hypothesis sections, and no conclusions appear at the close of this formal study; the conclusion-drawn-section ...empty.

TWENTY

A community sprouted up at Lake Sinai when a small group of survivors organized themselves. In another life-time they were sheepherders who clung to the solitude and remoteness others had given up when technology advanced. They loved the simplicity of their lives. After the quakes, they banded together in their locale taking care of each other. Instead of a mountain, part of the lay of the land they always knew, a huge lake now became their domain. Prior to the quakes, these people lived very simply using their sheep for food and trade. With virtually no sheep after the disaster, they were no longer sheepherders.

They spent most of their time after that day burying

family members and searching for survivors. The majority of the group was very young, and didn't know how to lead. With no direction and few sheep left to work with, they floundered in all their activities. They started to talk about the fact that they didn't see airplanes flying over anymore and no cars drove through. This is how they determined that whatever happened with the earth quaking didn't just happen to them locally. It happened everywhere else, too.

During their searches for survivors they stumbled on a damaged truck full of "radio equipment". En route the day of the quakes, the front end of the truck fell into a crevice. The driver hit his head on the windshield and died. The sheepherders were the first to find the truck. Recognizing the value of the new radio equipment, they salvaged it for future use, even though no one in their new collective group knew how to use it. It took them four years of studying the radio equipment manuals before the sheepherders figured out how the amateur radio system worked.

Barely surviving at the edge of the new lake, the sheepherders hoped for any opening the radio could provide. Mostly, they wanted to know what happened elsewhere in the world and to help project what their future may hold. After a long time and after many tries, they made a successful transmission. The diligent team in Jerusalem monitoring all the standard frequencies 24/7 heard the faint signal. The remaining sheepherders in the Sinai Peninsula learned about the global disaster. They lived very isolated before and after the tragedy. Once they learned about teams, a very simple logic, they planned to build their own community of teams to help each other and rebuild their lives. But still they argued.

The arguments divided them. No one could agree on how to execute a plan which would be good for everyone. It wasn't until the children began to swim in the new lake that the resort idea came to life. The plan to build and run a resort by the lake, would give them all new lives in a community setting to help them stay together. As if by a lightning strike, they all realized that everyone didn't need to worry about food anymore. A team could have food for its focus. This would stop the few people who horded major finds, to share. Everyone else dispersed into other teams and suddenly, as if by magic, they made progress. The four year cycle of arguments ended. They began building.

The only place close by to search for any of the

items needed was St. Catherine's, the ancient monastery now in ruin. The legends around the monastery were many, but only one stuck after the recent disaster. The tree spoke of as "the burning bush" was said to be within the walls of the old place. Part of the legend simply said "that's why St. Catherine's was built, to protect the old tree." Built in approximately 530 A.D. located at the foot of Mt. Sinai, now most of the monastery laid under the water of Lake Sinai. The remaining section on land, hung on cliffs at the water's edge, difficult to get to. Because of the location, the ruins were just found two years earlier. The sheepherders never went back because it was so dangerous. The last time, two of them died when they stepped onto loose rocks climbing the high cliffs to the ruins.

New teams in place and plans to guide them, the sheepherder's scavenger team, set out for St. Catherine's. They brought back broken pieces of ceramic tile, marble, and brick. The torn paintings and manuscripts would be built into the design of their new lodge, along with dented chalices which all lay in the decaying rubble of the demolished ancient holy place.

The most tragic find that day were the residents skeletal remains. Found altogether in a single space, suggested when the quakes started, they all gathered together for safety. The ground disrupted so violently with the quaking, the room they took refuge in, trapped them. When found, the deteriorated crushed remains were four years old. The sheepherders knew no one survived, because they didn't see anyone after the tragedy. Before, they would see the residents outside the walls of the monastery taking walks and hunting.

Finding the remains disturbed the sheepherders. They laid their families to rest four years earlier. This brought back vivid memories of the tragedy. They worked very hard to let go of their grief; the shock of finding the room with all the skeletal remains together, tormented them. They left not wanting to deal with their feelings. However, after a day they decided to go back to try to bring themselves closure once again, because leaving the skeletal remains behind without doing anything proved too difficult. Arguments erupted again, helping them to recognize their need to do something, other than ignore their sad discovery. They went back together with all the teams to hold a memorial service and set fire to the room.

The difficult proximity of the monastery, plus the fact that no buildings stood upright, brought no hope for them to use the old place as living space. They planned to scavenge the piles of brick, concrete and tile.

Slow but positive progress brought a new image to the desert skyline next to the lake. Created in sections, the lodge grew in size to twenty guest rooms. Additional bungalows at the water's edge became the homes of the sheepherders themselves. They transmitted a need for multiple items, which they had no way to scavenge for. Their question came through loud and clear, "Where can we buy what we need to finish the lodge?"

An obstacle not yet encountered prior to this transmission from the sheepherders: no money for exchange. Gold no longer backed up the destroyed financial institutions and all computers were out of commission. The Filternet was lost, since computers no longer worked. All were reminded, about the day when the old internet exploded in a series of viruses set into action by international terrorists and commercial vandals. Their collaboration failed and they lost control ending the old internet in the year 2048. The viruses held all the transmissions open while the blackout virus wiped out all connections permanently in a singular moment.

The government controlled Filternet became the

new expensive commercially run and politically regulated tool after the internet died. This followed other U.S. Government run businesses like, banks, health services and aviation services. Gangs infiltrated lobbyist groups with the eventual election of top ranking legislators coming from mob affiliated politicians like an evil affliction. In years after, this change expanded globally wiping out ties to all country's initial constitutional documents drawn up by their forefathers. Trusting in God at a public and government level was lost worldwide.

Rosalie heard about the questions which came through from the sheepherders in Sinai regarding scavenging for building materials. Money never came up before their question. Only survival provided everyone with a focus to this point.

The sheepherder's location became their issue. Scavenging, with only the monastery in close proximity and no major cities in ruin near enough to their home at Lake Sinai proved to be a challenge. Although the monastery provided some very unique discoveries, this fact stopped them from being able to find what they needed to complete the new lodge. This was different from all the other active global teams which proved to be successful.

Waiting to hear back from Jerusalem, the sheepherders scavenge team set out on their weekly trek to the monastery site. During the prior week's trip, they found two destroyed automobiles, which they thought to be useless for the current endeavor. However, over the weekend, after discussions with some of the other teams, they decided to go for another evaluation of the car parts. When they dug around the buried second car, they encountered the top portion of a garage door. It appeared to be upright and intact. As they removed the gravel, they saw an edge to a huge platform-type rock used as a driveway next to the top of another garage door. The door, below the driveway level looked as if a garage was underground. The only conclusion, the ground, underneath the garage behind the door, shifted during the quakes. They found it buried about eight feet lower than the platform-type rock driveway. More and more digging brought the scavenge team to a fabulous and very valuable discovery. When they cleared away the gravel and huge boulders from in front of the garage door, they pried open one piece. Inside, an undamaged hover-car lay in its underground cocoon. After they removed all the pieces of the garage door, the team stood around the car and looked on in astonishment. Not a scratch on the hover-car, just dust from the seepages through the door during the quakes. No one in the group knew anything about how to work or drive this type of automobile, but all knew the advantage of finding a treasure of this magnitude.

TWENTY-ONE

After the transmission from the sheepherders, the first thing Rosalie thought, *trade or barter. That's how it worked in the beginning, so now we're beginning again. Perfect.* She wrote up another document with all the details logical for a barter system for the regular Amateur Radio schedule now simply called ARS. She considered many different aspects for this new world beginning; part of which included education barter for ongoing use by the universities. This barter system allowed for exchanging students to study in the specialized fields they chose or for training aboard a tall ship. Transportation to other universities aboard the tall ship, helped teams in areas where scavenging showed fruitful, due to the old distribution centers loaded with products to barter for items like water and canned meat. The need for manufacturing, still non-existent, due to the multitude of "stores" produced for the millions on Earth prior to the disaster. Someday, many years after the disaster, manufacturing would need to begin again. However, recovery using existing products through scavenging in the destroyed cities remained key to the survival of the few people left on Earth. All teams worldwide followed the directions Rosalie wrote. She prepared suggestions for reading on ARS of what to look for and how to store multitudes of products specific to their locales and what they could share for barter.

Rosalie's new plan for this would work globally, and also gave the sheepherders a way to succeed. It will help them to visualize how to maintain a smaller single team of sheepherders and for that team to focus on caring for their diminished herd to use as their stock for trade.

Rosalie initiated the transmission to the sheepherders. "Trade and barter will be our next phase of recovery. Until you said you had a need for something other than scavenging, we didn't introduce an exchange for anyone. In my directions, as you will hear, I've covered so many new avenues for barter. It will be very exciting and should put wind in your sails."

"Miss Rosalie, I don't mean to interrupt, but we've found something. We don't know how to use it or if it still works, but it is in perfect condition...a hover-car. Do you think we will be able to barter somehow using this vehicle?"

"Oh, how exciting...by all means, this is a perfect beginning. Along with using your sheep to barter, I'm sure we'll be able to help you work out a plan. Once you decide what you need to finish building your lodge, we can have another conversation to figure out the details and who around the world can be part of your barter plan. In the meantime, I'll set up a global transmission to begin the ideas for Trade and Barter." The sheepherders signed off the transmission and set to work.

This spark from the team in Jerusalem revitalized the sheepherders and promoted their success as they worked to finish their resort lodge. The bartering success brought many levels of change to the new lakeside community.

With the lodge and its adjoining community

complete after ten years, visitors trickled in. At first they enjoyed the lake and brought their own masks to be able to see the new view underwater since the lake was never there before. Barter and trade, provided a way for its new patrons to make payment for exchange of a stay at the lodge. Because of their fascination with what they saw on their first visit, a couple men returned a couple weeks later. Huge caverns were discovered by these divers during their second recreational dive.

Considered as gossip, no one believed the stories. They passed from the few visitors at the lodge on the edge of the beautiful new lake, to people they met along the way back to their teams. These stories turned into new legends about the caverns, "they were haunted by the ghosts of the past". Since the resort's patronage grew very slowly, the news of the caverns being haunted remained local for a number of years.

Rosalie heard the stories about the caverns not too long after they were discovered. The mysterious stories intrigued her. She often spoke to her longtime friend, Anatole, about going there to visit the resort and dive to the caverns. So often in fact, she took diving lessons, to learn about scuba gear. She planned to visit the lake and decided to be ready when the opportunity presented itself.

The small and isolated resort and nearby community of former sheepherders, will provide the solitude she looked forward to and read about in the library brochure, which she found after the lodge opened. The unusual hand written advertisement showed up on the library's main bulletin board. With an artistic sketch of the new lake, everyone walking by was drawn to it. After a few weeks, they found out it was left there by a person bringing in a barter delivery. The appeal of a quiet restful vacation spot, reinforced by reading the brochure, helped her fulfill her dream of visiting there since she first learned of its history. This would be her first time off in ten years.

Those past ten years flew by because her work during that time turned into passion. The more she learned the more she wanted to learn; a pattern she followed her whole life. To visit the Lost Mountain Lodge promoted not only a vacation, but a chance to learn about the sheepherders and see how they adapted their new circumstances into new lives. Whenever she thought about the recovery, she realized the rebuilt scientifically diminished world, created a world of survivors attentive to education and scholarly values, but this space was different.

These citizens appreciated their saved lives while they lived in a new and very different world devoid of anything similar to their past.

She packed for her vacation, ready to meet the sheepherders, who lived a new profession because of the changed lands. They built a different livelihood for their families at the memorial to Mt. Sinai, a major new resort for Lake Sinai.

TWENTY-TWO

Rosalie tried to convince Anatole to come along with her on vacation, but even though their friendship grew into a brother-sister bond during the many years since they met, somehow going on vacation didn't fit into his plans. Their conversation turned his way, as usual, because he claimed to be too busy to leave for two weeks.

"So why don't you come with me to see what's there? We hear so many tales about shadows and shapes and unusual caverns to explore. Just think about it, Mt. Sinai, up-side-down! It's a fascinating idea to explore."

"No, I'm too old for that."

"Old; you're only nine years older than I am. Besides, it's right up your alley, rock digging."

"You know I just don't like the idea of "under water". And besides, you've been taking scuba lessons planning for this ever since the sheepherders gave you a free hover-car trip for you to visit. I'm sure they didn't expect you to wait ten years before you used it, but now you're going. I haven't prepared like you did, because I just don't want to go diving."

"Okay, okay; well, I guess suggesting it will be interesting to meet all the former sheepherders in person won't make a difference either."

Anatole shrugged his shoulders and shook his head in the negative, confirming Rosalie's statement.

She scheduled her vacation with the resort. The hover-car shuttle, set in place so many years ago after its discovery at St. Catherine's Monastery, arrived just before dawn Saturday morning. The shuttle service began as part of the first barter arrangement for trading shuttle services for building materials to complete Lost Mountain Lodge.

While enjoying the ride down through the Sinai Peninsula, she saw how much area still needed to be recovered, even after thirty five years since the day of the quakes. Rosalie's mind wandered to what she perceived as the joyous part of the tragedy; the changed mindset of the surviving people. The change…people believed in people again; they simply cared again. She remembered once the shock and the sadness passed, everyone came together in unity. When communications started, all people learned from their past mistakes and now understood the benefit of unity. The English language, adopted in over a hundred twenty countries before the earthquakes, helped to unify people through ARS. Because everyone spoke the same language, the instantaneous cooperation in Jerusalem, fell into place. The survivors communicated as if they knew each other for a long time. The unity developed even stronger when the countries around the world learned how Jerusalem organized their teams. The dissention of people, the undervalued arts and sciences, and the wars prior to the catastrophe, now existed only as historic facts.

During the long drive she reminisced about the day Anatole found her in the rubble. When she regained consciousness he reassured her about her ability to heal and to be all right, *Certainly, God would not allow you to survive so horrific a day, to let you die here in my fumbling hands. After all I'm an archeologist. Old bones and rocks are my life. My abilities to mend human flesh are limited; I have to believe He intended you to live since the steam didn't kill you. So let's get past that and let me get back on track with organizing myself to find more survivors like you. I believe I find things better than I do anything else. Just like organizing my teams to work through their day-to-day tasks when uncovering a new bed of relics...* Rosalie remembered how he rambled on and on that day, keeping her mind off the pain and the fear. His chatter about archeology showed her the true love of his life; she chose to trust him and found him to be an honest compassionate man, with massive depths of endurance and patience.

TWENTY-THREE

There it is; the sign pointing toward Lake Sinai, the driver slowed the car for the turn.

Her excitement grew. The hover-car turned toward the vacation she planned for so long; a peaceful, quiet and restful two weeks.

The countryside, with its massive lush bushes, burst into an expanse of green when the car turned toward the secluded resort parking lot. The bushes hid the resort from the main driveway. When the car drove around to the entrance she admired the architecture and beauty of the Greek tile pieces. The tiles covered the outside and inside of the archway overhead and the floor of the circle driveway. When she stepped from the car, she smelled a floral scent which she never smelled before. *I'll have to ask about that.*

All the hours she rode, she now realized she remembered nothing of the scenery. She spent the whole time reminiscing; that's all she remembered of her day, except for a couple places which she thought the destroyed countryside still needed to be recovered. Her revived thoughts of bygone days became her treasured memory. The shuttle driver hardly spoke, so Rosalie enjoyed the solitude during her ride, which gave her a gift of these remembered thoughts.

Rosalie checked into the resort. When she communicated with the hotel to make her reservation, the hotel manager promised all her choices would be in her room upon arrival. Although the people she communicated with in the past were no longer working in the hotel, the person who took her reservation did recognize her name.

Her simple homey room presented a perfect view of the peaceful lake. "Perfect, just perfect," she mumbled as the bell man opened the windows and she again smelled the fragrance, the same as when she first got out of the car. "What is that wonderful floral scent? I've never smelled it before."

He smiled, "Its Starry Wild Jasmine. Someone brought us a small plant several years ago. It seems to like our climate. We've had good luck with it. None of us had ever seen the plant or smelled the fragrance before. It was part of a small barter, when we received some tiles from Southern Greece."

"Oh, it's really so pleasant."

"Thank you, Ma'am. I hope the room is what you expected. This is one of our nicest rooms with a clear view of the lake." The gentle warm wall colors with floral accents in the drapes and carpeting, exactly what she requested, felt like the management decorated just for her.

After she unpacked, Rosalie fell asleep in the cozy large-pillowed lounge chair by the window. She woke hungry a couple hours later and called the hotel operator to learn about restaurant facilities. The operator said, "We have a new room service dinner; are you interested?"

"That's perfect. I'd like to rest a while longer." She ordered and waited for the food to be delivered. Her waiter told her about the facility and the surrounding properties, including the diving facility at the shoreline. Tomorrow

Rosalie planned to discover the area to determine how to spend her vacation.

Rosalie remained true to her plan to stay away from the beach, since she knew the scars on her legs caused many questions. She remembered her first diving lessons without a wet suit. Never in a million years did she believe her classmates would be so inquisitive. There, as part of the barter program from other countries, the small class knew nothing of her history because all of them were new students at the university. They asked questions about the steam scars which melted parts of her skin so many years before. With so much to discover there at Lake Sinai, Rosalie knew she wouldn't need to lie on the beach or swim and endure the questions which brought up painful memories.

Again drifting off into memory, she thought about how her legs healed, when Anatole nursed her back to health. The scars took the shape of the bandages he placed on her legs that horrible day. She saw the discouraged look on his face, after he removed the bandages. The look told her more than she wanted to know at that moment. Wrinkles in the fabric of the torn up jacket and part of a local band insignia imprinted on her calf and shin.

Anatole's makeshift bandages left an unexpected brand. Not knowing what to do for the burns, he just kept pouring water over the bandages to keep the skin cool. He did this several times a day without taking off the fabric strips. When several survivors started to help him with other tasks and just after Rosalie came out of her unconscious state, he decided to remove the bandages. His exact words stayed with her always, *Oh Rosalie, I wish I was a doctor.*

The telephone buzzer disrupted Rosalie's daydreaming. "Hello... yes, this is Rosalie Danforth...Yes, I requested information about a diving excursion. Great, thank you; I'll pick up the information later." Rosalie placed the telephone headset back into the old style cradle, and then cozied up in the lounge chair by the window and settled back into her reminiscent daydreams. *This is so pleasant; I should have taken a vacation a long time ago. It's so nice to think about the past in this quiet and subdued atmosphere. Let's see, what was I thinking about when the phone interrupted me? Oh, yes; I remember...*

The knock on the door startled Rosalie, "Room Service." Rosalie remembered she called them to pick up the dinner plates when she finished her dinner. Once the waiter left, Rosalie opened the window even wider for the breeze to come through; she laid down on her bed.

The next day would be full of new things while she discovered the lakeside community. She remembered another day of discovery; the day she found the study. The study gave Rosalie the reason to attend the university in the first place. The earthquakes buried the study along with plans for her future and then revitalized her life when they were eventually found again. Rosalie drifted to sleep.

TWENTY-FOUR

When she woke later in the evening, Rosalie decided to go out to socialize. She spent all the time since she arrived resting and wanted to get out and do something special. Because she didn't want to spend her vacation alone, she called the concierge.

"You'll enjoy the Car Door Piano Bar off the main dining room which faces the lake. It's a charming spot and many local patrons enjoy the music and the social time together with the hotel guests. After nine o'clock every evening, the crowd is lively and fun!" he boasted.

"That's an unusual name, why car door?"

"You'll see Miss Rosalie. It's very well named."

Rosalie decided to take the advice of the concierge and dressed for a special occasion. When she walked into the bar, she broke into a smile. Antique car doors decorated the walls as art and were parts of the tables. The chairs around the piano and at the tables made of automobile seats, provided comfort for an evening's seating and the automobile décor fostered a festive feeling.

When she sat down at the piano bar; everyone introduced themselves and broke into conversation about the weather, their drinks, and what tomorrow will bring for the small group of tourists. No locals were in attendance that night. Rosalie kept her disappointment to herself. She hoped to speak with family members of the sheepherders, who created the unique Lost Mountain Lodge. Even with her letdown, the light banter gave Rosalie exactly what she needed, a relaxing evening.

While she sat and drank champagne with the other hotel guests, Rosalie remarked, "I'm a bit cold. I didn't expect the air from the lake to keep the room so cool," her sleeveless dressy sequined top with its low cut front and back, along with the chiffon slacks she wore, provided no warmth. Several people in the group nodded in the affirmative.

A man, handsome and dressed well, but not appropriate for a formal evening, came up behind Rosalie, and placed his jacket around her shoulders. Startled, Rosalie turned to see the man turn away to leave. She caught his arm and he turned to face her.

Startled by her immediate attraction, she gazed into gentle blue eyes; like Paul Newman's in all those ancient movies she watched as a child. Her mind sprinted through the memories of the virtual HD Conversion Center (HDCC) late night offerings before the quakes changed their lives.

"Why did you do that?"

"I heard you say, you were cold. I thought offering my jacket was a good thing to do. I wasn't cold and I didn't need my jacket because I was leaving." He sounded a little irritated by her question.

"Forgive me, was I abrupt? I was just surprised and wanted to say something, but didn't know what it should be."

"Just thanks, would be enough. Enjoy your evening." He turned and walked away.

Rosalie thought this action to be just a simple

random act of kindness, but the moment stayed in her mind all evening. *Once I find out who he is, I'll return the jacket and thank him appropriately, but I'll have to do it the day after tomorrow, because tomorrow I have my first dive scheduled in the caverns.*

When she awoke with the sun already high in the sky, she saw on her bedside clock that she overslept. *The assigned group you will dive with will leave 11 a.m. sharp;* she recalled the concierge's words. Already 10 a.m., she needed to rush.

Thank goodness I got a quick breakfast at the café. Lunch will be served on the boat for our group about 2 p.m. This lunch timing is a good schedule for me, since my breakfast was so late. Rosalie arrived at the boat just in time. Almost ready to leave, she jumped on board and waved to the captain. He glanced over his shoulder to acknowledge her. He looked familiar, with a hat visor pulled down low, hiding his face. *I probably met him yesterday, when I checked in or walked around the hotel.* She adjusted her balance to the movement of the boat when it left the dock.

Rosalie mixed with the group; fourteen people in all including the captain and crew. With little conversation going on, it was clear everyone was anxious to start, just nods and smiles exchanged. They admired the clear water in the lake and enjoyed the warm breeze when the boat picked up speed. Rosalie's dark shiny hair blew freely as she turned her face toward the sun and squinted. Soon the clear lake water became dark when the boat approached the caverns. Mesmerized by the dark blue depths, all were silent. The boat slowed to a stop. Mt. Sinai up-side-down, the outcome of the cataclysm which lay below them, used to shoot high into the sky. All the passengers leaned over the sides of the boat to see the detail barely visible in the dark blue below. The amazing beauty existed here for just thirty five years.

Several people, probably the crew, began moving around the boat while everyone else viewed the fathom below. Eager to prepare for the dive into the caverns, Rosalie turned to locate the diving equipment she brought with her from Jerusalem. That's when she saw him, *there's the man who loaned me his jacket last evening. I wonder why he's watching me.* Rosalie, startled by his gaze, became unnerved by this man's stare. She decided to take matters into her own hands. She walked over to him to thank him for his courtesy the night before.

"Hello, remember me, from last night?"

"Of course, I remember you; you still have my jacket."

"I planned to return the jacket to you tomorrow, since I knew I'd be tied up with my diving plans today."

"Yes, this diving excursion was set up for me, too, several weeks ago."

Surprised by his reply; "Aren't you Enrico, the captain of this boat? I saw you as I boarded; you drove the boat away from the dock."

"Oh that…since I've been here several times diving, Enrico and I are now friends." Pointing toward the bow, he said, "That's Enrico over there. He lets me, the amateur sailor, take the boat out before the waters get dangerous. It's part of my escape to begin my vacation. I just arrived yesterday. I saw you while I ate my dinner last night, and when I walked by you and your friends, I heard your comment. After that, exhaustion set in; yesterday was a major travel day."

Rosalie found him easy to talk to, even though their initial meeting ended so abruptly. "I understand. I arrived from Jerusalem yesterday. I collapsed into sleep for the whole afternoon, just waking to go out for some socializing."

"Jerusalem…I'm going there next. I'm going to visit the university. I've been communicating with the team that made the DVD discoveries years ago and I want to meet the leader. She appears to have a solid grasp on so many of the studies documented there. I've been talking with her, but now since I'm so close, I thought taking time to meet face to face would be appropriate and beneficial for our working together. I extended my vacation this time around, to include the extra stop. I don't plan to get over this way from Volgograd again for a while."

Shocked by the words she heard, Rosalie stumbled, "Thomas…you're Thomas?"

"Yes, that's my name, but how would you know that?"

"I'm Rosalie."

"You're Rosalie?" He looked surprised, "I expected…well…someone older?"

"I'm old enough. Why didn't you tell me you were

coming to see us? I would have arranged to be at the university, not vacationing."

"I love to surprise people, so I just show up. It's always been very effective for me. I see everyone in their true working environment and style," he said with a devilish grin on his face.

"Oh, I see. Well, how long are you planning to be here vacationing? I'm here for two weeks. I don't want to cut it short. I have been planning this trip in my mind since I heard about the discovery of the caverns years ago."

"Perfect, I'm here for two weeks, too. We can get to know each other outside the work environment. That will be a true benefit for both of us; we won't have to waste time getting to know each other upon my arrival in Jerusalem."

Rosalie smiled at Thomas and turned to listen to the instructions from the diving coordinator. The first instruction was to separate into groups of two, because they use the buddy system.

Unexpectedly, Rosalie felt a hand grasp her hand from behind. Thomas chose her for his buddy. She turned and smiled her acceptance and held his hand tight.

The dive was even more incredible than Rosalie ever imagined; they drifted through the depths, two by two, while they followed their leaders. The caverns went on forever. The water, so clear, the sun's shadows streamed through the currents, while they floated with the vast black backdrop of the depths below. Not once did the water get murky. There were no particles of any underwater disturbances; just pure beauty, as if viewing rows of paintings in a museum. These moments fulfilled Rosalie's dreams.

The day ended with a beautiful sunset over the water when the boat drifted to a stop at the dock. All embraced as they departed while they expressed their goodbyes. This day again proved that since the global tragedy they all became family, in this new world of peace.

Thomas lagged behind to speak with Enrico in private. "I'd like to plan a special surprise for Rosalie. I enjoyed this day with her, and want the feeling to continue with a special private dive with the two of us and a guide. I could tell how much Rosalie enjoyed this day; so giving her another fun day would be great for both of us. I'd really like to get to know her better."

"Sure Thomas, I'll arrange this for you, but it will

need to be day after tomorrow. You need to rest tomorrow since you're not used to diving all that much. At least, 24 hours between dives is important for your health and safety." Thomas agreed, and said goodbye in a rush so he could catch up with Rosalie. He wanted to invite her before she left.

New to the idea of a relationship with a woman, and not knowing how to flirt, even though in his fifties, he liked how he felt when he was with Rosalie. Nervous about what to say and do next, Thomas' naiveté, probably obvious to Rosalie, became an obstacle in his mind. Building on their common love of diving, became a logical way to start a relationship for Thomas. *She is so independent and so involved with the world rebuilding.* Unlike Thomas, hidden away in his simple work in Volgograd, where he dreamed about meeting someone to spend his life with.

"Hey there, Rosalie; wait for me," Thomas sounded like a teenager; he caught up to her just when she stepped onto the dock.

"Hi Thomas; I thought you already left and didn't say good-bye. I was kind of sad, because I thought we had such a good time together today. I'm glad to see you're still here."

"I can't believe you'd think I'd leave without saying good-bye. We had more than a good time together today. We had perfect day. And with that thought in mind, I'd like to invite you to another planned day of perfection, day after tomorrow."

"What do you have in mind, Thomas?"

"I arranged with Enrico for a special guide to take us again to the caverns. It will be just the two of us, the guide and Enrico, of course. The guide he's arranging for us has done more than a 1000 dives here in the caverns, and knows many out-of-the-way spots, which we can enjoy discovering together."

"Oh Thomas; how fantastic! Do we have to wait? Why can't we go tomorrow?" She hugged Thomas without realizing it.

Thomas explained to Rosalie how Enrico wanted them to rest. "His advice is important, since he is the expert," Thomas made his explanation while he clung onto Rosalie's hug. *This is a good place,* he thought.

They rested as prescribed by Enrico. Rosalie slipped into her relaxed slumbers. She slept in, ordered room service for breakfast, fell back to sleep after breakfast which confirmed Enrico's prescription to be correct for the extra day of rest. Upon awakening late in the afternoon, she stopped by Thomas' room to return his jacket. When she knocked on the door and received no answer, she surprised herself by the strong disappointment she felt. She decided to take the jacket to the front desk; they took care of the return for her. *I wonder where he is,* she thought. She turned in for the night and in her mind planned her morning tasks, as she drifted off to sleep.

They planned to meet for an early morning breakfast; Rosalie arrived first. She sat daydreaming, while she waited.

As Thomas arrived at the breakfast table in the café, he thanked Rosalie for returning his jacket, and explained, "It's the only jacket I brought with me. I need to keep track of it." Rosalie smiled as she remembered how he described himself several years ago, when they first communicated via their initial ARS. Hearing this about his jacket, fit in with her understanding of the type of person he was. She believed him to be studious, quiet, and practical. *Yes, the jacket fits all that.* She expected his hair to be light, not the dark brown with a touch of gray at the temples. He looked quite distinguished but she envisioned him to be more rugged looking, even though he appeared to be in good shape, as if he exercised regularly. Their ages appeared to be close; but they never spoke about that. *His deep voice suits him, as well; I really never noticed on ARS.*

With so many new thoughts about meeting Thomas, the fact that she kept thinking about him since they met, surprised her. She never daydreamed about anyone this way before. *I had a boyfriend when I was thirteen, but that short lived relationship didn't last. I was totally into my science fair project, and he just wanted to party. Dating a few times, and even though socially we were a good combination, I wanted a different ideal for myself. After the quakes, even Anatole never had a romantic place in my heart; it was all gratitude and love like for a brother.* Feeling about Thomas this new way surprised Rosalie and became an unexpected happy distraction, even though her inexperience created awkwardness.

"Sorry I'm a bit late. I overslept. I guess it's funny; I practically slept all day yesterday. I did go out late in the afternoon to set up some surprises for you for today," he disrupted her daydreams and enticed her with his secretiveness.

"You didn't have to do that; I'm already excited about today's adventure. I can't imagine anything else could top that. Well anyway, I'm sure it will enhance the day, whatever the additional surprises are; that was very sweet of you."

"I just want this to be a perfect day, and from the looks of the weather, we're already off to a great start. Have you been outside yet?"

"No, not yet; I am so hungry, all I could think of was food, so I got here early. Coffee held me over until you arrived. I've already downed two cups."

They ordered and ate breakfast. Both very thoughtful while they scrutinized each other across the table smiling, yet comfortable in their momentary silence. They walked to the shoreline together. Enrico greeted them and introduced Rosalie to Doug, his partner and their diving guide for the day. Thomas knew Doug from previous trips to the resort.

Rosalie learned Doug came from Norway and dove every weekend with his grandfather while growing up. When they talked about learning to work in teams from

ARS so long ago, she smiled. She knew many people listened to the broadcasts, which she set up to help clear the chaos, but when she heard Doug and Enrico's tales of survival, the stories brought her work from long ago, back to life for her. Their story closed with a sad note about Enrico's little friend Rubble. During their preparation to leave on the boat's maiden voyage to their new planned home at Lake Sinai, the lumber stored at the top of the stairs crashed down during a storm. Rubble heard the rumbling lumber on the stairway and ran outside. The lumber trapped the dog at the bottom of the stairs. The impact crushed his little body. Enrico found him and laid him to rest behind their shack and from then on he talked incessantly about Rubble. His chatter lasted for days, and stopped him from working on readying the boat for the trip to Sinai. They didn't leave as planned, Enrico got lost in his grief for his little friend. Doug began to talk about the grief he felt for his grandfather and soon Enrico's chatter calmed. Eventually, they made their way to the new lake. It took them two years to get there.

"Let's get started, shall we? We have a full schedule today. Thomas' plan is for you to see many things, Rosalie. It will be a beautiful day!"

Eager to begin, everyone smiled when the boat pulled away. Doug drove the boat. Thomas sat beside Rosalie. Together they enjoyed beauty which surrounded them.

TWENTY-FIVE

Doug took the foursome to a different place on the lake. This surprised Rosalie. She thought all the openings to the caverns to be in one distinct spot. This new place, a very secluded section, resembled the ancient fiords in Norway which existed for centuries.

Thomas planned for Rosalie to see some old ruins just ahead. Enrico pointed out the ancient monastery, St. Catherine's, in the distance. "If you look closely, Rosalie, you'll see an odd perspective. Several buildings obviously in partial rubble above the ground, yet as we drift closer, you can see part of the other half of the building under water. It looks like it's hanging from a ledge," he concluded.

The overgrown foliage in the ruins near the edge of the water added to the strange look of remote desolation. Rosalie remembered the sheepherder's descriptions from so long ago. They explained the difficulty of trying to get to the ruins for scavenging, *now I understand the effort it took for them during those salvage years.* She reminisced as she looked on in amazement.

Although the mountains were not very high, the walls of the shifted cliffs ran straight down into the water, an eerie effect created by the wall-like cliffs. The boat drifted and it gently touched the cliff walls. The noise of the wood against stone shrieked in the total silence. The sudden quiet after that became even more pronounced. They heard just the slight shuffle of the water against the boat as it slowed to a complete stop. The lake was absolutely still. They sat in silence, while the foursome encountered this sudden indulgence of utter tranquility and peace.

After a few minutes, Doug and Enrico started to move around the boat to prepare for the first dive of the day. They went through the riggers to check the oxygen levels in all the tanks, the appropriate battery levels, and the necessary radio transmitters, which assured communication between the divers and the boat.

Rosalie and Thomas began to suit up. While Rosalie dressed in her bright blue suit, she remembered the day the salvage team presented her with birthday gift boxes wrapped in old newspapers. The bright blue suit and scuba tanks, found during year two after the disaster, became her surprise birthday presents. These items found during the initial scavenging were stored for future use.

When someone from the old salvage team heard of Rosalie's interest in diving, the team retrieved the items from storage and wrapped them up for her birthday gifts. "I didn't know such a beautiful color in a wet suit ever existed; I've never seen this color blue before." She danced around holding the bright blue suit next to her body, thrilled beyond words. She embraced the most perfect part of the gift, scuba gear. The double re-breather tanks, a system defined in the early 2000's were still brand new because the tanks stayed sealed in the original packaging. The new scuba tank set generated gas to breath. She learned to use the system during her scuba lessons over a couple years' time. The items, as all products, ceased to be produced since prior to the global tragedy. These treasures she now possessed came from her friends and she was very moved by their thoughtfulness.

Doug offered assistance with her suit-up, which pulled her back from her daydream. "I don't believe I've ever seen a wet suit in such a unique color," his remark made her smile.

"It was a gift from my family team in Jerusalem. When our dead body team disbanded, the last few people on the team came up with a new idea for a team, Educational Recreation. They were ready for something upbeat and fun, after so many years of sad and grisly work. One of the first things they suggested, a place with lessons for regular and under water swimming. Because we'd already heard about Lake Sinai, I kept talking about diving in the lake. For me it was just a dream about a future possibility. Then for my birthday about two years later, I received this wet suit, and the re-breathers," she ran her hands over the tanks as she spoke.

Doug smiled, "I can tell you really treasure the items and the people who gave them to you."

"Oh yes; I do. Then on top of that I helped the shepherds with the 'barter' systems around that time. My diving didn't seem so far-fetched after all, especially when they gave me a free round trip shuttle in the hover-car, because I helped them get started... and well, here we are!" looking very contented, she gestured a wave with both hands pointing to their surroundings.

Enrico interrupted, "The tanks are ready; Doug, will you show Thomas how to check the lighting gear for all of us. I want to explain a couple things to Rosalie and since you've been here before, Thomas, you won't need this part of our instructions."

Doug stepped to, as if to reply to a ship's captain, "Aye, aye, sir." Enrico picked up a hose and threw it at Doug in jest.

Rosalie sat down next to Enrico. "I want to explain about the water currents here. I also want you to understand the legends started about this spot so you won't be startled by what you see, while Doug guides you through the main cavern opening. Although most of the time there is steady wind here at this spot on the lake, I am grateful for the total calm today. Your first dive will be very special. When you get to the cavern opening, you will see how massive it is, and it will appear like a black pit. The contrast at that point is striking. Doug will direct you to spend a few minutes there for you to take in what surrounds you. The sun's rays dance in the water very unusually at that spot. We attribute it to the shifting currents which rush downward into the cavern. The constancy of the dancing sun rays with the astonishing mixture of shadows, bring on the appearance of ghost-like creatures which shift around the cavern opening. These shadows can be mesmerizing. I want you to be prepared for the moment to grasp everything around you."

"Oh Enrico, I've heard the stories about ghosts in the caverns. Of course, I never understood until now, what or where they were. I looked for things like what you described on our first dive with you the day before yesterday, but I never saw anything. Although, that day thrilled me, I was somewhat disappointed when I thought about it later that evening. I'm so excited. Can we leave now?"

"No, I have just a little more to tell you. The cavern opening is not too far from the surface; however, like I said earlier, the contrast is great. Light to extreme dark are only a few meters apart. Once in the cavern your lights will be essential. Follow Doug's directions on when to turn them on, so you don't waste any batteries. At this point, the journey turns from the sideways cavern opening to the cavern turning straight downward. Hold Thomas' hand for a feeling of balance and continuity. Doug will place tethers between you, Thomas, and himself at your waistlines while you're spending time at the cavern opening. This will assure your small group will stay together during your downward descent. Remember, at this point, it will be very dark." Rosalie nodded in agreement, "Follow Doug and don't let go of Thomas' hand, and you will enjoy the experience. Your slow descent will continue and you will notice light ahead of you. It's fascinating and mysterious because you continue downward. When you arrive at the light, you will be in another large cavern. The light comes from above, with apparent chasms which open to the surface. The chasms filled with water only a portion of the way to the top of each aperture. This allows the light into the cavern for us to view the new beauty that is now part of our lives. Okay, that's enough for now. Of course, everything is in reverse on your way back." Again, Rosalie nodded to Enrico to indicate she understood.

Rosalie, Thomas and Doug completed their suit-up activity, with lighting gear, tethers and radios checked. Doug immersed into the water first, with Thomas and Rosalie to follow; their adventure began.

TWENTY-SIX

The trek downward, exactly the way Enrico described, hypnotized Rosalie. Dazed by the beauty, she followed Thomas in a slow downward drift. The shifting light shadows appeared from everywhere and surrounded them, as if playing a game of tag, but so quick and just out of reach, no one able to win the game.

"It's time to move away from this large cavern. We go down from here," attaching the tethers, Doug said, "Rosalie, hold tight to Thomas' hand. We'll talk very little from here on. It's a waste of oxygen."

Rosalie nodded, "Absolutely Doug."

"Are you ready Thomas?"

"Yes, Doug; let's go!"

As much as she wanted to continue onward as directed, Rosalie felt disappointment to leave these amazing flashes of sun rays which jumped within the moving water currents.

Thomas grabbed Rosalie's hand and pulled her forward into the cavern to keep up with Doug. She looked back as they moved away from the dancing lights which reminded her of the kaleidoscope she treasured as a child.

The cavern below loomed massive and black. Rosalie clutched Thomas' hand; she knew her eyes were open, but she saw nothing. Just at the moment she started to feel a touch of panic, Doug told them to turn on their lights. This made Rosalie feel a little more at ease for the drift into the dark abyss.

They coasted downward with the current and soon Rosalie thought she saw faint light below. The light got brighter and brighter each minute. Once they entered another room, the light extended up so high it appeared to be higher than the old church cathedrals she remembered from her youth.

Doug circled the room and pointed out several spectacular light chasms while they drifted. The far end of the room showed a dimmer light, probably due to a division inside the cavern which stopped light getting through from the apertures high above. Rosalie guessed foliage or a portion of a hill also stopped the light. Doug motioned with a hand signal to follow him into the dimmer portion of the room. Near the end, Doug turned on another flashlight, and pointed the beam of light at a wall of the cavern and said, "Follow me through here."

Thomas directed Rosalie to go through the narrow passage first to follow Doug. Thomas swam close behind and held Rosalie's hand. Even knowing Doug and Thomas surrounded her, movement through the narrow stone corridor made her uncomfortable, a stifling feeling, almost claustrophobic. Her head touched the ceiling as the passage narrowed. She reached up letting her hand glide against the smooth rock and clutched Thomas' hand tight with the other. As they progressed, the water felt a little warmer against her wet suit.

When they turned a sharp corner and as if by magic, they encountered a bright new room. This room felt different; almost as if they were outside and not underwater anymore. As they followed Doug upward, the water felt even warmer. Thomas at Rosalie's side now, smiled. She could see his face with the additional light in the space. This room must be part of the surprise planned for Rosalie, because Thomas looked so excited, like he anticipated something new again soon.

Rosalie saw Doug touch the ground ahead of her when he walked out of the water. It's very bright now; the ground came up underneath Rosalie's feet. This, a surprising sensation for Rosalie, since she realized they were so far down underwater and yet, they came out of the water, into bright sunlight in the new room. She followed Doug with Thomas right behind her.

Rosalie ripped off her helmet and mask and hugged Thomas. "You're wonderful to arrange this for me. Thank you, thank you. What an experience; how was this discovered; who discovered it? I have so many questions; I don't even know where to start. Please tell me everything you know; I want to know it all," stopping her questions to catch her breath.

"Yes, sure, everything; we'll tell you everything, but now we rest and look around this room for a while. When we get back to the boat for lunch, we'll explain all the discoveries and who's been here to do it all. I'm so glad you are happy to be here. I wanted to share this with you. After meeting you in person, I knew you would appreciate everything about this place."

Doug checked over all the diving equipment; Thomas showed Rosalie around the room. A large space at least two people high at the highest point, with dirt on the floor, not really sand, more like gravel. The air smelled musty, but not stale. They rested and chatted about where the light came from.

The ceiling of the room glistened like an altar which held hundreds of candles and the candle flames flickered because the air moved them. The "flickering" rays of light shone through the ceiling apertures from the bright sun high above. The sporadic clouds which passed between the sun and the apertures, made the light in the ceiling dance. The unusual affect, occurred on sunny days. This room on a cloudy day, with dim minimal light shining through, couldn't be found.

Thomas broke the silence, "Let's start back to the boat. It's getting close to lunch time. We need some food before we go for the second part of our planned day."

"Please Thomas, just a few more minutes?" Rosalie begged. She lay back onto the gravel to look up at the ceiling full of streaking lights.

TWENTY-SEVEN

"Doug, how long ago was this room found and who found it? That dark corridor on the side of the huge cavern is virtually unseen," Rosalie pondered the question.

"Oh, that would be me; I found it. When Enrico and I took our first patrons down, we didn't know the caverns were there. They came back a couple weeks later because it was so fascinating. During the second dive with them, we stumbled onto the large rooms. We almost lost one of them, because he wandered off alone. After we learned the first cavern opening was so vast, we put together the speech Enrico gave to you on the boat earlier today. Oh, I'm getting off subject again…anyway, after those two dives, Enrico and I came every day to discover what's here. Mostly, it's me diving, with Enrico keeping tabs on me using long tethers. A couple older shepherds, who built the resort here, remembered how to create rope out of reeds. You know the old hemp strands used to create canvas in ancient times. That's what they used to create rope out of. Our shepherd friends helped create long tethers with that old "technology". We have since scavenged around finding a warehouse in Spain, right near the Barcelona ruins. We managed to get composite ropes from there. We are using those today. Sorry, I do like to talk and I get off the subject. Well anyway...fascinated by the shapes of the caverns, I scrutinized every inch. The location of gravel always caught my eye, since the floors of the cavern rooms appeared like buckets holding loose gravel. At first I thought it just odd looking. After I talked with Enrico and the local resort shepherds, their descriptions of caves in the Sinai Peninsula, gave me the logic that the cave ceiling was under my feet. I took that to mean the cave was up-side-down." Doug stopped for a moment and rummaged through his back pack. He pulled out a container of water, opened it and drank the full contents. Rosalie and Thomas waited with patience to hear more of his tale.

"About a year after the initial discovery, I checked

out the walls of the big room, touching each side and up-side-down ledge from top to bottom. I wanted to understand the find. On the last side of the room I found lots of loose gravel and rubbed so more would fall away. After a while I cleared the area, smoothed down to the final portion, just like a sand sculpture at the beach. That helped me understand I needed to follow this pattern to remove more loose rocks. Without realizing, I opened up a space. I came back day-after-day. Sometimes Enrico came down to help, but most of the time he kept close tabs on me from our boat for safety reasons. After the fourth day of moving the gravel, I noticed when I pushed the space, it moved away from me, instead of pieces falling downward. I shoved with all my strength using both hands. As I pushed, my arms fell into another space. Vivid light rays streaked between and around my arms surprising me. Just a second before the space fell in; the room became pitch black, except for my dim flashlight. Stunned for a second, my mind raced. The complex logic... I was so far down underground and yet there was bright light! So stupid, I pushed through and my scuba tanks caught on the opening. They nearly ripped off my back, but I managed to get them free. When I slipped into the next "new" room, a huge amount of gravel fell down behind me. The bottom surface dropped as if a temporary floor fell into place. When I plunged into the blinding light, more gravel and rocks followed. I was sealed in. The tether rope caught under the huge amount of gravel. I needed to untie it, so I could move around in the water. I did that and felt the angle of the underwater floor, which sloped upward to the light. Before the gravel sealed me in, my radio worked. Enrico and I communicated about progress. Now trapped in the new room though, my radio didn't work anymore. I believed Enrico could not hear anything I said to him. My mind went crazy! In the flash of a second, I thought of a hundred bad scenarios, all of which left me dead. I panicked! Feeling sorry for myself, I cried. After that I hyperventilated. I hadn't felt so out of control since Granddad died in front of me all those years ago. Come to find out later, Enrico did hear me, and started his rescue procedures. But in the meantime, I needed to get rid of the panic. My Granddad kept coming into my thoughts, so I started to think, *what would he do in this situation? I know, get into action. The light in front of me needed to be discovered. Hey, that could be a way out!* I followed the ground upward toward the light. After several steps I found myself walking out of the water, a wild and unique sensation under the circumstances. I think this kind of moment would be described as surreal. I stepped onto the mounds of gravel, almost like a mini-beach and fell to my knees. My tanks felt like they weighed a ton. I slowly removed my mask, only trying a couple breaths at first. I needed to know if I could breathe the air down there. Once I was sure, I removed my scuba tanks and turned off the oxygen to save as much as I could. During the scuffle of those last moments, I knew I breathed erratically, and used more oxygen than normal. I dropped down, lying on the gravel, rested and took long deep breaths. I looked up to the ceiling and saw bright light from the sun's rays streaming through odd looking holes. It was noon time, so the sun was high overhead. I knew that's why the room was so bright. I communicated what happened to me over my radio, but all I received back was noise. Enrico and I planned for emergencies; however, I always thought I would be a rescuer, not a rescuee. Rest was important. I remembered that from our plan. There was nothing I could do at that point. I told myself, *to rest now, will help me later. "*

"After a little time passed, I relaxed and fell asleep. When I woke-up the room was dim; the sun's rays no longer straight above streaming in. Near dusk, soon it would be dark, but still no word on the radio or signs of a rescue. I checked my flashlight; the batteries still worked. I used them sporadically. I slept as much as I could overnight, so grateful to see the light of the rising sun. With the light of morning, l started to dig myself out. I told myself to be calm and remembered my grandfather's words the first time I dove alone. He said *if your mind starts to feel panicky, keep telling yourself to be calm. Remember, you are in control.* Before I knew it, I fell asleep when the room became pitch black. A whole day trapped and still not rescued. When I woke up again, I set into action right away. I put on my scuba gear; my tanks were about half full. I monitored my time right from the start so I could be sure to have enough oxygen to get to the surface. I pushed aside, what I would estimate at about fifteen buckets full of gravel and spread it out flat toward the other end of the room. From there it wouldn't fall back to the space that I came through. Once my hands started to hurt, I used my flippers to push the gravel."

"The space I came through was marked by the tether still in place. I stopped the underwater work after forty five minutes. That was all the oxygen I could spare for my rescue. Fifty two hours passed, a long time to be trapped. The sun shone through the apertures again, brightness returned to the room."

"Oh Doug, you must have been terrified," Rosalie interjected.

"Yes, although I could breathe, so I knew oxygen was getting into the room from somewhere, probably through those odd holes in the ceiling. There was no water or food. I started to play out the scenario in my mind and scared myself. Why I couldn't keep Enrico in my mind, because I knew he wouldn't leave me there to die, I'll never know. I kept getting back to my grandfather's direction though. It was like he was there with me. I can't explain it better than that. It's how my thoughts went. Through the words I repeated in my brain, my grandfather said to me so long ago, I again fell asleep. I thought if I fell asleep, I allowed myself to escape the reality of the scary scenarios I created in my mind. About 3 o'clock in the afternoon, Enrico knelt over me, still in his scuba gear. Shocked by the sight of Enrico's mask in front of my face, I panicked. I shoved him away. He fell back into the water. After a couple seconds, I realized he was there to rescue me. I was coherent again. I hugged him. I didn't want him to disappear. Enrico reassured me it was truly him. I was never so glad to see anyone in my life. All the fear and panic were gone from my head, and I started to share the "find". This new room we could now share with our diving patrons."

"Wow! I guess I asked the right question," Rosalie jumped in. She smiled at Doug and reached out to touch his arm. "I'm so glad you're safe."

Thomas smiled, and shook his head in agreement as he reminisced about this tale he's heard more than once.

During the time Doug spoke about the room discovery, Rosalie glanced around and scrutinized the details of the amazing place.

Unprecedented rains fell over the past months in the Lake Sinai locale. When they first entered the room, Doug indicated in his quick explanation, that he didn't know if the room would be under water or not. Even though there was so much rain, the amount of water balanced out making their entry to the room possible.

After they laid there another ten minutes watching the ceiling flicker, Rosalie sat up. She knew it was time to start back to the boat. Her eye caught a washed away spot near the back of the room. No light shone on that spot, so no one noticed it earlier. Now, her eyes adjusted to the different light, it caught her attention. She walked to the area; she saw gravel washed away leaving obvious water erosion crevices from the recent rain. The floor declined toward that side of the room, so all the water that came through the apertures above ran down toward this spot. Rosalie knelt down to check out the erosion. She saw scrappy shredded pieces of what appeared to be bits of very old looking shoe laces interlaced in the gravel around larger rocks.

"Hey guys, look at this; Doug bring that fancy flashlight of yours." Thomas and Doug soon knelt next to Rosalie overlooking the spot.

"I've been at this end of the room dozens of times, when I first found the room. I never saw this before." Doug held the flashlight; Rosalie and Thomas removed the gravel which mixed in with the larger stones.

"From the looks of the water erosion, these rocks were probably buried before," Rosalie's common sense logic confirmed a possibility. When they removed more and more gravel, the wedged together larger stones took on a distinct rectangular shape, with the top one smooth on one side. The hole became about 3 feet wide when they removed more gravel.

"I have a small shovel folded up in my back pack."

Doug jumped away and messed up the progress when gravel fell back on the rocks.

"Whoa, slow down Doug, the gravel dust will choke us and take away our oxygen," Rosalie cautioned. "There's no rush; these stones have been here a very long time, I believe. I'm glad you thought about the shovel, my hands already hurt just from the little bit we've already removed. We'll make faster progress with a shovel."

After twenty minutes they managed to get the stones loose. The shoelace type threads, shreds of animal skin, were the size of ordinary strings. They held these stones together. At one time, they were obviously intended to hold the stones in place, with one outer bottom stone, almost like a casing.

"The bottom stone has broken into two, so this one here was a single stone before. Plus, the two longer stones look rather like trays within a case," Rosalie said. "Doug, do we have something we can cut these skin remnants with? I want to see what's between these longer stones."

"Yeah, I think in my pack. Just a minute, let me look; I'll move slower this time. You're right about the dust; it took a while for it to settle."

Rosalie noticed Thomas' grin. He watched her excitement. "I wish I could say I planned this as part of the day, but that would be pretty bold," as astonished as both Doug and Rosalie.

She leaned over and hugged Thomas. "What if we find something important? Wouldn't that be amazing?" Her almost inaudible whisper, attempted to keep the secret, even though they were about to bring something old out of its hidden burial place. She broke away from their cozy extended hug and accepted the knife from Doug.

Rosalie cut through the skin strings and captured the tiny pieces which fell apart. She handed each piece to Thomas. With the last string cut, she hesitated to look. She held her breath and looked up at Thomas and Doug. Her eyes sparkled in the sun rays, which streamed into the room through the apertures above. The silence of the moment deafened them.

"What are you waiting for, Rosalie?" Doug said, biting his tongue in anticipation. "Turn over the stones."

Rosalie picked up the broken tray-like top piece and turned it over. Surprised by its weight, she almost dropped it. The first glimpse of the chipped out wording on the rock made time stop for her. She said nothing. Rosalie's placement of the removed rock blocked both, Thomas and Doug's view. They strained to look over her shoulders. Silence...

"Do either of you know what language this is?" breaking the silence. "It looks like Hebrew to me, but I'm so nervous; I can't think. I mean it's logical, we are in Israel. Come on, what do you think?"

"It's old looking; yes, the symbols look Hebrew," Thomas said, as he stared and held onto Rosalie's shoulders. "I'm no expert though; I've seen Hebrew, and worked with some of the symbols for different translations when we found a buried temple in Volgograd, but that was more than twenty years ago."

"Can you believe the condition of the writings? I wonder if the words are etched, chipped, or burned out somehow. It looks so new and perfect, and yet," Rosalie speculated when she picked up the second larger tray rock, "this second rock is shaped different, and the writings although in good condition, are not chipped out by the same hand. This writing is more personal, like a note. Look there's a signature........ משה

"Whoa, wait a minute," Thomas said. "I think that word is Moshe. That's a familiar use of the name..." he hesitated, "Moses." He took a deep breath, "Can this be written by "the" Moses? Do you know how old this is if it is "the" Moses?"

Awestruck at this revelation, "Can this be possible? No, this can't be what we're all thinking." Rosalie still excited, but stayed focused to build in some common sense. "If this is "the" Moses, how and why was this hidden away? Where was this hidden away? Now that we found this in the cavern, where was it before? We're in the right locale for this to be "the" Moses...but what is it? As I scan the other words, I don't understand most of them. My friend Anatole taught me most of the Hebrew I know, but I'm not an expert when it comes to translations. Okay, now what do we do next?"

Rosalie tripped over words, her mind raced with so many possibilities. "If these stones are authentic and if I remember the Bible's book of Exodus my dad read to me as a child, God told Moses to build a tabernacle for the tablets he gave to Moses. The tabernacle was to keep the tablets safe and therefore this covenant between God and his people would be safe. If Moses built the tabernacle for the commandments, maybe he built a container for these parts hiding it away. How else could animal skin pieces still be intact as much as they are? We should look for more stones or a sealed type of place where these stones could have been hidden. And look, the bottom piece is like a case. See…it has carved fingers which wrap around, so maybe there's a top to the case. The ceiling of this room would be a place to start. Since Mt. Sinai is up-side-down, this room we're in right now, wouldn't it have been a cave?" She looked back and forth at Thomas and Doug, "This end of the room is darker and more solid than the middle and the other end, where the apertures let the light through," she pointed as she spoke. "Doug, where's your flashlight? Can you use it to scrutinize every inch of the ceiling? Thomas, you and I can dig a wider and deeper hole to see if we can find any other pieces. Let's start, we don't have much time. Enrico is waiting for us."

Grateful for the direction, Thomas and Doug jumped into action. After a few minutes Doug said, "Hey, look at this, over here in the corner. It looks like a jagged kind of square edge. Thomas, can you give me a boost up a few inches? I think I'll be able to reach it. Maybe I can see if it's loose. It's a different stone than the gravel-like smaller rocks around it."

Thomas gave Doug a boost up by leaning against the wall of the room and made a stirrup by holding his hands together and supported it against his own leg.

"I'm glad you're barefoot, Doug," Thomas teased, "I don't know if I could hold you if you weren't. My hands are   already   raw   from   digging."
Thomas leaned his right shoulder against the cavern wall; Doug reached up with both hands once he stepped into Thomas' stirrup. He touched a few small rocks wedged around the other larger square edged piece. Some of them fell to the floor right into the hole that Thomas and Rosalie just finished digging. "Hey, watch out Rosalie, I can't stop the gravel from falling."

"Okay, Doug."

Doug held the rock with his left hand and brushed away more of the gravel-like rocks with his right hand. The square edged stone began to feel loose.

"Oh no...LOOK OUT!" The stone broke away from the rocky ceiling and crashed to the cave floor. The deafening sound, with stones hitting stones in the small room stirred up dust into a huge cloud completely filling the space. Unbalanced after dodging the rocks, Thomas broke Doug's fall when he grabbed the open zipper edge on Doug's wet-suit. He fell onto Thomas. This stopped him from falling onto Rosalie; however, it stirred up even more dust. Now the room was silent and thick with dust, with not a word from Rosalie.

No longer able to see her, Thomas' sounded frantic, "Rosalie, are you okay?"

No reply.

He raised his voice, "Rosey, answer me." Thomas scrambled to his feet to move toward her.

Barely audible, holding her hand over her mouth and nose, "Don't move, Thomas; let's wait till the dust settles." Rosalie said, "Let's cover our mouths the best we can. This dust can't be too healthy. I can see another large stone down here now, which looks the same size as the etched stones, but let's wait, okay? We don't want to damage the stones by stepping on what we can't see. With all this happening; we can't take that chance," Rosalie's muffled voice whispered. Relieved, Thomas and Doug followed her instructions.

The dust settled after twenty minutes and Rosalie pulled the new piece away from the dark corner. "If more rocks fall from the ceiling, they're safer over here," pulling her flippers under her knees. "I don't know about you guys, but my knees hurt. This gravel has sharp edges. Hey look, the stone didn't break!" She scrutinized the ceiling stone. The same size as the first ones Rosalie found, it became part of their new collection. All three experienced adrenalin rushes moving the stones and grinning ear to ear as they tackled helping each other.

Rosalie pointed toward the unstable ceiling, "Since we dislodged this additional stone, more ceiling pieces will continue to fall. It's time to remove these discoveries to a safe place."

"I've been thinking about that," Doug said. "It does present a problem. Removing these stones will be dangerous, because we need to carry them through the water. Since they are so heavy, their weight will drag us down. We need to make two trips. In one trip we could lose them in the depths or one of us could be injured. In either case, we can't risk it."

They wrapped up the stones, the skin pieces and the remnants, and placed everything from the first part of their discovery into Doug's pack. Doug suggested the details of how they would get this heavy pack to the surface and constructed a plan for the second dive back to retrieve the last of the stones. Fatigue needed to be considered since they've experienced multiple stresses along with adrenalin rushes. Rosalie and Thomas agreed with Doug's plan and they knew it would be safe, as long as all the details were followed to the letter.

Rosalie, the first to reach the boat, followed their plan. The last radio transmission to Enrico told him the plan with very few details; he could tell they were very excited about something.

Glad when Rosalie showed up in the water next to the boat; he helped her on board. She hugged him in her excitement even before she got her mask off and talked very fast in muffled tones, "We found something; something important. Thomas and Doug are bringing the first load to the surface right now. It's very heavy. Oh my God, you just won't believe it."

"Rosalie, let's get your mask off."

"No, no, I can do that myself. There's no time, Enrico, please help them? Oh, Enrico; wait until you see it. You just won't believe it. You just won't."

Hearing the urgency in her voice, he got into

action, and in moments entered the water to meet up with Thomas and Doug. He headed to the cavern opening and saw them coming; their helmet lights directed him to their position. He saw how the drag of the object they brought to the surface, slowed them. The weight appeared excessive, because Doug and Thomas kicking stride looked strained. Enrico tied the tether rope which he brought down to them, around the pack. Once secured, he tugged on the rope three times, which Rosalie felt above in the boat. She began to pull the discovery to the surface. The three divers guarded the treasure as it drifted upward.

.

TWENTY-EIGHT

They stayed on the boat for lunch, giving them a chance to rest, but Rosalie, too excited, to even consider resting, danced with Enrico around the deck. After that she danced with Doug and then last but not least she latched onto Thomas. They laughed and laughed, because they needed no music. The rhythm came from their mood and the excitement of the moment.

"Can this be happening? Did we really find something important?" Rosalie asked Thomas as they made their final turn around the deck.

He grinned as he twirled her, "Yes, today really is happening. We found something very important."

When they settled down to eat lunch, they discussed how to get back to the cavern room to take pictures of the discovery site and retrieve the second stone casing.

"Oh Enrico, I don't have a camera. A few of us in Jerusalem bartered for them after the university in Russia brought back the simple technology. I was wrapped up in my work and never did get one."

Thomas jumped in, "Yes, we were all so excited when we got that working. It's funny. I have a camera, but didn't bring it with me. Two cameras will be necessary, to cover the site, plus the underwater trek."

"Don't worry," Enrico said. "I have both kinds. I take lots of pictures, but have never gotten any developed. I have them tagged in a bin in my bedroom closet. One of these days I'll get the developing done. But...we can use my cameras, and you can take the film to Jerusalem to get them developed for our documentation of the sight." Before Thomas, Doug and Enrico made the second dive, Enrico took pictures of the stones and the team, setting up with a timer so he could be included. Rosalie stayed on the boat with the initial stones. Enrico's underwater camera came from the Barcelona ruins when they bartered for rope. He used it for the first time to capture on film the underwater trek for documentation of the placement of the find. They returned to the boat with the last stone just before dusk.

For easy access, they kept the discovery in Rosalie's hotel room. The four of them worked from there to examine the stones and planned for what will be up coming. They knew the stones were old and the language was ancient Hebrew, but they had a lot more to learn.

While her companions went to clean up after the long day, Rosalie once again examined the stone slabs and wrote down her initial translations. "I can't believe I don't know more of these words." *Anatole will be able to complete the details. I know he will.*

As everyone arrived back at her room, she jumped right in, "The translation, well, from what I can tell, it's unbelievable. How will we be able to tell the world about this discovery?" Rosalie's question left them all to ponder the idea.

Even though the translation from Rosalie's minimal bits of Hebrew knowledge only showed several words for each line, they believed the discovery was important. The stone casing and the personal etched note raised questions in their minds. They all pondered the "what if" idea.

The carved out words on the stone with the rounded edge at one end, with a list-type of writing, showed a different carving style than the note from Moses. This suggested the possibility of something more than the Ten Commandments Moses brought down from Mt. Sinai so long-ago.

בצע את עשרת הדיברות, חיים על פני כדור הארץ ישגשגו לנצח. כפי שהובטח בכתביו של אלוהים, להרוס על ידי מים לא יקרה שוב. אם עשרת הדיברות מוזנחים, פעולה אחרת תתרחש - ההתפשטות של כל המינים הפוכות. חיים יתחילו שוב אם האהבה וטוהר של לב כדי להמשיך.

First primarily... Earth...long time.

Pledge... of God... devastation... water...anew.

First ten rules ...bad...spread...classes... turn around.

Life ...start...love...humanity.

The second tray-like piece is written more uniform like a note, and the verbiage went lengthwise on the stone shaped in a rectangle.

אלוהים נתן לי הוראות לתת רק את עשרת הדיברות לשבט שלי

ולבנות אוהל אחסון.ארבע הנבואות הן כמו לדעת את העתיד. אלוהים
כיוון אותי כדי לשמור אותם נסתרים. יהיו רק עשרה כללים לעקוב. ידע
של העתיד טמון נסתר. משה

The words, more personal, as if specific to just the person reading:

"God instructions first ten rules to my tribe build storage tabernacle. The foresights ... future. God directed me to keep them .... Only ten rules to follow. Knowledge of future forgotten. Moses"

"I know my translation is lacking. My friend and colleague, Anatole, our expert in Hebrew and Archeology can provide clarity for us. We can take the stones to Jerusalem University to have them authenticated. The exact translation can occur there, too. You know every time I examine the stones, I get more excited. It's hard to keep focused."

All grinning, Thomas, Enrico and Doug nodded in agreement. Still in awe of what they found, hearing Rosalie's calm and logical plan provided relief for the three men. She provided directions easy to follow with a matter-of-fact attitude, as if to say, *this way is logical and just makes sense.* They were also thrilled to hear her growing excitement. It suited the occasion.

"Several major discoveries are on file now at the university. To add another treasure to the collection will be easy for the experienced staff. This will be the safest place to keep the discovery intact," she concluded.

Thomas excited and eager, "If it's true and these are four prophecies that Moses received on Mt. Sinai, this will be a debatable discovery. After all, so much history was based on the major fact that there are Ten Commandments and nothing else. These prophecies wrapped and hidden on the mountain, to surface after so many years and after a cataclysmic global tragedy can only be speculated about. The Jewish people believe in even more commandments within their religious writings. These prophecies may be more significant for Christian believers. Ultimately though, for those of us who believe in God, this discovery must be the will of God." Exhausted, they all dispersed for a well-deserved rest and agreed to meet the next day.

To wake up without the alarm relaxed Rosalie even more than the few hours she slept. Excited, she couldn't fall asleep for several hours, and woke up easily, even though she slept so little. With important decisions to make, they agreed to get the rest they needed and waited to meet until lunchtime. Rest will be key to making good decisions and plans; however, she was too excited to sleep. For privacy and to be able to discuss the situation freely, Rosalie arranged for the four of them to lunch in her hotel room.

They agreed another trip to the site where they found the stones would be necessary; however, they will search on the ground above the room, not through the water route in the caverns. Thomas nodded in agreement, "Yes, with direct sunlight hitting the top of the room, there should be a way to reach it from the outside. Let's plan for an overland trip. Enrico, do you know of any paths around the caverns?"

"I spend most of my time on the lake, but I know a few. We'll find our way. I'll set up food and gear for tomorrow through the lodge concierge and ask to have it included with your room barter, Rosalie, as if we're just going on a picnic. I don't think we want to ask anyone about the paths, because they'll want to know why. We don't want to talk about this discovery yet, it could be very controversial."

"Yes, we need to talk about where to store our discovery long-term, now that we decided all the other details. In addition to what I said earlier about Jerusalem, with my close ties to the university, and since it re-opened as the global archeology university, it's the perfect place for the stones to be housed. We can utilize the facilities there for appropriate authentication as I said. I will direct the testing for authentication with Anatole. Our security procedures will be worked out through the specific practices he has in place for the existing archeology department."

Thomas added, "I'll ride back to Jerusalem with Rosalie and the stones, since I planned to visit the university prior to our discovery anyway. This will give some added security for Rosalie, even though this area has a history of being safe." Rosalie smiled; pleased with the idea she would continue to see Thomas for an extended period of time. Rosalie and Thomas glanced at each other smiling several times, which confirmed to Rosalie, Thomas felt the same as she did.

Doug and Enrico left after lunch, and promised to leave a message about when and where to meet the next day for their excursion to the hills.

Rosalie and Thomas spent the afternoon alone together. During this time he told Rosalie about his tragic and lonely past. Rosalie acknowledged with a sympathetic hug, now understanding the limp she saw in Thomas' stature as they walked together.

Even after all these years it was still difficult for him to tell the story. Her thoughts drifted through all the details, *and isn't it funny, both our parents were teachers.*

TWENTY-NINE

Rosalie woke with a start. *Was the dream a message? It felt like a message. Now how silly is that? I think in facts and what is, not on the possibilities in a dream, but I remember... Dad telling me that sometimes God speaks through dreams. Just like Jacob waking up, and he knew God was there, but didn't know it until he dreamt it.*

Her dream lingered in her thoughts, and felt odd to her. The very specific dream with details which included herself, Thomas, Enrico, Doug, Anatole, Red, and someone from Spain, drove her thoughts. Three new people in this obscure place, brought together quite by accident, who started their lives in many different corners of the world, and now they were part of Rosalie's life. Her dream about them altogether with Anatole and Red invaded her normally factual thought process. Their backgrounds and tales of sadness after the day of the quakes; all very unique, never before overlapped or connected in any way. Yet, here they are in her life and now in her dream. The simple dream presented nothing about the new discovery. A familiarity with everyone implied their relationships would be forever and also served a purpose in some way. There were two other faces which showed in the background, in beautiful very colorful draping costumes. When Rosalie thought about the dream, the details jumbled up. With these scattered thoughts, she held onto the dream as if putting it into her back pocket. She knew somehow the knowledge and involvement of this dream, with Red and Anatole and the university, meant something for a benefit to all their work. The puzzle which haunted Rosalie became a strong tie to the person from Spain. As far as Rosalie knew, she never met anyone from Spain, her whole life, and… *What about the faces in the background?* Through the next few days, Rosalie pondered the vague, yet unique message left with her from this dream. *Maybe I'll tell Thomas about it later.*

Rosalie looked at the clock on her nightstand. It would go off in a minute, so she turned it off. After she thought about her dream so intently, she knew she wouldn't fall back to sleep. Her mind raced. *Did yesterday happen or was that a dream, too? Have we really found something important and historic? Am I going to wake up soon?* She got up and prepared for the trip to the overland site hoping her thoughts were just thoughts and that yesterday's discoveries were real.

THIRTY

They started out early after meeting at the boat, which took them most of the way. The rarely traveled trails above the caverns were difficult to get to, because the adjacent sheer cliffs shot vertically straight up into the sky. Their walk started just beyond the ruins at St. Catherine's monastery.

Rosalie's thoughts drifted back to her original ARS calls with the sheepherders. *They spoke so much about St. Catherine's Monastery. It's so amazing to now see what they spoke about, and how difficult their scavenging must have been. When we get back to the lodge I'll ask to speak with the people I spoke with on the transmissions. I should have done that when I first arrived. I hope they're still around.*

"Hey Rosalie, grab my hand. Hey, earth to Rosalie,

see my hand; grab it." Jerked back to the reality of the moment, Enrico's hand flashed back and forth in front of her face.

"Sorry, I was daydreaming." She reached up and seized his extended hand. "My mind is exploding with so many things, everything is disjointed and amazing. We found something so incredible. Something no one else on earth even knew existed. I can't believe it and yet, it's like I knew we were supposed to find it." She stepped up on the rocks and slipped a couple times. Enrico's strength proved helpful as she stepped to the weeded area above the cliff's edge.

They followed as close to the edge of the trail as possible. Past the cliffs, the trek became easier. Enrico took charge, because he visited the trail once before. "Hey listen up. I'm not sure whether the ceiling of the room is strong enough to hold our weight, so…just watch where you step...nothing sudden or erratic. Since light shows in the room really clear, we should be able to recognize the openings."

Once they examined the top side of the ceiling, and nothing proved unusual, Enrico took pictures of the site from every possible angle. Doug carried their picnic lunch and they took time to eat while on solid ground. When he opened the picnic backpack, he grinned, "No wonder this was so heavy on my back. Who thought of this?" He pulled out two bottles of very old Greek white wine.

"Oh, that would be me," Rosalie said, "Don't you think we should be celebrating?" Grinning ear to ear, her happiness overflowing, everyone began to enjoy the lighthearted moment. "We need to toast to this day!"

Over lunch they laughed and enjoyed their wine and food. Doug took lots of pictures. These once-in-a-lifetime moments with their exuberance needed to be recorded. They took a few minutes to brainstorm, and were confident they did not miss anything important before starting back to the lodge.

The next few days were all about the excitement of the find with a little rest fit in. Grateful for the time, Rosalie's mind reeled; she planned out what would be done first upon arrival back home in Jerusalem. Since her vacation turned into an adventure before she even started to relax, tomorrow will be a walk along the beach, a nice dinner out with Thomas, Enrico and Doug, then blessed sleep. She planned to repeat the pattern for several days.

THIRTY-ONE

Enrico and Doug came by the hotel to send Rosalie and Thomas off. "These few days have been so full of wonder and excitement," Enrico said. "Thank you for coming to Sinai, your enthusiasm opened our lives again."

"We'll keep in touch with you on a regular basis, so you know what we plan for the discovery," Rosalie said as she hugged them. "We'll work through the details right away."

Traveling to Jerusalem started Rosalie and Thomas down a new road together. Instead of two separate lives, the way they arrived at Lake Sinai, now their lives tied together in ways they never expected.

The shuttle ride home allowed for extended conversations. They learned more about how and why their lives progressed the way they did. Their obvious ease with each other, made it sound like they finished each other's sentences and brought laughter and silliness into their banter. Especially sensual for Rosalie, she never felt this with a man before. With this comfort around him, she relished his teasing. The closeness she felt for Anatole for all these years, different and more like a brother, never intertwined in her thoughts like these new feelings.

With ARS, Rosalie and Thomas exchanged information for several years; however, they didn't know about each other personally. One fact jumped out at both of them, this new relationship they discovered, was like no other they experienced before.

They arrived about 2 p.m., which allowed time to look for Anatole. When they found him in class teaching and not available, they set up a secure space in the archives library for the stones and animal skins placement.

The twosome worked quickly, placing the artifacts for viewing, in a safe place. They found a glass top table, more like a cabinet, which allowed viewers to see, but not touch, the stone casings. They also found a battery operated "vacuum" container, to limit any more deterioration. This space in the archive basement next to the old chamber which housed the CD/DVD's discovery provided a perfect resting place for the cabinets. Being locked away during the day, will be the initial status. At night the main building alarms would be set. Confident this would be enough security prior to any announcements; Rosalie confirmed the need for extra security set in place later.

"There you are; I heard a few people say they saw you coming in a couple hours ago. I really missed you." All smiles, Anatole rushed over and picked her up in a bear hug swinging her around. "Two weeks is too long for you to be away without even a word. I should have gone with you like you said. I hope you had a chance to rest. Was it as beautiful as you told me it would be?"

Happy to see her friend, Rosalie couldn't get a word in edgewise through Anatole's ramblings. She laughed, "Okay, you can put me down now. I'm glad to see you, too, but I have someone I want you to meet." Anatole finally saw Thomas.

Shocked to hear Thomas' name, Anatole grabbed his hand and shook an extended shake, "What brings you to see us in person?"

"After my vacation I planned to come to Jerusalem. I wanted to meet Rosalie and you and the rest of your team. With so many years of ARS talks, I thought it was just time. Since the multi-hover-car-find a few years ago, moving around the Middle East between survival communities became easier, especially after my technical team in Volgograd reversed the engineering of the unusual cars. I took advantage of the hover car shuttles set up by the lodge and started visiting a couple years ago. That's when I met Enrico and Doug. Suddenly meeting Rosalie unexpectedly two weeks ago, my restful vacation went up in smoke, to coin an ancient phrase." With Thomas' curious explanation leaving him puzzled, Anatole turned to Rosalie expecting details from her.

"Anatole, I have something to tell you. Do you want to sit down so I can tell you the story from the beginning? We may as well be comfortable," Rosalie directed them to the couch, excited to tell him every detail. Rosalie sat across from them near her desk while she told the whole story.

Anatole jumped to his feet, "You mean they're here? The stones are actually here? Where did you put them? Why are we sitting here?"

"Okay, sure, you can see them now. Since you were in class when we arrived, Thomas and I set up a place in the secure area of the archive rooms in the space next to the old CD/DVD room."

"Well, what are we waiting for?" already out the door with Rosalie and Thomas close behind. Anatole still unaware of the personal connection between Rosalie and Thomas; they smiled at one another and understood Anatole's excitement. There will be time enough later to tell him about their feelings for each other since they're only still discovering what these feelings are themselves.

Gazing through the glass cabinet window, Anatole kept repeating, "Are you kidding?" Then again while he checked it out from another angle, "Are you kidding?"

"Thomas, Enrico, and Doug all agreed with me, bringing the discovery here to the university would be the best way to go, especially because our archeology department has such a great background since the disaster. The tourist community built at the lake has no facilities. As far as we all knew, it's the only growing community from there at the lake all the way south to the Red Sea."

"Look at this style verbiage. Why would Moses

not bring this portion of God's prophecies back to his people? There's a huge difference between this and the second stone. The word etchings are burned not carved. The numbered prophecies are…formal with precision edges to the word carvings. The second stone, with the more crudely written "familiar" note explaining why it's here, from Moses to whoever finds these stones, is written as if in a hurry and with less precision. Do you realize if we authenticate the stones and the workmanship and the animal skins to be that exact age we'll be changing history as we know it? This can have so many ramifications. God wanted us to be accountable for our actions. This is so unbelievable, but here it is in front of our eyes!"

"I know, Anatole, we've been talking about this for two weeks now. I'll work on developing the pictures we took at the site, and place them into this display. Once the authentications are completed, anyone who will view the discovery will understand where we found them," Rosalie said.

"Then…Enrico and Doug will have their hands full. Their business will have huge demands on it, something we've never experienced in more than thirty-five years, at least not that we're aware of. The barter recording alone will be daunting. They'll need to expand. We already suggested they start building a second boat to be ready for the possibility of the change if we have success with the authentication, and deep down inside me, I believe we will," Rosalie finished her explanation looking weary. "A thorough plan is required. We need to sit together to brainstorm all our ideas and come up with a good set of next steps."

Thomas noticed how tired Rosalie looked and jumped in, "Hey, I think it's time for me to get you home. This has been a long exciting day." He held Rosalie's hand and smiled at her. For the first time, Anatole noticed the closeness between them and was taken aback by the thought. He tilted his head questioningly and looked into Rosalie's eyes.

Rosalie didn't want to make a specific explanation, even though Anatole's look was clear to her. She needed to take care of everyone's fatigue; they all needed rest. "Anatole, at first I thought we could set Thomas up with one of the student apartments at the old airport; you know, the cute apartments built for our younger survivors once they grew up, giving them a home of their own to experience. But after I thought about it a bit, I realized he needed to be closer for the demands placed on him for our work. Would you please arrange with the dormitory set up crew, for Thomas to utilize a room while we continue to work on the authentications? Or, do we need to go through Red? That will give him close proximity and a little space for himself. Both your apartment and mine are too small. He'd have to sleep on the couch. At least, in a dorm room he'll be close by and he'll be comfortable," Rosalie smiled at Thomas and shook her head in the affirmative as if to get agreement from him. He followed her lead and nodded.

"No problem at all, I won't involve Red, she'll be involved enough when we get started," Anatole said. "Do you want to go there now to get it all arranged?"

"No," Thomas replied. "I'll take Rosalie home first. That way I'll know where she lives for future reference. I'll be back in a little while. Where can I meet you, Anatole?"

Anatole didn't like someone else seeing to Rosalie's needs, however, he agreed. "Okay, I'll meet you right here, outside Rosalie's office. You'll be able to find your way back here easy enough. I know you've never been to the campus before, all you'll have to do is back track."

Amy E. Zajac

"Thanks Anatole; I appreciate that."

Rosalie hugged Anatole and gave him a kiss on the cheek. "Goodnight, Anatole. I'll see you in the morning. Let's say ten o'clock, okay?"

"Ten it is. Sleep well; tomorrow will be a busy day," he smiled at his best friend.

Thomas and Rosalie walked away arm in arm. Anatole watched them until they were out of site. His mind raced; so much for him to take in with all the news of the discovery and now a relationship for Rosalie. He never planned on that. *Maybe she'll talk about her and Thomas tomorrow.* Anatole took a deep breath and sighed. He pondered the unexpected scenario and walked to his office.

THIRTY-TWO

Red, the designated Dean of Students, Dean of Sciences, and creator of the new university publishing program, dropped by Rosalie's office to check on her dearest friend who returned from vacation the day before. To her surprise, Rosalie's office, overflowed with students and faculty, and appeared to be the hot spot of the day...*so much for a nice quiet talk.*

"Excuse me; may I get through please; excuse me; excuse me; excuse me; may I squeeze through; excuse me I'm looking for Rosalie Danforth. Is she here?"

"Red, is that your voice I hear? Get back here; just follow my voice. Hey, everybody; let Red through."

"There you are; what's going on?" she hugged Rosalie. "I thought we'd have a nice quiet chat about your vacation. Instead, I find total disorder. It didn't take you long to get back to work." Rosalie smiled and before she answered, Red saw Thomas sitting behind Rosalie's desk. "Hey, who's that?"

Rosalie placed her arm around Red's shoulders and pulled her over to meet Thomas. "Red O'Leary, meet Thomas Stojan from Volgograd Provinces University.

"Thomas…the person we've been talking to for years? Is that really you? Did you cause all this chaos?"

"Hello, Red. I'm so happy to meet you in person," he shook Red's hand. "But no, I'm not the cause of the chaos. Anatole's testing of some old artifacts Rosalie and I brought back from Lake Sinai yesterday has everyone in a furor. She has a lot to tell you; there just hasn't been time to get to you yet."

"Yes, Red," Rosalie grabbed her arm, "Let's get out of here, Thomas can handle all these questions and well-wishers. I have so much to tell you." She turned to Thomas and kissed him affectionately, then started to leave.

Red saw the feeling behind the kiss, "I guess you

do have a lot to tell me. Come on, let's get out of here."

After Rosalie's quick update of the details of her vacation, Red looked at her in disbelief, "Incredible. I send you off for vacation for two weeks, and you come back with artifacts to change the history of the world and you find a man for yourself along the way."

"I know it's a lot to take in; however, the last two weeks have been the most perfect two weeks of my life. Come on, I want to take you down to the archive rooms, so you can see the stones in the display cases we set up."

Deep in thought, Anatole examined the stone with the personal note from Moses etched into the rock. He was surprised when Rosalie and Red walked in. "Oh, it's you two; quick close the door and lock it behind you. All I did was set up a few tests this morning in preparation for this afternoon, and all the staff went crazy. They made every assumption you could imagine and clamored for information. Putting two and two together, a couple of them figured out it had to do with your arrival yesterday. There were several more conversations and I swear the whole campus went into speculation-mode-extraordinaire," His frown noted his annoyance.

"Oh Anatole, I know you're upset by everyone trying to get involved, but what we have in our hands is the chance of a lifetime. This little bump in the road will pass and we'll still have these moments to remember."

"You always know how to defuse me," he smiled at her. "Well Red, what do you think of what our girl has brought us. Can you believe it? With my first view of it yesterday, it appeared to be authentic. Now seeing it again today, I'm even more convinced. We'll get the detailed testing done later. Right now I'm going to scrutinize the initial translations Rosalie did, and get them into university documentation as our first step."

"Rosalie's told me about it; I haven't seen it yet, though," she smiled at her friends.

"Well, get over here. You won't believe it, even when it's right in front of your eyes; besides you're going to be part of this you know," Anatole said grinning ear to ear. "I can't remember ever having this much fun! Jerusalem and Lake Sinai are now really back on the map. I've been waiting for years and years for an opportunity like this and now Rosalie just dropped it into our laps," he hugged her and didn't want to let her go; he hadn't realized how much he'd missed her. She brought him the greatest gift of his life, and he knew he'd never be able to express how much this meant to him.

THIRTY-THREE

Red organized a team of graduate students enrolled in Master Studies to work as an extension of the primary testers, Anatole, Rosalie, Thomas and Red. This allowed bandwidth to accomplish a multitude of tasks which go along with such a tremendous discovery.

Just like everyone else, Red's mind reeled once she saw the artifacts in front of her. The teacher in her plunged into idea-mode, "I'll use a couple students to help me document our plan from which we'll create a new curriculum for this study. It will be built into another overview class of "how-to" for a major ancient discovery. A win for the initial students who work the study and another win later for the university's added class, presented with a true life scenario attached. What do you think, Anatole?"

"A great idea...it will enhance our curriculum. Be sure to keep Rosalie up-to-date. You know she'll have suggestions," he joked.

The translations written by Rosalie while at Lake Sinai, changed once Anatole and Red's expertise became part of the mix. Mostly word style made the differences, because their knowledge of writings "of that time in history" augmented the translation of the note written by Moses.

The translations took about two months to complete. Scrutinizing every word, by comparing to multiple sources of ancient literature, Bibles, and writings from as far back as were available. Many years before, hundreds of Hebrew and Greek Bible translations and old publications found by the salvage team were brought to the university library. With these documents at their disposal, Anatole and Red utilized many of them to compare to Rosalie's initial translation. The graduate studies team, worked around the clock, to stay on schedule. This allowed for celebration of successful changes when their work passed each planned milestone.

"Hey Rosalie, I'm glad you stopped by. I've tried to group these stones and I'm not having any luck with it. When you described it the other day I thought it would be a breeze, but I'm stuck. I was thinking a symmetrical pattern would be the way to go. Are you sure these fit together?"

"Don't get frustrated, it really does work. There are small indentations on each end of the stone with Moses' note, with opposite protrusions on one of the long stones. Have you tried putting these together with the other etched stone in the first group we found?"

"No, that hadn't occurred to me. When I spoke to everyone, we all talked about a single covering because the others were held together with the animal skin," Anatole replied with Rosalie shaking her head in agreement.

"Yes, I remember; it's just something about these protrusions right here." Pointing at the stone, "I know we found them separately, but maybe with all the upheaval during the earthquakes, they were separated, falling apart."

"Yes, that's it! Watch this!" Anatole pulled his gloves back on and gently placed the stones with the note and prophecies at the center. The other stones fit together as part of an outer wrapping.

THIRTY-FOUR

The graduate studies team prepared all the necessary tools in a clean room. They chose a room with no windows then placed a series of very secure locks on the door. This provided the security for the tedious, multi-level testing to be accomplished. First, dimmer lights, appropriate for as little deterioration as possible of the animal skins needed to be set in place. These were installed after the salvage team found the stored lighting kept at the old Jerusalem airport. Oxygen was bad enough for deterioration; they removed as many factors, as possible, to eliminate decomposing.

Red gathered the graduate studies team together, "Since you're all qualified for the position, you'll draw straws." When she heard grumblings, "I know you all want to be part of our actual team, but we can only use one person." All the students came from other countries in a barter plan. They knew there wouldn't be many chances like this opportunity; each chose a straw. Sili, the youngest student at the university jumped out of his seat, "WOOHOO, it's me! I got it!

Since Jerusalem University reopened years before with the archeology and associated sciences curriculum, Anatole, Red, and Rosalie were the experts. They will attend all testing sessions with Thomas and Sili as part of their team. Positive calculations, documentation, witnessing, and photographs were vital to the work from the first moment of testing to the very last moment of testing. Validations, peculiarities, failures, test restructuring and re-testing required all signatures to show completion. The expected timeframe for a positive testing procedure to be fulfilled was twelve weeks. If any of the participants missed a testing session, the session would be postponed. That way they held to the criteria set up prior to the tests inception. They allowed no chance for anyone to question the validity of the data, since this first major new discovery will be held up to major scrutiny by global collegiate teachers and professors.

The final testing preparation meeting confirmed all the information discussed up to that point, and included Rosalie's last instructions directed to the student on their team. "Sili, the final step will be for you to write up the summation of the outcome for the overall team. You have a huge opportunity here since the information will be locked in the basement vault with all the stones. You will work through the details of the testing, to put them into writing. We will be your proof readers, questioning every statement you make. The analysis of your words will be done by all of us, Red first, Thomas next, Anatole after that, and then me. This helps us by having fewer questions during each test iteration. By the time we've provided all details, the presentation will be read by the rest of your university special studies team. Once no more questions arise, we'll pass the summation to the ARS Network for transmission to university leaders worldwide. After that, our planned University Consortium will bring all the scientific leaders together. This will provide an opportunity for viewing and also receive validation and sign off of the testing data from the global universities' leaders. So you see, Sili, your work here will be placed into history, forever."

"I'm so ready to start, Rosalie. My whole life I've wanted to be part of something. I'll be forever grateful for this opportunity. When do we begin?"

"A few more details need to be ironed out. I'll let everyone know in a couple days,"

Rosalie was excited to start; however, she thought about the words in the prophecies. They were vital and important to all mankind. She felt the same way when she learned about the studies she rediscovered in the found CD/DVD room all those years ago. That room provided the "edge" for the University of Jerusalem to open first before any of the other universities around the world. The study about diminished propagation of all animal species, which could not be explained by the scientists, and left the scientific conclusions..."empty", still ate at her whenever she thought about it.

Rosalie sorted through the details of the study in her mind along with the prophecies found at Lake Sinai. They somehow complemented each other. Rosalie decided to spend an afternoon comparing the details of the pre-testing and wording of the "found" propagation study. For Rosalie, the details matched each other "in theory".

Rosalie presented the scenario to Thomas during dinner the night before the testing started. She wanted to see his reaction and she knew it would feel good to bounce this idea off someone else. No one but Rosalie, in the testing team, knew the details of both, and would not know to connect the two together. It's almost like the stone casing found at Lake Sinai, which required the insides before the actual box could be built. One was connected to the other.

All day Thomas looked forward to the quiet dinner he and Rosalie planned for just the two of them. Every day they ran in different directions to accomplish their planned tasks, which allowed them no time to spend alone. They met at seven o'clock in Rosalie's office.

"Do you know where you want to go?" Thomas asked. "What do you feel like having for dinner?" Their hug lingered a long time. Rosalie was content to stay there forever.

"Let's go to my apartment. I have everything we need for Chef Salad and wine to go with it. It will be relaxing and quiet."

"Oh Rosey, that sounds perfect. I'm relaxing already. Let's stroll the long way, shall we. It's a beautiful evening, one to be enjoyed. I'll help you when we get there."

"You haven't called me Rosey since the day in the cavern room when the stones fell from the ceiling. I like it. No one ever called me that before, not even as a child." She hugged his arm as they walked.

During the evening walk, a perfect quiet time together, Rosalie told Thomas the theory she formulated which involved the old study at the university and their new discovery. The premise fascinated him. Once the details of the testing were complete in about twelve weeks, Thomas and Rosalie agreed to evaluate the study. They would attempt to tie them together more formally, than just in theory.

When they arrived at Rosalie's apartment, there was no more talk of the discovery or studies or tests.

THIRTY-FIVE

All were present at ten o'clock as planned. They started with the stones all put together including the outer box casing. The geological tests showed positive and all updated introduction documents signed off. These first tests just for the outer casing took two full days to work up and document.

"Tomorrow the first step will be to remove the casing. Thomas if you will help me lay out the casing with the tablet and stone note removed and placed in order, then we can test the protrusions first," said Anatole.

"Wait a minute," Thomas interrupted. "What

protrusions? I didn't see any protrusions."

"Remember, last week, Rosalie helped me get the stones in place. The protrusions on the outer stones, fit together with the original stones from the floor, with the protrusions on the one internal stone to attach to the outer casing. See here, how perfectly they fit together," he pointed to where the stones connected.

"You're kidding!! Really?," He looked at Rosalie, and talked faster than usual. "Rosey, where's my briefcase? I haven't seen it in a few days; I've been so involved with all the testing detail preparation. Do you know where it is?"

"Well," taking her time to answer, "I believe it might be in my office, in the corner next to the easy chair. I think you placed it there a couple weeks ago. Don't worry, it will be safe. My office is locked. Why are you worried about it all of a sudden?"

"I believe I have a picture you will all find interesting. I put it there about a year ago. I received the picture from Ethiopia when one of my student's cousins sent it to us for validation. Give me your keys quick." Rosalie reached into her jacket pocket and located her keys. She tossed them to Thomas. Heading out the door of the testing room, "I'll be right back. Don't close up the stones yet. I want you all to see this picture. Don't go away," he held his hands up in the air shaking them forward in excitement. Curious about Thomas' enthusiasm, everybody waited.

Running through the halls, Thomas almost passed Rosalie's office door. Fumbling the keys, he dropped them as he tried to get the right key into the lock. After he got the door open, he grabbed his briefcase. Thomas ran back to the testing room and pulled out a disheveled stack of papers. He flipped through the stack and tossed each sheet on the floor until, almost at the bottom of the stack, he found the picture.

Thomas handed the picture to Rosalie saying, "Look at the bottom of the page, at the edge of the large stone," sighing as if relieved. He watched her face, as she recognized what he told her to look at.

Total surprise and then shock on her face, Rosalie jumped out of her chair, "Where did you get this picture, Thomas? Look Anatole, look here," she held the picture in front of his face.

"Thomas, why didn't you tell me about this before?

When I figured out that the pieces fit together, you didn't mention anything."

"Rosey, I've been caught up in paper work for the testing. I haven't seen the stones since we set them up in the viewing cases," catching his breath.

"What am I looking at?" Anatole asked.

Rosalie pointed at the picture. "Look there," she said, "the same protrusions, see there…just like in our stone casings, exactly. See?"

Anatole grabbed the picture, scrutinizing it closely, "Yes…I see. Okay, Thomas, where did you get this? Who took the picture and what is it?"

THIRTY-SIX

"About two years ago, one of my students, Vasily, started to communicate with his cousin, whom he originally thought was lost to the quakes. One day out of the blue Vasily received an ARS message from his cousin, now a celibate monk in Ethiopia. He lived in the ancient city Aksum."

"Over and over again, Maadiah asked his cousin to bring me to see a special set of stones he found in rubble during the clean-up in years prior. Maadiah, ordained by an elderly monk who survived the disaster, taught him everything for the Monk's order while Maadiah grew up at his side. About a year after the old monk's death, Maadiah found the odd stones, shown in the picture he sent to Vasily."

Thomas and Vasily, not able to arrange to get to Ethiopia delayed everything, so Maadiah sent the picture through a walker nomadic group. It eventually arrived via a hover-car delivery after about six months. "When he sent us the picture, he explained an Ethiopian legend about the Ark of the Covenant. The Ark, sent to Ethiopia in the tenth century by Menelik I, the son of the Queen of Sheba and King Solomon, remained in Africa. According to the legend, the Ark was first placed on top of a mesa in Lake Tana, where the monks watched over the relics; eventually it ended up in Aksum. The chosen protector of the Ark was the Ethiopian Orthodoxy, a Christian religion which incorporated Judaic traditions. The legend explained because this protection occurred, Ethiopia and its people were granted divine protection for everything except misrule and poverty. The resting place for the Ark of the Covenant for many centuries was a small chapel next door to the St. Mary Church of Zion. The Ark, seen by a solitary monk guardian, chosen for a lifetime post to guard God's Covenant, remained within the fenced-in grounds of the chapel. No one, except the chosen monk ever saw the ark. It was thought since only the monk was allowed past the curtains, because, should anyone else view the Ark, they would "become ill and die". Never seen for centuries the shroud of mystery around the Ark of the Covenant remained in their imaginations."

"Aksum mostly destroyed during the catastrophe, with a handful of survivors, included the child Maadiah and the elderly monk. The monk always believed in the Ark legend even though he, like everyone else, never saw it his whole life. He searched and searched for the Ark; he never gave up. The Ark needed to be saved. When the old monk determined Maadiah learned enough, he became an ordained Monk, to fulfill his life. Maadiah went on with the old monk's search, yet never believed anything was ever there, because legends are not real; however, it gave him a focus. One day he found the unusual stones while he dug in the old rubble inside the crevices at the outskirts of the village. The rubble inside one huge crevasse needed to be removed, to make space for more storage. The other crevices close by were already utilized; they needed more space. When they dug in the unused crevasse, the rubble they cleared produced the stones. Maadiah found the pieces in an unexplored section."

"The legend's chapel, stood near this spot, prior to

the day of the quakes. The chapel disappeared, so the new monk believed it fell into the crevasse. Maadiah made this determination, because of the multitude of details his old friend taught him before he died. Maadiah sent the picture to his cousin."

"Thomas, I'm entranced by your story," Rosalie jumped in. "Do you realize this picture may be possible added proof to authenticate the stone casings found in Lake Sinai?"

"And vice versa, our stones found in Lake Sinai may authenticate the stones found in Aksum," Thomas finished the thought, "that's why I was so excited when I heard you mention the stone's protrusions."

THIRTY-SEVEN

All agreed the testing needed to be placed "on-hold" until they determined if the stones in Aksum could be brought to Jerusalem for testing and validation. This required a team to travel to Aksum to confirm what the pictures showed. The perfect transport would be the rejuvenated tall ship the old scout team brought to Tel Aviv-Yafo, about a year ago. It took several weeks to plan out their travel.

Rosalie left the travel plans to Thomas and he reached out to Vasily. Thomas knew it would take time for Vasily to get to Jerusalem from Volgograd. It will be important for him to connect with his cousin. While they waited for Vasily to arrive from Volgograd, Thomas worked out a plan with TJ and Friday, the co-captains of the tall ship. They agreed to take the team to Ethiopia and also wait with the tall ship to bring them back to Israel.

In the meantime, an ARS message was transmitted to Mitsiwa, where a runner traveled to Aksum to tell Maadiah, his cousin Vasily will come for a visit.

The group traveled by hover-car to Tel Aviv-Yafo where they boarded the tall ship for travel. The necessary time planned for the round trip, twelve days, included overland travel in Ethiopia. No one paid attention to scenery during the first leg, their conversations so intent on the discoveries and the possibilities of what they'd find in Aksum.

Rosalie, Thomas, and Vasily, met Maadiah outside Aksum; the happy reunion exploded with laughter and old Russian chatter which Thomas remembered vaguely from his childhood. Vasily and Maadiah's parents grew up together just outside St. Petersburg. As missionaries, Maadiah's parents, moved their family to Ethiopia not too long before the quakes. Maadiah's father, originally from Ethiopia, understood the need for religious involvement in the small towns of his home country. This move back to Ethiopia fulfilled his father's life's dream, when Maadiah turned five years old.

Excited about their arrival, Maadiah insisted they see where he found the stones before it got dark. "We don't use electricity in the caves. With so few of us working in our teams, we kept the bits of electricity working with batteries for personal living spaces. We knew we could work in the caves during the daylight hours using torches in the lower levels. Rosalie, amazed at their use of the crevices, now major caves, "Our work's cut out for us; there are so many rotten pieces of wood mixed in with the rocks in the crevasse. We'll plan to start excavating the area first thing in the morning when the light in this spot will be best." They planned to find more evidence to support the stones discovered by Maadiah.

After they saw the crevasse, Maadiah took them to see the stones. The year before Maadiah arranged for one of the survivor teams, contractors, to build a small special container made out of some local petrified wood. The very hard wood gave the artisan contractors a local and unique framework for the cases.

"All the Aksum survivors believed the stones belong to the Ark of the Covenant. The new case box created for the stones became part of the alter in the open air church set up and used for these last thirty five years.

Our local people's faith rejuvenated when I found the stones. Up until the discovery very few survivors attended the Sunday services I carried on since my old priest friend died. After the discovery of the stones everyone I knew on all our local teams, started to attend my services Sunday mornings. The legend came back to us all, even though they were just stones and not the commandments themselves. Everyone in Aksum believed the tablets which were inside these stones would be found someday. We bonded, and told each other we all needed to show God we believed, even if by just attending services together every Sunday. Just one person refrained from joining our Sunday service, a very old woman and friend named Kabibe. She lived a quiet reclusive life since about five years after the disaster, because she had difficulty walking. She also struggled with an asthmatic condition she suffered with since her youth. All the current first aid team members took turns to visit her on their regular schedule. Her positive attitude shined through to everyone who came with food and sundries." Maadiah opened the beautiful box.

"I knew it. They're like our stone casings." Thomas held up one of the pictures they brought with them from Jerusalem to compare.

"Yes, see how the top stone tucks, as if to attach to another stone. We don't have that stone here, yet we know how it should be, because we have a matching complete set in Jerusalem," Rosalie marveled at the same workmanship. "They're exact, look here." They all admired the precision of the details carved into the stone casings found in the caverns at Lake Sinai compared to these stones found in Ethiopia's quake rubble. "Maadiah took great care to keep the stones safe even though the village's condition progressed little during the last thirty five years. Somehow though, these few people made it through the struggles of living in the small out-of-the-way village while they paid tribute to the past by caring for the stones."

Rosalie, Thomas, and Vasily worked for days in the logical spaces near the spot where Maadiah found the Ethiopian stones. Nothing...

They interviewed everyone in the village being sure not to miss any idea. Nothing...

Rosalie chatted with the people from the village, explaining the reason for their visit and that their stones matched the ones they were currently testing. It was only after these more intimate conversations that Maadiah and the people of Aksum gave their permission when Rosalie requested the stone casings go back to Jerusalem with them.

Preparing to return home, Thomas worked with Maadiah to package up the casings for the trip. To confirm the similarities between the two sets of stone casings will provide another page of history to be confirmed, not only for the people of Aksum, but for the whole world.

The village of Aksum fascinated the visitors from Jerusalem, especially the fact that religious strengths were woven through the threads of its history.

One final fact shocked Rosalie as she said goodbye, "Maadiah, your village progress outwardly appears to be slower and behind other places we've encountered and learned about. How did these few people survive? They're so happy and positive."

"Oh, Miss Rosalie, this is a recent change for us. My old priest friend, kept me focused and busy. Together we lived for each next day, but the others clung to negativity and the insurmountable grieving for so much loss, which I have to believe, can be attributed to our remoteness. Anger took over several of the men. I remember a bad fight between two of them, when I was a little boy. One man was killed and it scared me. I remember they fought over their few belongings because most everything was gone. The adults stayed to themselves after that and no one helped each other at all. With no family for most of us, the situation hung over all the survivors like a horrible message from God. He'll continue to destroy us if we fight, so keep to ourselves. I was the only small child, so I don't remember how my old priest friend resolved the anger with the adults. All I had to build on was the knowledge given to me by the old priest. He helped me to learn that anger, envy and hatred were wrong. Through all this he educated me. We didn't learn about the "team idea focus" through ARS, because no one who knew about amateur radios survived here. Approximately ten years ago we learned about the team idea from a visitor who walked through. The idea changed the demeanor of our village. The new thoughts helped everyone to stop worrying about the old losses they'd held onto for so long, and it was then we organized ourselves into small teams."

When Rosalie heard the story told and she understood her simple idea reached so far even after twenty five years, she could hardly believe her ears. *There it is again; it's so amazing that after all those years the simple team idea reached so far, and helped so many people. I can hardly believe it! My simple idea reached this remote village. WOW, wait till Anatole hears. This is so fantastic!*

"Everyone in the village involved themselves with the new team focus; except for the eldest survivor, Kabibe. She stayed alone, and took on no new team tasks. Since she was the most positive person in the village, her focus didn't need to be adjusted. The struggle no longer existed about who would provide her food; the task fell to the appropriate team, instead of passing off the task to anyone who would take it on," Maadiah's pride for his village family came through with his simple explanation.

This last bit of knowledge became the perfect item to close their visit to Aksum. Goodbyes completed, the trek on foot to the nearest transportation terminal, about twelve miles in Adi Abun, became the next venture. Adi Abun's survivor teams created a bus route to Asmara in Eritrea, and from there to Mitsiwa on the coast. Rickety old school buses in very poor repair maintained a weekly route.

Now when they traveled home they carried the added weight of the stones. Their walk to the bus would be slower. The tall ship and its crew waited at Mitsiwa to take them home to Jerusalem.

Their search for additional stones came up short. They found no evidence to support their hopes and theories for finding whatever was within the cherished stone casings. The three travelers walked silent through the unusual countryside. They headed toward Jerusalem with only the casings... a partial treasure.

Rocks and dried clay spikes shot high toward the sky, obvious remnants of the changed terrain from so long ago. However, these juxtaposition rocks and dried clay now bore weeds and bushes and trees in the spaces where a seed eventually grew, and gave an odd appearance to the aging ground.

"It's almost like an evil forest of grass and weed-covered crazy shaped rock monoliths shooting into the sky," Thomas commented as he shifted his carrying task to Vasily. "Have you noticed the odd shadows? I'm glad it's sunny today. This place would be scary in a wind storm." They all nodded in agreement as they walked the rugged terrain.

THIRTY-EIGHT

Maadiah surprised the travelers when he stepped out from behind a rock formation just when they turned a corner in the shabby roadway. Out of breath, he waved them down in excitement.

"You won't believe it," he yelled. "A miracle in sadness, that's what it is; a miracle in sadness," he dropped to his knees just in front of Rosalie.

"Where did you come from?" Vasily said. He stepped forward to hug his cousin.

Pointing south, "A shortcut through the old crevasses, it's not easy to travel so that's why we built this road to get over to Adi Abun our closest neighboring town," Maadiah said, still breathing heavy.

"What miracle?" Rosalie asked.

Speaking a hundred miles an hour, Maadiah explained the elderly woman, Kabibe, died in her sleep overnight. "She lay in her bed, so apparently her heart failed. Found this morning by two members of the First Aid team, when they took her some food for the day. Extreme sadness overcame everyone, since this was only the second death in our village since the fight about thirty four years ago, but excitement is keeping us off balance in what we're thinking."

"The first aid people who found her looked around Kabibe's living space. Near the back where she slept, she built herself a small personal alter. With very old drapes created by a local tribal fabric drawn to the sides, the stone tablets remained hidden. The first aid team ran through our village, telling everyone. They were sad about Kabibe, because she was such a sweet old woman, who never bothered anyone, but they were so excited about the old stones they found. They were literally dancing from person to person as they told us, presuming they knew what the stones were because of the old legends we all knew and grew up talking about," Maadiah took a breath.

"What stones? What stones?" Rosalie jumped in.

"Kabibe must have found the stones a long time ago, and never told anyone. When I think about it now, it was probably about five years after the quakes when she started to stay to herself complaining about her knees." Maadiah speculated. "Knowing Kabibe, she thought since she found the tablets, she was now the guardian, and never left them alone or allowed anyone to view them, as the legend told us for so long. She was always so proud of the fact the last solitary guardian monk chosen for the chapel near the church of St. Mary of Zion came from her family. Her belief in the ark and all its tradition remained strong throughout her lifetime." Maadiah took another deep breath, "These past two weeks Kabibe has been very agitated. Since the moment you arrived to look for more information about the stones. Our first aid team talked about it with the rest of us. The excitement must have been too much for her, because her secret was too difficult to keep to herself. Her body just gave out."

Thomas interrupted, "You're saying that Kabibe, had the Ten Commandment tablets all this time, and no one ever saw them?"

Maadiah nodded his head saying, "Yes, we can't believe it either."

Awestruck by Maadiah's words, Rosalie stood silent, covering her mouth with her hand, tears streaming down her cheeks.

"Please come back to help us. We don't know what to do. Kabibe believed the Word should continue as in the ancient times, where no one saw the Covenant. However, we talked about it this morning. The world is different now. We're all starting new. Wouldn't it be better to share this gift from God with everyone? Please come back to help us."

"Of course, we'll come, Maadiah. Let's get started right now," Thomas said, "Before Rosalie floods out the road with her tears." Everyone smiled at the joke; the levity broke the intensity in the air.

No one touched the tablets, they remained where Kabibe placed them in her personal alter. As they walked in, the First Aid team moved her body from the small sleeping berth to a stretcher. "A service and funeral procession to the village cemetery will occur tomorrow; please attend with us. After that we'll work through all the details of how to proceed," a calmer Maadiah focused on Kabibe and the respect he felt due her. "Her diligence protecting the Ten Commandments deserves recognition. Now, through our reverence at her death, this will be accomplished. We need to remember she kept God's gift to the world safe for so many years."

Maadiah left the room with Kabibe's body. Vasily went with him to comfort his cousin and to learn more about Kabibe. He saw how important Kabibe's actions were to Maadiah.

Rosalie and Thomas stayed behind. Dim light streamed through the single window. Dust floated in the air and passed through the streaming light because of the extra movement of the visitors and unusual activities in the room that morning. The drab musty room with scarcely any personal items of Kabibe's anywhere, provided the ominous backdrop for the unlikely archeological find on the morning of her death. An old cushion from a couch or a chair lay on the floor at the foot of the altar worn down after years of Kabibe kneeling before God's Covenant. The drapes created from old African ceremonial costume fabric extended to each side of the tablets and were worn where Kabibe touched the fabric to draw the drapes closed over the tablets and then open again. By having these drapes, and just like everything Kabibe believed about the legend during her youth long before the disaster, no one except the guardian should see behind them, "lest they fall ill and die". Once she found the tablets, Kabibe took the place of the guardian. She stayed alone as Their caretaker.

The tablets, exactly like the tablet Rosalie's team found in the caverns at Lake Sinai, endured time well, because of Kabibe's constant care. She found them after they broke out of the stone casing. This casing Moses created to keep the tablets secure per God's direction. He just did it twice, when he separated the Ten Commandments from the prophecies. Then he buried the four prophecies on Mt. Sinai before he presented God's Covenant to his people awaiting him in turmoil at the foot of the mountain.

Rosalie and Thomas came into the room together, and they were both stricken with the need to whisper. "Do you feel the need for reverence?" She tapped her lips with her index finger as if to tell herself to not speak.

As soon as Rosalie saw the drapes, she reached over and grabbed Thomas's arm, "Look at the drapes," she whispered, "They're the exact pattern and color of the costumes those two people wore in my dream. Do you remember? I told you there were two people in my dream who wore very beautiful and colorful costumes." She pointed, "That's the exact fabric."

"You're kidding, right?" Thomas whispered back.

"No, I'm not." she cried and smiled at the same time. "God brought us here. I know it now. Oh God, we'll put it back together for You. We will. I promise." Rosalie's thoughts raced. She wanted to explain to the people there in Aksum about the prophecies and the note from Moses, but thought it was too soon to bring it up, since the stones back in Jerusalem had not yet been tested for authenticity.

Together, they sat staring at the tablets; awestruck and frozen by the undeniable treasure standing in front of them. They made no effort to move and waited there until Maadiah came looking for them.

After Rosalie and Thomas saw the Ten Commandments their thoughts once again rushed into speculation mode. They wanted time to discuss all the different possibilities. Thomas also wanted to learn more details about Rosalie's dream, especially now, since Rosalie spoke about the African fabrics, but there was no time.

The religious yet humble funeral service completed, the grateful villagers gravitated to Rosalie and Thomas. Overwhelmed by what they found in Kabibe's room, they soaked up every bit of information Rosalie and Thomas offered.

"Rosalie, we want to set up a chapel to display the relics we found in Kabibe's bed chamber. All the people in our locale will be eager to see the word of God, right in front of them," Maadiah embraced the idea of sharing the tablet stones.

"I understand your excitement about the discovery. I've gone through something similar not too long ago, but this is a very big discovery, Maadiah." Rosalie's mind juggled through scenario after scenario concerned about the limiting idea Maadiah suggested. "This discovery is so much bigger than a chapel in a small village. What do you think of this idea? Thomas, Vasily and I could take them back to Jerusalem. There is a much larger population there and also in the communities near Tel Aviv-Yafo. We can exhibit the discovery showing more of the world how your village kept the word of God safe, since, and before the day of the quakes. Plus the world will want proof."

"But Rosalie, the legends were clear and world-wide, even before the quakes tragedy. When we re-state them, along with showing the stones, people will know."

"Yes, Maadiah, believers will accept this as a fact, but this is so large a discovery we want everyone to 'know' what they're seeing is truly the word of God. In Jerusalem we have facilities with tools and testing procedures which will allow us to prove the validity of the claim that these stones are genuine. The world's population may not believe the claims of a small group of villagers."

"But our Aksum villagers and the people in Adi Abun deserve to spend time with the stones; how can we just let them go, even with your logical suggestions?"

"Yes, I know that will be difficult. Let's plan a special event prior to the stones being removed. We can include everyone from both Aksum and Adi Abun. Please speak to everyone who will help you decide what you'll do. I'll meet you in an hour so we can start planning." Maadiah nodded as he walked away. He scratched his head as though many questions still existed for him.

When they met an hour later, Maadiah told Rosalie the villagers of Aksum all agreed to her idea with one

FOREDESTINED

stipulation. "I will travel with the tablets and continue to stay with them, as long as I live. We will continue our tradition of guarding the commandments, but this time as a guardian in residence," Maadiah's gentle smile showed his contentment with the new idea.

"Maadiah, this is perfect! I feel so proud for you and your village family. We have so much to talk about and prepare for. Let's get started," she smiled and held out her hand.

With Maadiah's new role of guardian as placed by his people, to guard the Covenant of God, he spent a good part of three days working out a plan for the ongoing guardianship. Being the last monk in Aksum, the neighboring Adi Abun priest will train a younger Aksum man in the order of monks, to ordain him to follow in Maadiah's footsteps, the guardianship of the holy relics. The plan will continue with the newest priest always training another prior to his leaving for Jerusalem to begin the journey of service to God just as his ancestors before him. Since the low population of Aksum did not provide many men to take on the role and if no Aksum person would be available, an Adi Abun person would take over the role. The most significant difference, this role of

Guardian will no longer separate the Ten Commandments from the world. As soon as possible arrangements would be made for a specific building to hold the treasure of the ages, allowing all to pay homage to God's written word. There will always be a priest from Aksum or Adi Abun in attendance during viewing times as a memorial to the past.

The new vision promoted a world which rejoiced in sharing the Covenant of God. This priest will be the symbol of the past, to preserve the past, but to rebuild a world by sharing God's words. Rosalie, Thomas and Vasily's visit to Aksum was not a coincidence.

THIRTY-NINE

With Rosalie, Thomas, and Maadiah's suggestions, Aksum's contracting team created two containers for the Ten Commandments to travel in. The other casings stayed in their already separate container and the new boxes were made from the same petrified wood. Having three containers helped with the weight issue during transport. Even after their hurried completion, all marveled at their beauty.

To share the news, Maadiah sent a runner to Adi Abun, twelve miles away. Aksum villagers bonded with the small population left in Adi Abun when over the years the villages helped each other during floods. The people in Adi Abun also followed the legend of the Ten Commandments and now will share in the joy and view Them before they are taken to Jerusalem.

Everyone arrived from Adi Abun, in full costume of their ancestors, the beautiful shemma cloth used traditionally by Ethiopians; the same draping fabric from Rosalie's dream. Maadiah and the priests from Adi Abun held multiple services of Thanksgiving throughout the day. Reverence and awe encompassed every conversation and the jubilant party lit up the village streets all night. Many people slept outside, others slept in make-shift tents and still others never slept at all. New stories came alive around the fires built to warm the crowd, how an old woman took away a legend and created a new story to pass to the future; the story of Kabibe.

Leaving early the next morning, the procession marched at a constant, but slow pace. The people of both villages supported the expedition for the whole twelve miles to Adi Abun. The proud people chosen to carry the relic cases proved tireless. Even though they completed their leg of the journey, because they felt so privileged, they didn't want to relinquish the duty to the next scheduled eager participant.

When the procession dispersed at the outskirts of Adi

Abun, all the Aksum and Adi Abun villagers returned to their homes. Only Maadiah accompanied Rosalie, Thomas, and Vasily to the bus terminal. The scheduled bus left on time without drawing attention to the four travelers with the valuable pieces of history in tow.

FORTY

Their mode of transportation, the tall ship, and its crew, awaited their arrival in Mitsiwa. The ship allowed for small cabins for Rosalie and the relics. Thomas, Vasily, Maadiah and the co-captains with crew all slept in the crew berths. When the boat crossed the sea and moved toward Jerusalem with the discovery of the age, excitement and anticipation came out in the conversations between the travelers and the crew. Although the crew didn't understand the traveler's upbeat attitudes, they enjoyed their enthusiasm.

The journey to Jerusalem provided Maadiah a chance to see new places and experience the amazing tall ship crew as they climbed high in the rigging every day. At every turn, he was awestruck.

The last day of travel, Rosalie spoke with Maadiah away from the others; they sat up front at the bow. She planned what to tell him and didn't want the tall ship crew to hear. Maadiah nodded in agreement once he heard her unusual introduction.

"Maadiah when we get to Jerusalem, you will be privileged to be one of a handful of people to see and learn about something none of us even knew existed until recently. Its discovery is how we found you and the stone casings you discovered." Rosalie waited for confirmation Maadiah understood what she said; he nodded again.

"I traveled for a vacation to Lake Sinai. It's at the site of the old Mt. Sinai. There are caverns there, which can only be seen by diving deep into the beautiful clear lake. I met Thomas for the first time during my initial dive. We hit it off and went again with a new guide a couple days later. During the second dive we found some tablets. One tablet is a message to whoever finds the tablets, and the second tablet contained etchings of four prophecies that no one ever knew about until now."

Maadiah stopped Rosalie by raising his hand, "I'm not sure I understand; did you say there are prophecies that go with the Ten Commandments?" He dropped to his knees.

"How can this be?"

Rosalie explained everything she and her team knew so far. "Now, with the good tidings because we found the Ten Commandments, the world can accept the reality of where they're stored and that there are even more discoveries that go with original ten. God intended for everyone to live by His Ten Commandments, plus His four prophecies to understand we are accountable for our actions throughout our lives and through the centuries."

"I want you to understand, you and your line of priests will watch over all the tablets from God. I didn't want to tell you in Aksum, because I believed it would cause confusion for the people in your village. I believed when they heard about this in the world announcements it will fall into place easier for them once the testing and the world organizations confirm the authenticity. Do you understand why we waited to tell you?

"I do understand Miss Rosalie; I appreciate your caring about my villagers. You're right; it would have thrown them off, not believing such a discovery was possible, because they believe Aksum was the chosen resting place before the time of the quakes. As I said a couple days ago, now we can begin again."

Their trip by tall ship completed, they docked at Tel Aviv-Yafo. That's where Vasily left the expedition to catch transportation to Volgograd. Thomas will travel back to Volgograd in another two weeks for Vasily's graduation. At the same time, he will arrange for someone else to take his position. Thomas plans to stay and work with the Jerusalem team. Grateful goodbyes expressed and extended hugs for his cousin, Vasily waved and disappeared around a corner.

After the short fifty mile hover-car ride to Jerusalem, Rosalie, Thomas, and Maadiah arrived in the middle of the afternoon again, just like last time. They kept it simple with no fanfare; they just worked to get the relics set up in the safeguarded room with the stones and casing from the first discovery at Lake Sinai.

Rosalie was overwhelmed each time she came into the presence of the tablets. Her whole life she believed they existed, yet somehow there was always the question *"Where were the Ten Commandments hidden?"* Now, there right in front of her, was the written covenant. When she dreamed the mysterious dream while at the resort at Lake Sinai, the messages tying so many unusual people and events and details together got under her skin. She held onto the feeling and thoughts from the dream and each step of the way used it like a confirmation, as if she had advance notice.

FORTY-ONE

Rosalie sought out Anatole and Red in private. She found them in the hallway walking to their offices after they finished their teaching for the day.

Surprised she already returned Anatole hugged her, "No Thomas escort this time?"

Rosalie, relieved by his joking in standard Anatole tone, "Oh, he's here; he's occupied by something important at the moment," she minimized the explanation and bolted into telling their amazing story. She reached toward Red for a hug, "Just like last time, I have to say, you won't believe what we've brought for you to see," she smiled and spoke in a serious tone while she walked with them into her office. She closed the door behind them, "We have found...well,"...Rosalie stumbled in her words, trying to stay calm within the excitement of telling her friends. "We've found the one thing that all Jews and Christians hold in faith, but have never seen in all their lives. Can you guess?"

As they listened to her, Rosalie could see both their minds worked at a frantic pace to be the first to say the answer; they both hesitated, and said nothing.

Anatole reached for Rosalie's hand; holding it tight, "Tell us, I know your face is too serious to be joking."

"You're right about that, this is no joke. We found the Ten Commandments tablets, now set up next to the other display of stones, downstairs."

Both stunned; they stood frozen in their silence.

FORTY-TWO

"I got back as fast as I could. So much happened; some I expected and some not. I spent one day at the university after Vasily's graduation and I met with the Board of Directors confirming that he would be the perfect person to take my place for the technical team advisor. They agreed. It was that night I planned for a quiet evening, just packing and catching up on some sleep, because no one in the mainstream knew I was back. Surprised when someone knocked on my door at 3 a.m., I almost didn't answer, but she kept saying, *Professor, Professor, I need your help.* I recognized her, a new member on my technical team, who joined just prior to my leaving on vacation. She spoke very fast, I could barely understand her. I calmed her down and told her to start again from the beginning. She'd been working on a project she'd picked up from a graduate who went back to France. He'd been working on it for a year prior to her starting it. They were re-engineering the electronic circuit used by many products in the past. This circuit allowed for the communication through the PDS and other major electronics." Thomas smiled, "No one told her what she would see when she had a successful test. Working alone that night, her makeshift PDS test system lit up with a fuzzy screen and she froze. It scared her and she didn't know what to do or think. She never saw a working PDS, because she was six months old when all the technology was destroyed. She rushed over to my apartment to get me to help her."

"Her meticulous work brought the circuit to life. Now with Vasily as her leader, they'll make great progress as they focus. Vasily won't be coming to Jerusalem after all; he'll stay to work with his new team, to expedite the findings and hopefully additional discoveries."

"That's great news! It's so perfect it happened when you were there," Anatole shook his hand in congratulations. "Glad you're back; we're ready to start the testing. The radiometric dating procedure is in place. I'll be leading this, because of my past experience working archeological sites prior to the catastrophe. We've accommodated the Lake Sinai stones and the Ten Commandments as a complement, so we'll save time."

The team set to working around the clock in shifts. Success at every level occurred daily, leading to the completion and the astounding positive results. All the master studies team was walking around with smiles on their faces giving added incentive to the testing team to finalize everything to share with the world.

"Even though I believed in my heart that the tablets and note were authentic, now that our tests confirm it, I can hardly believe it. Do you feel that way, too?" she hugged Thomas after the final test results were confirmed.

"There's no way to describe this excitement. I keep saying it to myself, this is historic. When I try to wrap my mind around the past months, I keep thinking I'll wake up and none of this will have happened."

Across the room Anatole sat staring into the relic cabinet. "This is my life's dream. It's as if I was placed here to do just this. All my paths led here; like all my family issues set me in the right place at the right time."

Rosalie and Thomas enjoyed their hug and looked over at him as he spoke. "I think I'll just go on smiling forever. I could never have a more perfect fulfillment for my life."

Red, Sili and Anatole left the group after the final results came through. "When you finish the first draft of the summation, I'll start the proof reading right away. All the documentation will need to be ready for presentation at the consortium in three months."

"No problem, Red, I'll be finished this afternoon. I've been making notes every day so it will come together quickly. I'll bring the first draft over to your office in a few hours."

"Hey you two, let me know when it's my turn to proof read. I'll be over in the ARS Center. It's my afternoon to cover the messaging station," he waved as he walked off.

"I know we only have a short time, but we can do it all," Red smiled as she waved at Anatole.

Open to the whole world population, the initial invitation went out right after they returned from Lake Sinai. "I can't believe we only received seven responses. I know it was just an announcement of the prophecy discovery, but I thought more people would be curious. I think a brand new invitation is in order, now that we found the Ten Commandments. Don't you think?"

"Of course it is. I know the first response was disappointing, but this is a whole different story," Red shook her head. "Just you wait and see. They'll jump at this chance. The very first historic discovery since the disaster; they'll be here Rosalie, they'll be here."

"I know you're right. Yes, and they'll be able to see the actual proof. The displayed testing will be a huge part of the presentation to the consortium."

"Hey look everybody," Anatole ran through the door, out of breath. "Look at all these messages. I haven't counted them yet, but they're acceptances. It's so great…they're all coming! They were in my in-box waiting for me at the ARS Center."

Red took the mound of papers from Anatole's shaking hands and started counting, while Anatole hugged Rosalie. "Oh Rosalie, this is so thrilling!"

"Wow, I guess we just needed to give them something to be excited about. So far, we have 243 positive new responses in a matter of hours. Can you believe it?

Now our consortium will be fully attended," Rosalie reached over and squeezed Red's hand, laughing and crying at the same time, still caught in Anatole's hug.

University classes being suspended for an extended period gave the staff and students time to prepare and decorate the halls, the streets and even the pathways where new lanterns were strung for the events to come.

Additional apartments were put together out at the old destroyed airport, to house the visiting consortium participants. Many airplanes were never used during the initial creation of apartments. The additional spaces extend the original housing built several years before and will later be used for more dormitories at the university.

Jerusalem teams organized the food for the large groups, tours for the relics, and transportation for all attendees from Tel Aviv-Yafo. Two hundred fifty people will arrive in Jerusalem in three months; almost doubling the amount of the whole population of the Jerusalem survivors.

FORTY-THREE

Thomas knew the very last thing Rosalie checked every evening before she left for the day was the locked case. As she closed up, Rosalie's dream of a romantic proposal came true when she saw the small decorative antique box waiting for her.

She picked up the unusual box. Made of wood with miniature floral carvings, the box decoration was different than anything she ever saw before. Tears flooded her cheeks. She looked around for Thomas and thought, *where is he? Doesn't he want to be here when I open this? It has to be from him. No one else would be this creative.*

Simultaneously to her thought, Thomas burst through the door with Red and Anatole at his heels. He saw her holding the ring box.

"I was going to be here when you found it, but my sidekicks here slowed me down and when I tried to make excuses why I needed to be here with you, they cornered me and wouldn't let me leave until I told them what could possibly be so important. I relented and told them. They finally let me go so I could see you open the box!"

Out of breath, he knelt in front of her. Anatole and Red, arm in arm stepped up behind him and awaited the next few moments. Their grinning faces noted their approvals prior to the question! Rosalie smiled through her tears.

"My dear Rosey, since our special day diving together at Lake Sinai, you have been first in my thoughts. Please say you'll spend the rest of your life with me as my wife and friend."

Rosalie's tears of joy ran down her cheeks. Her clear acceptance leaped from her when she kissed Thomas tenderly. "Yes, yes, yes, I'll marry you. I love you, too!

She opened the unusual box. The old style ring's large sapphire gem glistened even in the dimly lit relic room. Rosalie gazed at Thomas and then back at the ring, the question written all over her face, she didn't even need to say it out loud, "Where did you get this gorgeous old ring?"

"The ring was my mother's. It was found by one of her students during the clean-up. Her body was documented as a death by fire; her valuables were underneath her body. We lived on the bottom floor of the apartment building, and she was in the back porch, trying to get out. When she fell, what she carried dropped underneath her. A pair of surgical scissors from her father, he was a doctor, and the ring from her grandmother."

"I never knew any of this information until about six years after the tragedy. When I first arrived from Sochi, I wore a full beard, having grown it during the long trek. My mother's student never noticed me working on the library and religion team and I didn't know her that well to recognize her. As a whim one day, I shaved my beard. She saw me a couple weeks after that, and we had the nicest reunion. We talked for a long time about my mother. After that, she searched the old records that up until that time eluded me. Within the information about my mother's building, was a small box containing the scissors and the ring inside this beautiful wooden designer jewelry box. I've treasured it all these years and hoped someday I'd meet someone to share it with. Today is that day, Rosalie. I saved this ring for you. I'm so proud you'll be able to wear it."

Thomas took it from the box and slid it onto Rosalie's finger. A little large, but so beautiful, she didn't care. Rosalie beamed. Her excitement spilled over to everyone; she repeated her affirmation. "I love you, Thomas! Yes, I'll marry you."

They hugged each other and turned to Red and Anatole. Red predicted, "This shared moment will be one of those memories we'll hold onto forever."

FORTY-FOUR

The University Consortium 2087, with its initial simple plans started ten years prior, now required a whole new schedule. After the discoveries of the ancient relics, the agenda grew twice in size from the original plans. The Ten Commandments alone proved to be historical from any vantage point. Rosalie's teams' discoveries on so many levels gave a whole new dimension to the festivities.

The "new" meeting space put together for a number of years with scavenged furniture and old airplane seats saved from the devastation so long ago became the planned location for the consortium. One of the children who survived in Jerusalem grew up to be very creative. He made lamps and built the chandelier for the main room auditorium. The new upgraded room would seat six hundred. The chandelier, built with PDS screens retrieved for this unusual usage, was made with reflective shining pieces. Everyone who entered the new auditorium marveled at the remarkable use of old PDS screens. Jerusalem's team became artists in their work over the years of recovery.

Chosen as mistress of ceremonies for the largest crowd in Jerusalem for over 35 years, Rosalie began, "In the recovery age, a different communication style flowed with simple and honest exchanges of information. This new honest approach started growing in Israel, Egypt and Russia, then extended to the new U.S., Europe and Australia. The new communication, a direct opposite of the global political rhetoric introduced in the early-2000s, where educators', scientists', ministers', and doctors' knowledge no longer commanded respect. Politicians no longer ruled, or owned technology which produced government regulated industries. No more "shortcuts" around education. Curriculums were rebuilt and universities reopened. The few educators who survived, took on the challenge to rebuild."

"All countries within ARS now understood each other. Their openness through the education and religious organizations adopted solid foundations when old technologies and old political governments ceased to exist. Suffering and basic humanity took over the world. The new world order built on the solid religious and educational premise grew through hope and people's goodness after the disaster. Everything was new, because almost all records of governments, hospitals, big business, religion, universities, and schools were lost after the cataclysmic changes on that day."

"Indifference was no longer the norm. Gang's and political influence no longer attracted people. The underworld figures and former gang members removed from the global political limelight, no longer promoted fear about education and learning. Catatonic lethargy now transformed in the overall populace to kindness, caring and compassion."

"No surprise to any of us is the facet that every society on earth paid the price for this massive blunder by humanity. Its arrogant political attitude overrode facts and predictions which provided the time to prepare the world's population or even prevent the mega-tragedy altogether."

"Looking back, after so many years, we're reminded of the sadness we all felt for the huge loss of life, but we learned. The societies that believed in the political platitudes released a disaster onto all of us. Now we believe in each other, in compassion, in truth, and in the value of educating ourselves."

Rosalie's calm and clear statement confirmed what everyone already knew, but hearing it for the first time at the University Consortium, provided a solace and confirmation that what occurred during the past thirty five years was good.

"The next item scheduled for the agenda, *The Ten Commandments*. All our global experts confirmed the testing data prior to the opening ceremony. The literature we distributed to each of you upon arrival will help to initiate discussions for the exciting and now verified discovery."

Rosalie started this topic, beginning with the simple facts about Kabibe and the village where she and Maadiah lived.

"During the years of turmoil after the quakes, Kabibe found and cared for God's word. She kept the tablets safe away from the troubled world, and only upon her death did anyone else see them."

"Maadiah chose to remain with the relics today, rather than attend the Consortium." Rosalie's reverent speech full of hope told how willingly Maadiah's people chose to share the Ten Commandments with the new world beginning again. "They decided to lose the ways of the past and open the beauty of God's word to all, instead of hiding them away."

Next on the agenda, Rosalie introduced the discovery team; most of whom were familiar to the crowd through ARS over the years. "Two people on my discovery team you don't know are the boat captain, Enrico Toffoli and professional diver, Doug Magnusson. Please welcome them to the stage. They've just arrived from Lake Sinai a couple hours ago." Rosalie waited for the applause to finish. "These are the final two people rounding out my team. Their roles as catalysts for part of a discovery found in the Lake Sinai caverns are well noted in the documents being distributed to you now."

Enrico, a natural speaker with great anecdotes to share, joked with the crowd while the document packets were distributed. This added joy showed the camaraderie felt by all at the opening day ceremonies held in the new university center auditorium.

"I'm hearing conversations starting out there," Rosalie shaded her eyes with her hand. The spotlight was too bright to see the audience, but then silence came back over the crowd. "This is where we are going to rock your world! We found something so incredible at Lake Sinai, words can't really express it...During a diving adventure at the lake, Thomas, Doug and I found stones from exactly the same time and locale as the Ten Commandments and with the same etching. They are four prophecies. Along with them is a carved note in a different writing style. It is a note signed by Moses." The totally silent crowd startled Rosalie. She stopped speaking.

A man in the first row stood. "You're saying the testing of these additional stones are valid and that they are real?"

Relieved to hear the question, Rosalie took a deep breath. "Yes, all are validated. These are the real thing! The pictures and documents you have in your hands provide you with every detail we have.

The final translation, placed into history for Moses'

note written as follows.

אלוהים נתן לי הוראות לתת רק את עשרת הדיברות לשבט שלי ולבנות אוהל אחסון.ארבע הנבואות הן כמו לדעת את העתיד. אלוהים כיוון אותי כדי לשמור אותם נסתרים. יהיו רק עשרה כללים לעקוב. ידע של העתיד טמון נסתר. משה

God gave me instructions to give only the Ten Commandments to my tribe and to build a storage tabernacle. The four prophecies are like knowing the future. God directed me to keep them hidden. There will only be ten rules to follow. Knowledge of the future lies hidden. Moses

The final translation for the four prophecies...

בצע את עשרת הדיברות, חיים על פני כדור הארץ ישגשגו לנצח. כפי שהובטח בכתביו של אלוהים, להרוס על ידי מים לא יקרה שוב. אם עשרת הדיברות מוזנחים, פעולה אחרת תתרחש - ההתפשטות של כל המינים הפוכות. חיים יתחילו שוב אם האהבה וטוהר של לב כדי להמשיך.

Follow the Ten Commandments, life on earth would flourish forever.

As promised in the writings of God, destroyed by water not happen again.

If the Ten Commandments are neglected, other action will occur – the spread of all genders reverse.

Life will begin again if the love and purity of heart to continue.

"The genuine four prophecies matched the Ten Commandments and all the stones measured to be the correct age according to our radiometric dating tests. The note from Moses also tested true in the correct timeline and translation of the old Hebrew." The undertones in the crowd started as all these items were stated and eventually thunderous applause took over the room. Cheers and singing from every corner began the pandemonium with people standing on their seats toting signs. This commotion lasted more than an hour and was reminiscent of the long ago exuberant crowds in New Orleans Bourbon Street. Usually these bashes were just prior to Ash Wednesday opening the forty day Lent preparation for Easter.

"These tablets are set up together with the Ten Commandments we brought back from Ethiopia. Starting tomorrow morning you all will have a chance to personally view the relics." Thunderous applause abruptly stopped Rosalie's speech. A repeat of the earlier reaction, first clapping and whistling, then shoes stomping, hugging, and dancing in the aisles. Thomas walked over to her and hugged her around her shoulders, while they waited to continue. After ten minutes, they calmed down enough for Rosalie to start again.

"Noted in your packets, each person is scheduled for ten minutes to view all the tablets. We suggest you arrive ten minutes prior to your appointed time."

"God intended the rules for his people to be seen, but in His time. Similar to the story of Esther, God's plan for the newly found four prophecies which Moses hid at Mount Sinai to be used 'at such a time as this'. (Esther 4:14) The Aksum people swore an oath to continue involvement forever. A single priest will serve as a constant guardian while people of the world view the relics. They will, on an ongoing basis, prepare a single person for a life's commitment to God's Covenant. This will allow them to be part of their new role as guardian."

The consortium's first day continued with afternoon introduction speeches for each country's university representative promoting their program successes and plans for the next ten years. This was the original part of the consortium's long term plan, amended now with the discoveries and propagation studies.

The consortium's second day introduced the studies and surveys re-authored by Thomas and Rosalie which corroborated the third prophecy. Although controversial, the studies and surveys showed proof of the path designated by the prophecy historically because propagation of the species did diminish.

"These studies too will be part of the new history validating that the word of God still holds. Yes, it "holds" even though Moses kept the four prophecies secret. Humanity would know the true facts of what God intended for his children today," Thomas' enthusiasm grabbed the crowd. "It was by God's direction, God's divine plan, that Moses separated the commandments from the prophecies. He brought the commandments down from Mt. Sinai to his people, the prophecies laid in secret, hidden on Mt. Sinai, to be found by Rosalie's team. His plan for the earth's cleansing occurred and the people of earth began to live the lives He intended. Hence, propagation would begin again. Although at this point in time, there is no corroboration of propagation re-start, however, all the other facts prove accurate and do match."

Rosalie joined Thomas at the podium and spoke about the studies and surveys with a theory kindled by her

Bible research. "We pursued back-up for the discovery and all it entailed. I read Exodus and Numbers over and over again. God was angry during this time because Moses doubted whether or not his people would believe the words brought down from the mount were actually from God. In, *Ex. 4:14*, we learned that it was so much so, God appointed Aaron the spokesman instead of Moses. It is possible God was not just angry at Moses because Moses doubted his own ability to convince his people the laws were from God, but also, perhaps God grew angry at His people for not waiting until Moses came down from the mountain. They built an idol, breaking one of His first commandments before they were received. Again, part of God's divine plan brought to the path of His people who wandered for decades as a part of an intended contrition."

"The Bible, written by men, depicted a version of an action told by another man, and not actually what occurred, but from a memory of what occurred. Moses followed God's direction. Historically, Moses kept the four prophecies secret, which had to be part of God's plan. Now that the four prophecies showed us God's intent, logic promoted the idea that Moses followed God's instructions when he told the people what happened on Mt. Sinai."

"The rationale prevailed since Moses questioned why God directed them into the desert where there was no water. God provided the water for Moses' people later; however, because Moses and Aaron doubted God's direction, God told them they would not bring his children to the land they were originally promised, Num. 20:12."

At this point, the Consortium broke down into smaller seminars, led by Rosalie, Thomas, Red, Anatole, and Sili. The speculative discussions lasted throughout the consortium's second day and proved very insightful for all.

Day three of the consortium Rosalie introduced the surveys set up by the First Aid Teams. The information followed the lead from the Jerusalem Medical Center's Maternity Department data.

"When Anatole discovered the details and created a limited study, this data held true. Only two hundred forty three births were documented worldwide since the day of the quakes, in the countries which built communications through ARS. And...every one of the two hundred forty three births was conceived prior to the catastrophe. Women were not getting pregnant. Although some of the outlying countries, which don't communicate through regular channels, may support maternity activity, the highly visible countries confirm the data, no births were registered for an extended period. And as stated in, Jeremiah 3:16...*And it shall come to pass, when ye be multiplied and increased in the land, in those days, saith the Lord, they shall say no more, The ark of the covenant of the Lord: neither shall it come to mind; neither shall they remember it; neither shall they visit it; neither shall that be done any more.* Again, even though written by man, the Bible followed the action that God intended. With humankind not multiplying any longer and now we find the Commandments, and oppositely, if we continue to multiply and live politically and outside Gods law, the commandments stay hidden from mankind."

"However, He allowed us to find the commandments, so the question we leave here with, will be "Have the people changed enough to reverse God's warnings?" All were quiet as Rosalie finished the question. You could hear a pin drop yet there were about five hundred people in the room.

"As we gather at this consortium to confirm the theory that the Third Prophecy proposed action occurred, we the people of earth, the people of God, did not follow the commandments as stated. Even though we didn't know the "prediction" or that the four prophecies existed, we were not excused from following the word of God."

The consortium resumed with Anatole presenting all the outlined information of the newest discoveries and plans for the historic documentation changes:

"A new history book, being prepared for publication, covers the first part of history, of course unchanged and with a new section about how the four prophecies found at Lake Sinai and how Kabibe sheltered Moses' Ten Commandments received from God at Mt. Sinai now are part of our changed world. God's Word hidden and guarded for centuries, never to be seen by anyone except the priestly guards of northern Ethiopia hold a place in our history. The Ten Commandments history will show in its entirety in the new book showing the four thousand plus years, since it is the basis of history already lived. The four prophecies will show intact from this consortium date forward with an introduction chapter relating how and who discovered them. This will also include the discovery of the Ten Commandments in Aksum, Ethiopia."

"Madeline "Red" O'Leary and Captain Friday co-authored the new history book to be shared worldwide. The collaboration by Captain Friday of updated geographic changes along with Red O'Leary's historic overviews gave the perfect updates for the thirty five years since the disaster. Red's department at Jerusalem University will tackle the publishing of the new book, using old techniques with the scavenged printing presses found in 2075. This exciting endeavor will be done on a limited basis, as the number of books required worldwide is finite."

"Individual religious groups within the New World Religion Organization requested a sign-off for the new history book prior to its publication. This is a follow-up to the already accepted factual testing and authentications by the participants of the Consortium and has been agreed to by the University of Jerusalem, the discoverers, and the authentication team."

"The new world history book will contain not only all the specifics for the discoveries approved at the consortium, but also the world condition, the transition since the disaster with the teams rebuilding, the international university organization, and the world religion organization."

"The new history book will include the determination of the consortium, that the surveys completed about propagation, and the Third Prophecy's conclusion provided a clear reason why the studies so long ago proved, propagation of all species was depleted. Simply, God predicted this would occur if the Ten Commandments were not followed. With the greed and failure of all people to care for each other, we don't deserve to be able to continue to populate the glorious earth He provided for us. Earth's population, no longer increasing, clearly showed in the generational study, as promised, not only in Jeremiah, but also, in the discovered Third Prophecy."

"The New World Religion Organization took on the task to create an addendum for the 2091 Bible publication, planned for publication by November, with distribution to start January 2092."

Applause with accolades yelled from the audience, noted approval by the lengthy standing ovation when Anatole finished.

FORTY-FIVE

The New World Religion Organization, with major representation in attendance by its Board of Directors, planned for a special speaker.

The president of the New World Religion Organization took the podium, "Will Rosalie Danforth please come to the stage?" he said.

Surprised by the announcement, Rosalie saw this distinguished looking man for the first time at the consortium, as she crossed the stage to greet him. He shook her hand, "You may not remember, but we have spoken before. We had a lengthy conversation on ARS about thirty six years ago.'"

Rosalie looked puzzled, "I'm sorry; I had so many transmissions and I don't recollect your name, Reverend Samuels," she smiled apologetically.

"Oh, my dear, of course you wouldn't. Back during those years, I went by the name, Ren. A nickname tagged on me since early childhood. Your dad was my mentor and friend."

Stunned, she lurched forward, grinned happily and hugged him on stage in front of the crowd who waited for the ceremonies to continue. "You also weren't a minister in high ranking for the New World Religion Organization," embracing him in disbelief.

Ren smiled at her levity. "Yes, my life changed for the better, since the last time we spoke. I hope we can spend a little time together, to catch up."

"Why didn't you ever contact us again? We thought you were dead when you dropped away from the transmissions."

"Do you remember how scared I was on the last transmissions? Well, I just had to put all that behind me. It took me a year to get to Spokane and by the time I got there, I didn't want to think of my open fear again. Talking on the transmissions would have brought all that fear back to the surface. Plus I was embarrassed about it. I was out of control; not a place I was very proud of with all my iron man flight training. In my mind, I should have been able to handle anything. When I arrived in Spokane, I moved into action with the city council. They followed a great track, and I wanted to be part of it with your "team influence" already implemented there. Even though Spokane didn't have the major damage that occurred around the world, electrical and mechanical technology didn't work anywhere. Oh let's put that aside for now, we can talk about all this later...but now, let's get to business, we have closing ceremonies to accomplish."

Ren turned to address the consortium, "As you all know, we gathered at this consortium to learn about and validate recent discoveries made by Rosalie Danforth's teams, who you heard speak earlier. In years past, our ancestors took time to honor people through designated societies like the Nobel Prizes, Academy Awards, and the Princess Diana Awards for Peace. Since these awards no longer have a basis for honor, the Unified World Universities steering committee and the New World

Religion Organization have created a new world award. This award denotes the moral courage, and self-less qualities our new world society now holds in high esteem. The first Rosalie Danforth Hope Award honors its name sake as the first honoree. Her Teamwork Concept distributed via ARS shortly after the cataclysm brought our destroyed world out of confusion and disorder. For those of you who have worked with Rosalie, you have, I'm sure been touched by her ability to change a tragic or impossible situation into a positive workable everyday event. She distributes hope as if she was serving you lunch every day and gave us unity." Waiting for the applause to finish, Ren looked at Rosalie and also applauded. "Even though this award was in motion prior to the discovery of the Ten Commandments and the four prophecies and all that entails, her team brought even more reason to embellish this award ceremony. One fact just a few of you know, is before that disastrous day so long ago, my mentor for many years was Rosalie's father, Timothy Danforth. He influenced my life since I was in 3rd grade elementary school. I never met Rosalie in person until today; however, many years ago she spoke with me over ARS. She was in pain from the news that her father died, still she took time to speak with me. Consoling me in my own tragedy of being alone after the quakes, and she, quite a few years younger than myself, gave me the strength to move forward alone. She, along with her father, turned into my most memorable people. When I heard about the new award being created in Rosalie's honor, and she was to be the first honoree, I asked if I could be the presenter. I am here to honor a true humanitarian and educator for the new world associations of learnings," thunderous applause broke into Ren's speech. "I arranged with our tall ship team to pick me up in Minnesota as a barter arrangement. One of their team members, Jeremy, was escorted back to Spokane taking my seat in the hover-car which brought me to Minnesota. He started in medical school last week, a fulfilled lifetime dream. Then I had the pleasure of getting to know the whole crew while we sailed here. We picked up many people along the way, also attendees of this consortium. By the time we arrived, the ship was at maximum occupancy, with an additional 125 people. I recognize many of your faces today. The tall ship's crew was most gracious as we stretched the walls of their floating home."

"I spent the long trip reminiscing, planning and preparing for this speech, and also setting up the plan with a process for presentation of this award to our future honorees."

Stunned by Ren's unexpected speech and the monumental acceptance by the consortium, with tears running down her cheeks, Rosalie accepted the beautiful handmade award when Ren placed it in her hands. A piece of a PDS screen carved with smoothed out etched edges in the gentle shape of a wave of hope. The diamond dust glistened through the etching. Rosalie's name and details of the award carved similar to the note from Moses' note found with the four prophecies.

She smiled through her tears and waited for the applause to diminish. "I am so honored by your words of appreciation," she turned toward Ren and smiled. "Since, well, forever, all I've ever done was pursue the next step. I didn't understand until this moment, that my personal words and attitudes meant so much. Recently I heard several stories of how the team work came to different places around the world. I was warmed by how gratified each person's words explained the way this concept affected their life in some fashion. I did know the idea helped clear chaos, which we all needed so desperately. Our loss too unbearable to grasp in our minds, we needed a simple way to help us focus again. This gave us strength to move forward in an impossible situation. Thank you so much for this honor. I am humbled by your overwhelming acceptance and hope that I can meet each and every one of you."

Rosalie graciously hugged and thanked Ren as she stepped away from the podium, "I hope we have time to visit before you leave. I want to hear about what you've been doing for thirty six years."

"Oh definitely…I don't leave for a few more days. We'll make time," they embraced and left the stage together.

"Exhilarating, that's what it was; simply exhilarating! I'm so glad I am able to be here to see your presentations and your team enthusiasm. You changed my life the day you spoke with me over ARS. Now I am able to give you something as presenter of the new award on this historic day."

"Oh Ren, it's so good to meet you in person. Thank you for being here. Please tell me about your life after you left Colorado. I'm so eager to hear about it. It's like a gap in my history, now that I'm seeing you." He smiled while they walked together and he told his story.

"The trek to Spokane was long, lonely and difficult. The countryside ravaged by molten lava, already cooled in places, and huge crevasses difficult to find my way across. Food was scarce most of the time; water even more difficult to locate. I carried the Ham equipment for a while, but after I fell a couple times, the equipment became inoperable because of damage. I discarded it, to make my trek easier. So much damage and so many dead bodies everywhere I went; most of the bodies lay open and decayed. I just kept remembering what you said. *I'm only responsible for my little piece of the world.* This helped me to move forward, I walked away from my despair."

"I encountered birds everywhere. I guessed they were more able to survive than other species, since they could be off the ground during the catastrophic occurrences or they could land in trees up off the ground. Because I didn't see other animals alive when I climbed through and around lands destroyed or disrupted, the fact that I saw so many birds remained as one of my most vivid memories of my trek to Spokane. Huge flocks flew near me and scavenged in the big groups. As time went on though, I started to see fewer and fewer birds. In one place, I came up over a rise overlooking what I believed used to be a meadow; I saw many birds eating other birds. This scared me; that vision should have been in a horror film, not something you just encounter when you turn a corner."

"By the time I arrived in Spokane I hardly saw any birds at all, a huge change in the years' time. I suspected food being limited after the quakes because of so much disrupted land, that the birds were not able to sustain themselves. I remembered thinking, *'Why had God forsaken us?'*"

"At one point the land flattened out to normal, so then for a while, I made faster progress. I found a sign that read Interstate 80. Walking on the flat concrete felt good, but didn't last very long. A huge crevasse cut off the comfortable walking, so I started to follow the crevasse north, since it was too wide and too dangerous to cross. After many miles, it started to narrow, and I was able to jump across it, and again started to move northwest toward Spokane."

"Arriving in Spokane after a year, I made my way to the City Council to learn how to get involved. The rest is history, as they say; I changed my life by becoming a minister, becoming involved in the university and the new government, and working with the new world organizations."

Amy E. Zajac

"The new world with politics and commercialism destroyed, lightened the burden of the past. The loss of cynicism allowed positive unity to encompass the populace who survived. Simple lives fostered a rejuvenation of people caring for people. The survivors traded the loss of politics and commercialism for warmth and goodness."

After Ren's last words, Rosalie once again hugged her friend and said, "Thank you for telling me. I needed to hear your story. I'm so glad we had these moments together and I'm so glad you're here. I have news for you and you can share in my joy. I'm getting married to Thomas tomorrow, and now you can be here to celebrate with us."

FORTY-SIX

The perfect timing for the wedding, allowed all Rosalie's friends to be in attendance, including Enrico, Doug, TJ, Friday, Maadiah and Ren. These people became so important and a part of the new life which brought Thomas and Rosalie together. Some by building a boat in Italy and bringing it to Lake Sinai, others traveled in a tall ship making the world a smaller place, and last but not least, Rosalie's father's friend from her home town in the old U.S. All were significant for the celebration of the discoveries.

Both dressed in their own traditional ceremonial best, Maadiah and Ren performed the simple ceremony together. The dimly lit relic room decorated with candles and Jasmine flowers brought in special from Lake Sinai made the Ten Commandments and the four prophecies back-drop a perfect setting for Rosalie and Thomas' wedding. With Red the Matron of Honor and Anatole the Best Man, everyone shared joy for this union. All knew true love and respect brought these two people together in a changed world of honor, decency and hope.

Anatole gave her away in the old tradition, with Enrico, Doug, Glenn, Mike, Sammy, TJ, Friday, Jeremy and Sili the only other guests. Everyone else spent the time to prepare and set up a party for the reception in the flower gardens next to the ruins at the old university chapel. Rosalie and Thomas proclaimed their simple vows written together for their ceremony. Once their vows complete and with the traditional kiss now just a memory, the wedding party walked to the gardens.

They planned to spend their wedding night at a specially decorated university apartment. Red arranged the whole thing surprising them for their wedding gift.

Joy in abundance as all their friends, university

staff and students, formed a path of candles on both sides of a walkway from the gardens to their wedding night abode. It took them two hours to accept all their friends' good wishes while they walked to a perfect beginning.

FORTY-SEVEN

Rosalie woke early and slipped out of the bedroom on tip toes to keep from disturbing Thomas still sleeping. The sun just came up over the mountains to the east. The excitement she felt kept her awake half the night. After all that's happened and all the discoveries and confirmations, and their perfect happiness since the wedding six months before, their most perfect non-realistic dream may actually come true. *Thomas won't believe it. I'll remain calm. I'll remain hopeful and I'll make my appointment first thing this morning. Thomas can go with me; I won't tell him where. Then the surprise will be the ultimate.*

Walking into the doctor's office, Rosalie smiled at Thomas and reiterated, "This is just a routine visit. I just forgot to mention it. Since the appointment is so late, we'll head to dinner right after. This is a nice way to finish the day. Don't you think?"

Thomas nodded, "Oh sure, Rosey, good idea. I'm hungry. Do you think this appointment will take long?"

"No, probably not, once the examination is finished, I'll ask for you to come in and wait with me. I always have to wait here in this office. You know how doctors are," Rosalie didn't want there to be any reason for Thomas to suspect, but she did want the doctor to tell them both at the same time.

"Well, Rosalie, when you told me this morning, I didn't believe it," Dr. Saheed commented. "However, I'm ecstatic to tell you. You are pregnant. This is the first new pregnancy in Jerusalem we have documented since before the catastrophe!"

Rosalie focused on Thomas' face. Shock turned to disbelief turned to elation in a matter of seconds. "Why didn't you tell me?"

"I wanted to be absolutely sure, so coming here

together and surprising you seemed perfect!"

"Everything we've discovered though. Or should I be thinking that the fourth prophecy will start to turn everything around? My mind is reeling. I don't know what to think about first. How happy I am, how happy you are, or what does this mean for humanity and how can we search for others to confirm what we want to be true?"

Rosalie hugged Thomas. "Let's just enjoy our moment. We'll celebrate with dinner. Tomorrow we can start the discovery of what this means. Okay?! I don't want the reality that I'm actually as old as Elizabeth when she conceived John in the biblical writings to stay in my mind."

Thomas tilted his head, his thoughts racing, "I hadn't thought of that. Our ages never meant anything one way or another, until you said that. I've felt so happy and I guess young too, since the moment we met. You're right though, everything else doesn't matter. Tonight is just for us to splash around in the warmth of the moment. We're going to have a child!"

Thomas grabbed Rosalie and hugged her and then picked her up and swung her round; they both laughed in the joy of the moment!

FORTY-EIGHT

"We need to look for other new pregnancies around the world," Rosalie said. "It would be important to document the patterns for any species re-propagation if things change according to the four prophecies. After all, it can't just be me. I know there are others including other species."

"You're right," Anatole agreed. "I can start an inquiry just like I built the original pregnancy study, years back."

"Perfect, that will give us a good start. Can you get to it right away?"

"Tomorrow, I'll begin tomorrow.'

Rosalie planned the new study, and decided to follow the ideas of how humanity changed, with new pregnancies, with people coming together through kindness and with more fellowships growing. Thomas focused on the other species lost, or endangered. He started with the sea because one of the first animals to be discovered through the study was fewer baby turtles born in the late 1950's. These perspectives totally different than the work Rosalie and Thomas did when they first met.

Since no studies occurred for this new theory which presented itself in the doctor's office with Rosalie's pregnancy condition, setting up the initial documentation correctly from the start will help those who follow to make their hypotheses.

"Humanity will be easier to track since the global tragedy. Once censuses begin again, with so few people left on Earth, the simple process will be the line-in-the-sand concept," Thomas said. "To determine what remained of the other animal species and insects will be more difficult and will take decades to understand the loss and the statistics."

Thomas heard from Vasily that his old team started from scratch to build a small circuit. No one on the team was an electronics savvy person. It took years to learn and recreate the lost technology everyone knew would benefit humankind as proved that late night when the PDS came to life in front of a startled student. The new university computer connection will be the first set up in limited use. The announcement told the world, "Volgograd University recreated the circuit through an old process of re-engineering."

A week after the Consortium's conclusion, the Volgograd University Team made a global notification through the last daily ARS scheduled transmission. They did this to honor the Network of ARS Operators. The computer technology side of education began again in Volgograd, opening diverse communication long since lost at the time of the disaster.

When Anatole heard the news about the circuits successful re-creation, he made a list of all the things he missed from the past. The first thing he wrote on his list, PDS. When he stopped by to visit Rosalie, he talked more about the circuit than he did Rosalie being pregnant in her fifties!

"There has to be a way to use the circuit technology to bring PDS back to life. After all, there are three satellites still circling the Earth as far as we know. One of those satellites stored the PDS stationing central with over a hundred years of cinema movies and the old television shows in the HD Conversion Center (HDCC). I'm ready for a rainy Sunday afternoon of PDS while I lounge around doing nothing but enjoy the old stories. I remember my mother doing that when I was a boy." After Anatole left, his enthusiasm caught Rosalie in a whirlwind of reminiscences.

I'll ask Thomas about what the Volgograd Team will do for upcoming projects. Anatole was so right. Not having PDS anymore was sad. After all, just touching that amazing diamond polymer screen was always such a science fiction dream come true at our fingertips. Surprising Anatole with a timeline for possible PDS viewing would be a huge gift for him. He can look forward to it since the circuit is a reality again. How fun would it be to see an old Paul Newman movie? Isn't it fun to dream again?... I need to stop daydreaming I have work to do.

Rosalie's pregnancy flew by. She researched the materials she received from universities and hospitals around the world. Once Anatole and Thomas created a makeshift old style computer for Rosalie, the slow momentum changed to high speed. With this computer she worked at home and planned to do so even after the baby arrived. The piecemeal machine resembled the documented word processors developed in the 1970s, pre-personal computers.

Rosalie contacted the technical university in Volgograd, the initial starting place for the communication network for a direct feed from their computers to start. Working from home helped Rosalie to keep calm and focused on good health for her baby. Through Thomas' connection to the university at Volgograd, she received one of the first sets of chips created from the new circuit discovery by the Technology Team. She asked the Volgograd Team to keep two of the chips for placement at two facilities in Russia. Since her study needed current documentation to begin with, she chose the maternity clinics in Volgograd, Svetlograd, and Jerusalem to be connected with her home computer. Just finishing her eighth month of pregnancy, Rosalie planned to stay at home.

During this time she planned to read all the data she

pulled together in scattered volumes. This started a new "study" of humanity, along with the data recorded during the Commandment and prophecy testing.

Rosalie coordinated the existing data she pulled together with the new data from the three facilities as part of the beginning of the maternity study. All the earlier documentation from the three maternity clinics, Anatole bartered to be delivered via special courier, gave her a starting point. Rosalie coordinated the exciting new data with the old study her Jerusalem Library and Religion Team excavated years ago right before the university opened. To start with, Rosalie planned for her own understanding of all the documentation.

After the day the doctor confirmed Rosalie's pregnancy, more women made appointments at the Maternity department to complete pregnancy tests. Dr. Saheed realized the significance of the obvious change with so many new pregnancies. He kept Rosalie up to date with a weekly communication.

FORTY-NINE

Settling in for her first week at home, Rosalie decided to tackle the most recent documents first, basically working backwards. With so many new documents placed into her cataloged prospectus for study, she'd be reading for a full week.

Each day Rosalie read more and more about humanity through the information provided by the other universities and the newest counts of the pregnancies confirming the turnaround in human propagation. She sighed and smiled with her realization; *the population is beginning to grow again.*

Once she finished the reading for the new Maternity Study, Rosalie began reading the documents which provided the details for the commandment and prophecy discoveries and testing records. This special testing material and the detailed synopsis written for the consortium, took only moments, since she memorized it prior to the presentations. Her reading helped her to revisit how she, Enrico, Doug, Maadiah, Thomas, Anatole, Red, and Sili intertwined their lives throughout the discoveries, the testing, and the consortium. This reminded her of the dream which woke her up that night in the hotel while still on her vacation at Lake Sinai. The memory of her dream, as strong as ever, flawed as all dreams are, because *it was just a dream.* Rosalie shook it off as one of the human failings that everyone encountered along the way, but kept going back to it, *it's just that sometimes we believe in dreams.*

Rosalie never read the biographies of all the participants completed just before the consortium. Moved by their personal stories and how they came to be involved in the historic events over the past two years, reminiscent tears started to well up as she read everyone's sad tale.

The last biography belonged to Sili. Rosalie never heard his story since he came in through the university's special studies team. The drawing of straws, for this appropriate participant, from all the qualified students made the ultimate decision for who would be on the initial studies team. Rosalie found him easy to work with and always available. He wrote beautifully, almost in a prose style, familiar, yet showing appropriate detail for clarity. Surprised by what she read when she began, she never knew Sili's full name before.

Born on the day of the quakes, Silvio Romero grew up as a foster child. Near death in hospital rubble, survivors found him about a week after the catastrophe. His parents and doctor lay dead beside him. Silvio miraculously survived. One of the women in the group that found him, just buried her own baby, and willingly took Silvio to her breast. Able to nurse him with the milk intended for her own child, Silvio thrived. His parents lay dead next to him, so their identifications provided assistance when naming Silvio. The people who found him gave him his father's name.

Silvio spent his childhood being passed from person to person in a rotation through the group that found him.

Everyone mourned and dwelled on the sorrow for a long time. No one wanted to bother with keeping a child happy and as he grew up, no one wanted to help him and keep him in line. He became unruly and spoiled, because no one cared. Born during the earthquakes, he reminded everyone in the group of their families lost.

As the years passed, he grew out of the disruptive behavior and became very clever. Silvio listened intently to everyone, taking advantage of every possible opportunity offered him. At 18 years of age, he decided to leave the group he lived with, even though they were now working in teams and progress started about ten years before. He needed to be on his own, and he wanted to understand how to take care of himself. After a month of wandering aimlessly, he stumbled on an old monastery, half in rubble from the disaster. There he encountered an old priest. The priest became his friend and taught him mathematics. He had already learned to read and write, but no one ever explained anything about numbers to him. Silvio absorbed the new ideas like a sponge. Grateful to the priest, Silvio promised to stay with him until he died. There was no one else to care for him and give him the last rights, in which he so strongly believed. Silvio stayed several more years. During that time the priest kept teaching him, almost as though he attended college; however, Silvio did not know this at the time.

After the priest died, he cleaned and organized the books and papers in the old monastery's library. When he finished, Silvio moved on again. Someday he hoped someone else may come along and find this place and build again. He believed someone else may also find the spirit and love that Silvio found there.

Once again he met new people who gathered together in the rubble of what appeared to be a very large city. He started working with the Library and Religion team. Always much younger than all the people he encountered, he found this to be odd. His knowledge of so many sciences fascinated everyone as he worked to build up the local university with his team. The old priest taught Silvio about archeology. He loved the idea of anything old and ancient and wanted to learn the techniques of archeological scientific study. Again, like a sponge he read every book he found in the university. Silvio heard more and more about Jerusalem and its archeological curriculum. He decided to find a way to get to Jerusalem. A couple more years passed and Silvio made his move, getting into the University of Jerusalem as a graduate through a series of tests, and then made his way to the special studies team. The rest "was history", as they say. Someday he will return home to his native Spain to share the knowledge and glory that now fulfilled his life.

Rosalie's mind reeled. She sat quietly and processed all the facts she read, putting them together with the details of the dream. Now with Silvio...Spain...all the pieces fit. Her dream came true; He planned the whole thing. A true message from God and only now did Rosalie recognize it to be foredestined. Her joy brought tears, as she digested all the new information, *just wait until Thomas hears.* She wept until he arrived home when she shared the joy of their detailed gift from God.

The End

FOREDESTINED

ABOUT THE AUTHOR

Amy E. Zajac lives in Encinitas, California. She is a member of the San Diego Writers/Editors Guild (SDWEG) and the Writer's Alliance of Georgia (WAG). Her first book, *It Started With Patton Teresa Leska's Story A Memoir*, released 2012, is her mother's compelling story as a Nazi political hostage. Her other stories can be found in published anthologies, *Chicken Soup for the Soul From Lemons to Lemonade; The Guilded Pen; Hot Dogs and Cool Cats Animal Tales a la carte; and A Cup of Comfort for Divorced Women*. Contact her at azajac10@yahoo.com